TWO PENNY BLUE

R DAVID

The second of the *Plain Sight* novels

Published in the UK in 2022 by Athan Press

Paperback ISBN-13: 978-1-8380825-3-6
.ePub eBook ISBN-13: 978-1-8380825-4-3

Cover design and typeset by Spiffing Covers

For my Mother

For Auntie Gwlad

Contents

SERGEANT TIMOTHY ALLEN 24
GERHARD ALBRECHT HAUPTMANN 30 1

PRIVATE ALAN BEVAN 19
ERNST BRAUN GEFREITER 21 15

CORPORAL TOBIAS CARTER 24
FRANZ CLAUS GEFREITER 22 29

PRIVATE ELGAN DAVIS 17
ERIC DRUCKER FELDWEBEL 25 45

PRIVATE ALFRED EVANS 20
FREDERICK ENGEL UNTEROFFIZER 22 61

SERGEANT GEORGE EDWARDS 24
EWALD FRANK FELDWEBEL 30 75

PRIVATE DAVID FLINT 19
GEORG HOFFMANN GEFREITER 20 89

CORPORAL IANTO GRIFFITHS 21
FREDERIK KELLER OBERLEUTNANT 30 107

PRIVATE MARC HARRIES 19
HERSCHEL LANGE UNTEROFFIZZER 28 121

SERGEANT RHYS ISSACS 24
MAX LEITZ GEFREITER 19 133

PRIVATE MORGAN JENKINS 20
JOST MEYER GEFREITER 21 147

SERGEANT SELWYN KIMBER 29
GERWIN NEUMANN OBERSTLEUTNANT 34 165

PRIVATE GEOFFREY LLEWELLYN 20
JOSEPH NAGEL GEFREITER 22 179

CORPORAL GARETH LEWIS 22
HORST OBERMANN GEFREITER 19 191

LIEUTENANT GUTO MORRIS 25
EMIL ORTMANN VIZEFELDWEBEL 28 207

SERGEANT EMRYS MOSTYN 26
ALBERT POHL OBERST 39 219

PRIVATE STEVEN OWEN 19
EMIL ROTH HAUPTMANN 41 235

CORPORAL GORDON PRICE 21
HERSCHEL RICHTER GEFREITER 19 247

SERGEANT CYRIL PARRY 28
ADEL SCHAGER LEUTNANT 29 265

PRIVATE ARNOLD ROBERTS 18
ARNO STEIN FELDWEBEL 27 281

PRIVATE MERVYN TUDOR 20
FRIDOLF TELLER UNTEROFFIZER 26 297

SERGEANT HAROLD UPTON 24
ARTUR VOIGHT GEFREITER 19 313

PRIVATE TOMOS VINCENT 21
HANS WITT GEFREITER 22 329

PRIVATE ROBERT WILLIAMS 20
GOTTFRIED ZIEGLER VIZFELDWEBEL 28 341

A SOLDIER OF THE GREAT WAR
EIN DEUTSCHER SOLDAT 357

1

SERGEANT *TIMOTHY ALLEN* 24
GERHARD ALBRECHT HAUPTMANN 30

The sun bathed the peninsula and rose high over the sparkling sea that, today, didn't look cold (but it was, enough to take his breath away) and reflected on the glass of the lighthouse, cyclops of the night, and swept over the fields of yellowing grass where it warmed the backs of grazing cows who did not lift their heads. It sped toward the farmhouse and came through the half-open sash window of his bedroom to where he sat on the bed thinking of nothing, but bursting with eagerness for what the day might offer when a calm, adult voice said in his head, 'This is all you will ever need.'

He jumped as if pinched.

He should never have left the farmhouse by the sea that overlooked the beach and the scalloped bays. But Aled had no choice because he was four years old and grown-ups (not his parents) took all his decisions for him.

None of them could stay there, no matter what the voice said, even if they had all heard it or heard voices of their own telling them the same thing: they were in West Wales on holiday and two weeks was all they had. It was to be his last and only holiday with his aunties and uncles but he couldn't know that.

After a moment, still perplexed, he jumped off the bed and ran downstairs. He didn't understand what the voice had told him or why. He didn't know if he would remember hearing it, because it was his voice from many years hence and the future was full of uncertainty. Life is not an endless holiday, as little boys come to realise too soon. The bedroom remained full of sunlight and the warning went unheeded.

He lived with two aunties, Nesta and Delia – Welsh matriarchs of the legendary kind – and three uncles, Howell, Idris and Emlyn, in a shop in Trebanog at the top of the Rhondda Valley.

Howell was the eldest. He had never married. None of them had. The shop had been their parents' who had opened it in 1901. There would be no one left to run it after them, except Aled – and he would not. The valleys were not the future, not his future.

They had taken him in when he was eighteen months old. He didn't remember it. Trebanog and the shop was all he knew and, outside, was the steepest of hills down to Porth and the grey river at the valley bottom. The neighbours, some of them more uncles, aunties and cousins, called him 'Aled' or whispered 'Jean's boy'. It was his life.

They had decided, now he was old enough, to take him on a proper holiday during miners' fortnight when they could shut the shop. So, they all squeezed into the van that was used to fetch stock, with Howell driving, Idris next to him and the aunties and Emlyn sliding around in the back and Aled sitting on Delia's lap and then swapping over to Nesta because he was getting heavy. It was a long journey, *too* long in a van, but they stopped three times for a wee behind the bushes and to stretch their legs and once to eat corned beef sandwiches and hard-boiled eggs and drink tea from the flasks (which is why they stopped again not long after, to Howell's exasperation).

A buzzard circled overhead. 'Look,' Idris said and Aled shaded his eyes to see the imperious bird.

The van creaked its way through the lanes getting ever closer and, suddenly, there was the sea, just as Aled remembered it on their day trips to Porthcawl and Southerndown.

He spent every day on the beach, getting sunburnt and then quickly turning almost as brown as his hair. The uncles and aunties took it in turns to keep an eye on him as they paddled ankle deep, wistful in their years, while the other four sat on a rug above the tideline and dozed or went for slow walks to the far end and back. They called him for ice creams but he was already running when he heard it coming so that he could get to the front of the queue. The children jostled and bobbed, bare-skinned and rubbery, some of them glistening from the sea, holding out their hands for money from their parents, pointing and choosing from the garish selection on the ice cream van window.

Aled was so tired he nodded over the sausages and chips cooked by the farmer's wife. To bed.

Another day. He helped the farmer with the hay and played with the sheep dog until it ran to hide in its kennel. Always the cries of seagulls, the un-tuned orchestra of the sea and, once, in the dusk, an owl. It began to rain and toads appeared out of the bracken and waddled across the path.

The farmer told him, 'If the cows eat the bracken, they will die.' He didn't tell him what would happen if they ate the toads. When it got dark, there were glow-worms. But, next day, the sun was as hot as ever.

The voice didn't speak to him until the last day before they had to come home. In those two weeks, it was a perfect future remembrance of innocence, bookmarked by the strange event. There was so much space, in such contrast to the cleft of sky to be seen from the shop because the mountains were so tall and often shrouded with rain.

The voice couldn't make him remember the holiday either but, if he had listened, he might have thought about it during the long years of hindsight when his uncles and aunties were no longer; when everyone from his childhood had gone, including those he had yet to meet.

If that was to be.

So they left Pembrokeshire in the ancient van and rattled and groaned up onto the Heads of the Valleys road until they reached their valley and banked into a precarious descent. No one said very much and Aled slept. He didn't wake up until Howell stopped to let them out before he put the van round the back. 'There we are then,' he said, wearily, 'I'm getting too old to drive all that way,' and no one answered to reassure him that he wasn't because they all knew he was, as were they all, and he was the only one of them who could drive.

'We'll never get him off to bed now,' said Nesta. 'We shouldn't have let him sleep all the way back.'

'Let him stay up,' said Delia. 'It won't do him any harm, it's everyone else who's ready for bed, including me.'

'It's a long way in that old van.'

'I'm glad we did, though,' said Delia, 'aren't you? Do you think we'll be able to go again next year?'

'Next year will be difficult. We will have other things to think about,' said Nesta.

'Oh,' said Delia, 'will we?'

'Yes, we will.'

'Did you ever collect stamps, Uncle Howell?' Aled asked, as he lay on the floor of the landing with Idris, as his brother, Jack, had done before him. Aled didn't know he had a brother. Once.

Howell was resting in the armchair next to the window. He opened his eyes. 'I did, but that was, well…' He looked at Idris and smiled at Aled. 'I had some old and quite rare ones that my father gave me. Perhaps I'll dig them out one of these days. But after the war, well…'

'What war?' asked Aled.

'My collection was nothing like as good as Idris', nothing like.'

'What war?'

'Howell was away for a long time,' said Idris, before Howell could answer. 'He didn't have time for stamps after. That was my job.'

'Why?'

'You carry on looking at the stamps with Idris, there's a good boy,' said Howell, slowly pushing himself to his feet with the arms of the chair. 'I'm going for a bit of a lie down.'

'For forty winks?' asked Aled.

'Yes, for forty winks,' and Howell went into his bedroom, the one nearest the back stairs, and closed the door.

In a field of shattered tree stumps, Lieutenant Howell Morgan gently closed the German officer's eyes. To his left was a copse, green and untouched. The smoke filtered through it and a breeze stirred the leaves. It was quiet now and other soldiers walked past, slightly crouched, holding their rifles. They glanced at Lieutenant Morgan, on one knee. They could not hear what he said but they knew what he was doing. Perhaps their feelings were mixed, but they did nothing to disturb him.

Howell took the small *Book of Common Prayer* from his greatcoat pocket that he always carried with him and read: '*Father of all, we pray for you, for…* I do not know your name, fellow soldier, *and for all those whom we love but see no longer. Grant to them eternal rest. Let perpetual light shine upon them. May his soul and the souls of the departed, through the mercy of God, rest in peace. Amen.*' He closed the book and slid it back into his pocket. Then he added, because it came to him, '*But dead or living, drunk or dry, Soldier I wish you well*,' not for the dead man's future, of which none remained, but in hope of better days gone.

Howell leaned forward and gently lifted the soldier's head to free the strap from around his neck. 'Thank you,' he said, and hung the binoculars around his own neck. 'I will look after them, I promise.' Then he got to his feet and followed his men.

Howell kept the binoculars on his bedroom windowsill, polished black, every speck of mud removed and never allowed to gather dust, with the strap, supple with beeswax, coiled neatly alongside. Howell never took off the lens caps to keep the memories of what they had seen locked away. But, sometimes, he let Aled hold them, but not for long lest whatever was inside leaked onto the child's hands like contagion.

'They're very heavy, Uncle Howell.' They tingled and felt warm like flesh but with a metallic smell. Living but lifeless; inanimate but beautifully made.

'Yes, they are. Let me have them now,' and Howell would place them back on the windowsill and arrange the leather strap.

On the barrel was inscribed ALBRECHT Gerhard Hptm. It had been on the underside of the binoculars, half sunk in the mud. Howell could not have seen it as he prayed.

Every morning, Howell saluted the superior officer and he had never told anyone he did but, once they had finished with the formalities and because they had known each other for a long time, he was Gerhard.

Outside on the landing, Aled asked, 'Where's Uncle Howell? He said he was only going for forty winks. I wanted to play draughts.'

'Tomorrow,' Idris said, as he put the stamp album back in the glass-fronted cabinet.

'Can I see Uncle Howell's stamps?'

'In the morning, if we can find them.'

'Are Uncle Howell's stamps better than yours, Uncle Idris?'

'Some are, some aren't. They're just different.'

'Why?'

'Howell's stamps are older than mine.'

'Why?'

'He started collecting them before me. I think Auntie Nesta will want to get you ready for bed now. It's very late.'

Salute. 'Good morning, Gerhard.'

'Good morning, Howell,' Gerhard replied in his excellent English, respecting the language of the country of which he was a guest. Luckily so, because Howell's German was limited to the commands of capture, surrender and peace offerings of cigarettes when they had been obeyed.

'We had a nice holiday, Gerhard,' Howell told him. 'I think you would like Pembroke.'

'I think so, too.'

As he opened his bedroom door, Howell could hear Aled's high-pitched chattering downstairs.

'We're going to play draughts before the shop opens and then Uncle Howell is going to show me his stamps. They're older than Uncle Idris' stamps because Uncle Howell started collecting them before Uncle Idris did.'

'Did he? Eat your breakfast,' Nesta told him.

'Yes,' said Aled, shovelling cereal into his mouth.

In the kitchen, hewn from the rock beneath the mountain, Nesta asked Delia, 'Did you read Eve's letter?'

'I did,' said Delia, stiffening.

'What shall I tell her?' It might as well have been rhetorical for all the notice Nesta intended to take of what her sister said, but she waited for the answer.

Delia washed a breakfast plate. 'Can we talk about it later?'

'We can't ask anyone here,' said Nesta. 'It wouldn't be fair.'

'Wouldn't it? But does she deserve it, Nesta, do you think?'

Nesta put her sister right. 'It's not what we want, not out of choice, if we had a choice, but we don't.'

Delia soaped a teacup and didn't answer.

'If he went to school here, after primary school, what then? What if he runs wild?'

'Aled's a good boy,' said Delia.

'I'm not saying he isn't. But what could we do if he did run wild?'

'I don't know,' said Delia, handing Nesta the teacup.

'There's Mr Tanner and Mr and Mrs Hughes. They'll keep an eye on him, if it's needed, and it won't be. He'll be nearer to Jean.'

'Yes,' Delia replied, carefully, because they were not hopeful, but not even Nesta would say so if there was the slightest chance Jean might recover. 'But there's plenty of time yet before we have to decide.'

'No there isn't,' said Nesta. 'We've got to plan. It'll be on us before we know it.'

'But Nesta, we don't even know if that's what Eve wants.'

'Then we must find out, mustn't we?'

Delia handed Nesta the last dripping plate, feeling bullied by decisions, as she always was. 'Yes,' she said, reluctantly.

Nesta had taken charge (it was never in doubt) and would have been satisfied with nothing less. 'Then I'll speak to Howell and write back to her.' But the tragedy was more, unimaginable, and they would have given their lives to undo it. Powerlessly, they grieved.

Nesta cornered Howell when Idris and Emlyn were opening the shop. 'We won't be able to take him on proper holidays. What will he do during the school holidays?'

'We can still take him,' said Howell.

'I don't know which will break down first, you or that old van.'

'There's nothing wrong with the van.'

'Then you sit in the back of it all the way to Pembroke.'

'We don't have to go that far.'

'Howell.'

'He can play with the other children. Not all of them go on holiday.'

'Where? On the mountain?'

'What's wrong with that? We did.'

'He deserves a holiday every year, Howell, not just day trips to Porthcawl. And how old will you be when he's twelve or fourteen or sixteen?'

'Older.'

'*Old*, Howell.'

'You will be too, Nesta.'

'That's my point, isn't it? Too old for a growing boy.'

Howell didn't answer.

'He will be nearer to Jean.'

At the mention of her name, he retreated.

'Eve loves him, not like his mother, but she does. It wasn't the right thing to do, but with all that happened… Howell? Are you listening to me?'

Howell went out of the back door and up the stone steps to the outside toilet near the wire fence where the sheep kept trying to get in.

The mountain towered and, on its sides like a growth, a slag heap of greying shale, rock and stray lumps of coal had grown as if by pressure from beneath: a tumour from the mine, growing no longer and, now, it was simply there, with no plans to remove it.

He ached as he lowered himself onto the toilet, every joint cracking with Eve's name, grateful to be able to think undisturbed before returning down the steps, like Moses, to give his judgement. It was a pretence. Nesta had made up her mind and it would be painful to change it.

'But Nesta's right, Eve always loved him,' he tried to convince himself, as he strained. But it would break his heart. In one life, how many times can a heart be broken? 'We must ask Alan before we do anything.' He pulled the chain.

Howell left Idris and Emlyn to run the shop, and went for a walk up the mountain, slowly, there was no rush, but not to the top, which was too far and, there, the wind could howl.

He sat on the grass, which wasn't wet, and looked

over the houses below of faded red brick and dark slate roofs, a single line, close ranked, marching with side roads branching off but never able to venture far as the slope got too steep.

He didn't move as the sheep gathered around him and not when a lamb lay down on his foot; and not when his foot went to sleep, as did the lamb; and not until the lamb got up and wandered away after its mother.

When he got back, the shop was closed for lunch.

'You were a long time up the mountain,' said Delia.

'A lamb went to sleep on my foot.'

'Well, sit down before your food goes cold.'

A year went by and Aled's fifth birthday was less than a month away.

2

PRIVATE *ALAN BEVAN* 19
ERNST BRAUN GEFREITER 21

He parked the car near the stepping stones and walked, deep in troubled thoughts, with his head bowed and hands clasped behind his back, to the estuary where he could go no further. A sign said, *DANGER STRONG CURRENTS, It is an offence to swim in the river and may result in prosecution.* 'Well,' said Mr Tanner, 'I'd better not then.'

He sat on a bench. Tusker Rock foamed and, beyond, a smudge on the horizon, Somerset and Devon receded to the south west. Across the estuary, the dunes began. Further was Nottage, then Porthcawl, after which the dunes resumed; Kenfig, its remnant of a castle barely rising above the sand; Kenfig Pool; Sker Rocks and desolate Sker Beach; ten more miles, Port Talbot, the steelworks billowing clouds of steam and, over the refinery, two gas flares on masts: the fiery eyes, watching.

'He is lost there still,' he murmured. 'Poor boy… poor

boys. Why did I come here of all places?'

The waves roared and the wind was chilling off the water.

He forced himself to consider the matter. 'I must attend to it but I wish I could leave it be. There may be no need; he will soon be dead and there's an end to it.' He gripped his hands together until the knuckles were white. 'No, I will have to tell them.'

He shook his head and his crowded thoughts were distracted by yet something else.

As a young man, newly a teacher, he had been engaged to be married and dates were set and plans made. But she had left him for a former love who returned home from the RAF, as if he had been a dalliance. He tried to convince himself that it was better he knew before they married. But, for a long time, he imagined her coming back after seeing the error of her ways. He wanted her to; he would have put it all aside. Even now, when he heard a Vulcan bomber going over, loud… LOUD.

Suddenly, here was a new woman, late, when he was on the cusp of finishing his life's great diversion that had become his single passion.

He had not thought it possible, so *impossible*, it had never occurred to him. He was not vulnerable or lonely but, abruptly and without warning, she had made him realise how much he feared the empty days of retirement.

On the day they met, she held out her hand, and said,

'Good morning, Mr Tanner, I am Rose Davies.'

They shook hands. 'Good morning.' The impossible possibility struck him, dumbfounded him: her perfume, her eyes, her discreet cleavage and full breasts.

He wanted to know if she was married and regretted not saying, 'Good morning, Mrs Davies,' so she could correct him (oh, for *goodness* sake, she wasn't going to be *Miss*, was she – at her age? He didn't want a *Miss*. He didn't *want* anyone). He glanced at her left hand hanging by her side when he should have been smiling and looking into her face.

She noticed where he looked.

Married? Certainly. Divorced, widowed? He hoped. She looked at his left hand as he lifted it to touch her right hand clasped in his. It was a warmer greeting than he gave to strangers. No ring has ever been there he was telling her. But, don't misunderstand, not a crusty bachelor. Still hale. He couldn't squeeze enough ardour into a single gesture.

'Will you follow me?' He pushed open the door of his office and she went in. 'Please sit down.' He held his fingers, almost splayed, barely resisting a waggle, where she could clearly see them, should she have the vaguest interest in this man of late middle age who, untutored in the subtleties of the mating game, was making a fool of himself. He didn't know what he was doing – or cared – such was her effect upon him. He sat behind his desk and felt himself stir.

'Now,' he began, 'shall I tell you a little about us?'

'That would be very helpful, thank you, Mr Tanner.' She held her hands in her lap, her right hand covering her left.

'We're a small but growing school. We have three teachers presently. Mr and Mrs Hughes, who are married. They met at the school, as a matter of fact.'

'How romantic.'

'Yes,' he replied. He could not believe she did not already know of their history. She was from Bridgend. 'So why haven't I seen her before?' he wondered.

'Yes, their subsequent wedding most certainly was.' Subsequent to what? That terrible time. Why did he say that? 'They were married by a good friend of mine, Reverend Elwiss,' a friendship formed during and because of what happened.

'Yes, I know Reverend Elwiss or, at least, I know of him.'

'You do? Do you attend church, Mrs Davies?'

'Sometimes, but usually only for Christmas and Easter, although I used to take my mother more regularly.'

'Reverend Elwiss is always scolding me about attending more often.' So, their views on churchgoing were the same and not to be an obstacle – taking them carefully, one at a time, minor to major – which, if it had been, and she went every Sunday, his answer would have been, 'As often as I can.'

He continued. 'I take the children to the usual festivals, of course, and Reverend Elwiss comes into the school to take assembly quite regularly. He's from Hampshire, you know.'

'Is he? He's a long way from home.'

'Yes, but he's very integrated… now, uh, except for his accent. He gets ribbed about that, in a friendly way, and for supporting the wrong team although, to be fair, he is more of a cricketing man and it is the England *and* Wales Cricket Board, which a lot of people forget, so we're on the same side from a cricketing point of view… yes… and Mr Rees who joined us as a supply teacher and is now with us full time. Our pupil numbers are increasing, you see, and we need someone like yourself to help the teachers with the children, on a part-time basis, with reading groups, working with some of our less able children and helping with playground duty and so on. Do you wish to return to the fray? Is that it?'

'Partly. I used to teach in Maesteg.'

'Yes, I see,' said Mr Tanner, 'yes, so it says here.'

'We lived there for a while but I've moved back recently.'

'That's why I haven't seen you,' he thought.

'And after my husband died, I gave it up.'

A widow, a *widow*. Was she telling him? Her right hand still covered her left.

'I'm sorry to hear that. And what did you do after you stopped teaching?'

'I took some time for myself. Walking, trips away. I read a great deal, I've always enjoyed reading.'

'I used to teach English. That's how I began.'

'Yes, Mr Tanner, so I believe.'

'How did you know that?'

She smiled. 'I did my research. I always like to be prepared.'

He offered her the position.

'I embarrassed myself,' he thought. She was to begin her new job the following week and he meant to be guarded; friendly but professional. There could be no repetition. It had never happened.

He got up from the bench. With the wind at his back, his face was warmer. 'No, this will not wait. Do it today,' he instructed himself. 'Do not delay. Go and see them the moment you're back.' But his repressed longing had been aroused and he wished she was walking with him so that he could confide his dilemma and his stomach began to knot in anticipation. '*No*. I've only just met her. This is ridiculous.'

Eve Guthrie, who had been Eve Brown, but not yet divorced, would not communicate with her husband, even through lawyers, as he languished in Wakefield Prison, convicted of crimes of which she still refused to be told, but certain of his guilt and afraid to admit to herself that he was capable of them. Unlike Alan, of whose innocence she had no doubt, who had been given a sentence that was an eternity in the life of his remaining son and far beyond the mortal horizon of the Rhondda uncles and aunties.

Aled: she wanted him. Eve was galvanised until it became an obsession.

She wrote letters and asked herself, 'How many days is it since I sent the last one? I haven't received a reply.' (And became confused over which letters had been answered). 'Should I write another?'

Nesta replied, patiently and with understanding, regularly if not to all of them, never dismissive, because she knew – but not to admit to Eve – that it was a possible solution and the only one that had occurred to her. Invidious though it was for the boy and for them all. But not for Eve (although it was, if she could but see it. She could not).

Eve's letters asked, in differently worded ways: *How is he? Could I have another photograph? I'm sure he's growing so quickly.* To the purpose of it. *It would be lovely to see him again, it really would.*

She received a progression of black and white photographs which she framed and placed on the sideboard in the order of his growth, the boy rising.

Nesta gave snippets about what he'd said, how he amused them with his antics, the charming boy. But she was guarded. It would have been easy to tempt Eve into doing something foolish. Nesta half expected to see her turn up at the shop one day. Her probation had forbidden it, but that had come to an end and Eve's letters became more frequent and urgent. Time was short and her desperation to prevent a different outcome was the subtext of every word.

It was for more than the boy. She would be trusted again: an overwhelming demonstration of trust. The dark corners of her mindful prison would have some light.

How she would love him and how happy he would be with her; all the love to give she had never been able to bestow on children of her own (who might have had a streak of Roy). She wanted to give love and have it returned. 'Wanted' became 'deserved'. 'I deserve it,' she told herself. 'He needs me.'

She had not been to visit Jean. Nor Gwen who had gone back to Carmarthen. They had been friends. There was nothing left to say that had not been said and, to Jean, nothing that would be understood. So she didn't go, not even to sit with her wordlessly.

Jean would not recover; Alan would not be released. There remained between her and the boy only his ageing relatives.

The houses on Gwyn the Milk's fields were already shabby. They had not been as solidly built as Eve's with its three bedrooms and a box room, a garden big enough for a good-sized lawn and vegetable patch, now with a greenhouse of broken frames leaning in pieces against the fence amongst the weeds. Eve mowed the lawn. That was all.

Now, both to the front and back, she was hemmed in. Once there had been views and space for the boys to play. To either side, in the row of pebble-dashed houses, there were new neighbours. She was afraid they would discover her secret and barely acknowledged them during her comings and goings, except to smile briefly and say, 'Hello, how are you?' Occasionally, the weather.

Eve got a job on the trading estate with a small plant hire company keeping the books. It wasn't far from the factory where Roy and Alan had worked. Some of them recognised her when she walked past in the mornings and afternoons. But what could she say without beginning with an explanation that would be too long and self-pitying?

What had she known? She must have. How could she not have known?

She told herself, 'They worked with Roy. Why hadn't they suspected him of something?' It wasn't just her. 'Alan suspected and he was his friend. He didn't say anything.'

'But you were his *wife*,' hissed the apparition which had acquired Jean's desperate, maddened voice through the letterbox on that awful day when Eve had cowered behind the door.

It was unresolved; its shadow hung over the town. Children didn't walk to school alone and were met at the gates by Mr Tanner.

Doug Protheroe laced his fingers and pursed his lips. His bushy, grey eyebrows twitched in thought. 'Slim pickings,' he said, looking at the draft articles scattered about his desk. 'Disappointing. Couldn't you dig up anything juicer than this lot?'

'It's slow at the moment, boss,' replied *Herald* Andrew.

'When was the last time you spoke to Prosser?'

'Last week.'

'Then speak to him again.'

'I don't think he's got anything.'

'Well, if he hasn't, make it up.' Protheroe swivelled in his chair to look through the dirty window at the river outside. He rubbed a circle in the grime with his finger. The river was low and its banks were bleached. 'I hate this time of year. Everybody *has* to go on holiday.'

Herald Andrew left the office and went downstairs.

Protheroe heard him say, 'Come on Lloydy-boy.'

'And don't come back until you've got something,' he shouted after them. The door slammed shut making the glass rattle as if it was about to fall out and smash in the alley.

Protheroe went back to his meditation of the river, gnarly in his leather chair, as crumpled as a piece of old newspaper.

The post did not arrive before she left for work and, on the day the letter came, it was lying on the mat when she got home. She immediately recognised the handwriting and the Porth postmark. She tore at it and pushed the door closed with her foot.

Dear Eve, thank you for your letter, how it always began. *Would you like to see Aled? We think he's old enough now. Could you come on Saturday afternoon? I believe there is a bus leaving Bridgend at 1.15. Would that be convenient?*

Eve lived the days between in a trembling, sleepless daze. She endured every minute. Her manager at work told her to take more care because some of the invoices she prepared were wrong (he always checked them, not because he didn't trust her, he was just that sort of man). At home she went into rooms and forgot why she was there. In the evenings, she sat in the armchair (where she had cuddled Aled when he was small) and waited. She walked around the garden and tried to mow it but gave up, unable to concentrate. She forgot what hunger was and didn't eat. If it had been more than one Saturday away, she would have made herself ill.

Saturday came. She dressed in her best. Her fingers refused to help with the buttons of her blouse. She got shoe polish on the carpet at the foot of the stairs and didn't clean it up.

At 11.30, she left the house. At 12.00 she was at the bus station. At 12.15 she caught the earlier bus. At least she would be there. She would find somewhere to wait.

When the bus reached the top of the mountain at Trebanog, there was Aled's life in the valley below as she had not known it or been part of for over three long years. The bus began its descent into a foreign country. The sun followed until Nelson's Rock blocked it out. She got out at the bus stop before the one near the shop and went to sit on a dry stone wall that climbed up the mountain's side to where it became sheer and could go no further.

She waited.

Detective Prosser was fond of saying, 'No one tells me what to do, let's be clear about that, shall we?'

'Have you got anything for us?' asked *Herald* Andrew.

They sat at a small, round table in the corner of The Red Lion. Ellis Maynard would normally have been at his usual place at the bar at this time of day but he was detained elsewhere. Except when he made a nuisance of himself, the other customers forgot he existed, like an item of sticky furniture no one sat on.

'No,' said Detective Prosser, sipping his pint which he shouldn't have been drinking on duty.

'Is there anything at all?' asked *Herald* Andrew, 'something we could look out for, something rustling in the undergrowth?'

'No.'

'Come on, Gordon, you've got to give us something.'

Prosser held his glass halfway to his mouth. They both knew it was for show. These men owed him nothing and, one day, they would use the accumulation of small things against him. One word was all it would take (unless Phillips had other ideas: the great conductor) and he would be done for.

'Gordon?'

'Nothing leaps out that would interest you. It's the same old, same old.'

'Couldn't you dream something up – rumours would do; I don't need chapter and verse, do I? Is he cooking something up?'

Prosser's eyes darted and he emptied his glass.

'Another one?'

'Just the one, then.'

'You're going the same way as Jeffries,' thought *Herald* Andrew, as he picked up the empty glasses to take them to the bar. He came back holding three pints in both hands. 'Grab that one,' he told Lloyd.

Promises were easy in the pub.

'You won't ask him,' thought *Herald* Andrew, watching Prosser struggling. 'I know you won't.'

'I can't guarantee anything, mind,' said Prosser.

'No, we realise that, don't we Lloyd?'

Lloyd nodded.

As they left The Red Lion and Prosser headed toward the police station at the top of the hill, *Herald* Andrew said to Lloyd, 'That was a waste of time. We're going to have to dig something up ourselves. Let's try the hospital for starters.'

3

CORPORAL *TOBIAS CARTER* 24
FRANZ CLAUS GEFREITER 22

Salute: 'Good morning Gerhard.'

'Good morning, Howell. Did you sleep well?'

'Not well, no.'

'Unwelcome memories?'

'Yes.'

'You are closer to the end now, Howell. Forgive me for saying it.'

'There's nothing to forgive.'

'They are the cruellest memories, Howell.'

'Yes, they are.'

'The faces of men?'

'Yes.'

'You are afraid you might forget them?'

'I could never forget.'

'No, but you are afraid you might leave this world without honouring them. Your memories honour them,

Howell. Do not be afraid they will slip away when your time comes, they will not; there is more, I promise.' Gerhard smiled, 'Am I not the living proof?'

'I don't know if you're real, Gerhard.'

'I am as real as the men you remember, Howell.'

As Mr Tanner made his way to the vicarage, he rehearsed the words in his mind.

Reverend Elwiss' wife, Deborah, opened the door. 'Raymond,' she exclaimed, 'we weren't expecting you. Come in, come in. Ernest is in his study. Ernest? Raymond's here.'

He appeared at the study door.

'Tea and cake?' she asked.

'Thank you, but not for me.'

'It's no trouble, Raymond.'

'Go on, have some,' urged Reverend Elwiss. 'You know how much you enjoy Deborah's fruit cake. I'd like some.'

'Thank you, then.'

'Is everything alright, Raymond, you look as if you have the weight of the world on your shoulders? Come and sit down. What is it?'

'I'm on my way to see Bryn and Laura and I would like you to come with me. This matter concerns the three of you.'

'Oh?'

Deborah came in carrying a tray of tea and cake.

'Shall we drink our tea first?'

They sat in silence. Mr Tanner didn't touch the fruit cake.

'Come on,' said Reverend Elwiss, 'let's go. Something is troubling you and the fruit cake will still be here when we get back. I'll tell Deborah, she won't mind.'

They walked. 'I'm sorry to drag you out like this,' said Mr Tanner.

'I fear what you're going to tell us, Raymond.'

Mr Tanner sighed.

'I won't try to guess.'

'Please don't,' said Mr Tanner.

Herald Andrew and Lloyd hung about the entrance to Accident and Emergency watching the ambulances coming and going, trying to see if anyone was being taken in.

'There's one,' said *Herald* Andrew. 'Stay here and hide your camera. I'll ask that nurse.'

He sidled over. 'Is it serious?'

She gave him a frosty stare.

'No, I'm sorry, what I mean is, has there been an accident? My friend asked me to come down. He's worried...' he stood on tiptoe trying to see who was on the trolley as it disappeared inside.

'A car accident,' she told him, shutting the ambulance doors.

'Where?'

'I'm sorry, who did you say you were?'

'My friend's worried, that's all.'

'On the bypass.'

'A bad one?'

'You must go to reception, you can't come in this way.'

'Bad accident on the bypass. It might be something,' *Herald* Andrew told Lloyd. He stopped. 'Aye, aye, and what's this then?'

Bryn and Laura's small terraced house was their first home. Laura was pregnant and she was bulging. They were thinking about moving to somewhere with a garden and another bedroom, although Bryn was reluctant (knowing he would have to), as he had bought the house when he first started teaching, before they met. 'This will do for a while though, won't it?' he asked her.

'Only for a little while.'

There was a knock at the door and Laura was surprised to find Mr Tanner and Reverend Elwiss on the step.

They crowded into the front room that overlooked the rugby club. Even with net curtains, they were on show when a game was on. Bryn fetched a chair from the kitchen for Mr Tanner.

'What is it, Raymond?' asked Reverend Elwiss, having put up with his friend's testiness all the way from the vicarage.

Bryn and Laura looked at each other, squashed together on the tiny settee (she was always careful to be on the side of his good ear).

Mr Tanner was unsure of where to begin; his practised words fell by the wayside, as he feared they would. 'Well,' he said, and looked at the carpet. He was not their headmaster today.

'Raymond?' asked Reverend Elwiss, again.

'I did not tell you at the time because I don't believe it would have helped. Knowing who it was,' he said, carefully, 'might have made things worse. Rightly or wrongly, that was the judgement I made at the time.'

'Made what worse, Mr Tanner?' asked Laura.

'I know who attacked you Bryn, Laura. At least, I am almost certain of it.'

Laura's eyes widened. 'But…' she began.

'Please, if you would let me finish, Laura. I took my suspicions to Detective Jeffries. But, to my astonishment, he ignored me, he didn't even want to listen. I could not understand why, I still can't.'

'All this time?' asked Reverend Elwiss.

'You might not know him by name,' said Mr Tanner, 'but you will have seen him about the town and, I believe, seeing him, still a free man and not able to do anything about it, would have made things worse for you both – and, yes, Ernest, all this time.'

Reverend Elwiss let his hands flop onto his knees, 'I didn't mean any criticism, Raymond.'

'Why are you telling us now?' asked Laura.

'He was a former pupil of mine, not one of which I am proud, which is something of an understatement.

I suspected him for various reasons and I confronted him with them. He didn't admit it but he said enough to confirm what I suspected. Do you know Ellis Maynard?' He glanced at Reverend Elwiss, who was tugging at his earlobe.

'Somewhat by reputation – not this reputation, I hasten to add,' said the vicar, 'certainly nothing like this.'

Bryn shook his head.

Laura said, 'He's the one who's always in The Red Lion, isn't he?'

'That is Ellis Maynard, Laura.'

She leaned back and ran her hand over her belly. Bryn placed his hand on hers.

'I am telling you now, in answer to your question, because Maynard's long association with The Red Lion is soon to bring about his end. He has nearly drunk himself to death and is now in hospital waiting for the inevitable. I doubt very much if he knew what he was doing when he attacked you, as I'm sure he would have been worse for wear at that time of day, which does *not* absolve him in the slightest, and, unfortunately, some of the blame must lie with the newspaper.'

'*Some* of it?'

'Well, yes, Laura,' he said, anticipating her, unlike Bryn who would try to make sense of it, 'but the newspaper did not perform the act itself.'

'It might as well have done.'

'You are formidable, Laura,' Mr Tanner thought,

admiring her. He pressed on, wanting to get it said, 'I did not believe, up to now, that it would have served any useful purpose if you had known who he was, knowing, too, that the police had no interest in him and, after so much time, it would have made little difference if they had.'

'Raymond,' said the Reverend, 'it has been a burden for you to carry. That is all I meant.'

'If you had seen him about the town,' said Mr Tanner, 'what could you have done? It would have been salt in the wound, which is perhaps not the best choice of words.'

'Yes,' said Bryn, 'it would have been difficult.'

'It could have stayed a secret, for Bryn's sake,' said Laura.

'No, Laura,' Bryn said, 'Mr Tanner was right to tell us.'

'That isn't what I meant to say. But why couldn't it, if he isn't going to pay for it?'

'I understand,' said Mr Tanner, 'but, in a way, he is paying for it. But, now you know. Perhaps I should have told you sooner.'

'No,' said Bryn, 'you were right. What good would it have done?'

'I debated it many times. I did what I thought was for the best and you were always foremost in my thoughts. But the truth is out now. At least, it is between the four of us. I don't know if anyone else knows.'

'He wasn't on his own,' said Laura.

'Laura?' asked Reverend Elwiss. 'You've never said that. Are you certain?'

‘No. I don’t know. I thought there was someone with him.’

‘That would be important, Laura, if it could be proven.’ said Mr Tanner. ‘It never occurred to me that he did not act alone. But I mean to go and see Maynard in hospital and have him tell me the truth, if he will, if he can.’ He looked at Reverend Elwiss. ‘Will you come with me, Ernest? He might have need of you.’

‘What a dreadful symmetry…’ said the Reverend, shaking his head, remembering the wind in the trees as he crouched over Bryn’s unmoving body… *stop*. ‘Of course, Raymond.’

‘I would like to come too,’ said Bryn.

Laura turned to him, ‘Bryn?’

‘Yes, Laura. I can feel that. He’s kicking, or she is.’

‘Bryn, no, you can’t.’

‘Oh, my *pride*,’ Reverend Elwiss inwardly scolded himself. ‘That is truly admirable and generous of you, Bryn, the Christian thing to do.’

When Eve shifted her weight, the stones on the dry stone wall rocked and sounded hollow. Nelson’s Rock hung over her mightily. The mountains made emptiness vast and, on the other side of the valley, the sheep were white droplets on the plunging slopes. The houses trickled down to the river far below in the deepest of the V as if they were stones in a culvert. Her thighs were cold. The hour had almost passed. She tipped herself off the precarious wall.

Outside the shop, she hesitated. But Aled was inside. Her heart was beating out of her chest and she was shaking. The bell over the door jingled as she pushed it open. There were counters on all sides. To her right, next to the till, Idris sat on a stool with a pencil in his hand, adding up; to her left, Emlyn was slicing ham; facing her was Howell, with his hands on the countertop, as if he'd been waiting. They stopped what they were doing. It reminded her of the court.

'Hello, Eve,' said Howell. '*Nesta, Delia*,' he called. '*Eve's here*.' He lifted up the hatch. 'Go through.'

Nesta appeared in the doorway with Delia behind her.

She followed them down the passage to the back room.

'Please, sit down,' said Nesta.

Eve sat in the armchair next to the window.

'How are you?' Nesta asked.

'I'm well, thank you, and how are you?'

'We're all well.'

Delia went into the kitchen. There was the sound of cups and saucers being arranged. They didn't speak until Delia came back with a pot of tea.

Nesta said, 'The men have to mind the shop.'

'Yes,' said Eve, 'I understand.'

'Milk?'

Eve sipped, holding the saucer, balanced on the arm of the chair.

'Aled's watching television in the other room,' said Nesta.

Eve looked over her shoulder but the door was closed.

'Have you been to see Jean?' Nesta asked.

'Not recently. The last time I saw her, she didn't seem to understand what I was saying and I think it upset her.'

'She hears everything we say,' said Delia, vigilantly.

'Perhaps it is better she does not,' said Nesta, looking closely at Eve, 'until she is fully recovered.'

'*When* she is fully recovered,' Delia corrected her.

'I am surprised you haven't been to see her more often,' said Nesta.

'I didn't want to upset her again and there was no news.'

'No, there is no news to speak of.' Delia had that familiar alarm in her eyes, a concoction of powerlessness.

'Howell drives us down to see her on Sundays,' said Nesta. 'Not every Sunday, but most. Not all of us, not in that old van,' thinking of the never-ending journey to Pembroke and back, 'and somebody has to look after Aled. But I don't think he'll be driving for much longer so we'll have to go down on the bus.'

'Yes, I can imagine that would be difficult, every Sunday.'

'Would you like some more tea?' asked Delia.

'No thank you.' Eve's eyes strayed once more to the door, which she couldn't see without moving her head.

'I'll fetch him,' said Nesta.

The shy, beautiful boy, twisting his fingers, stared curiously at Eve, who was speechless, holding back tears.

'I don't suppose you remember Auntie Eve?' Nesta asked him.

Auntie? Aled looked at Nesta quizzically. 'No,' he said.

'You wouldn't, cariad,' said Eve, 'you were too little.'

'Why are you crying?' he asked.

'I'm not crying.'

'Yes, you are.'

'It's just so lovely to see you.'

'Can I go back and watch television now, Auntie Nesta?'

'Yes, go on,' she smiled.

'Can I?' asked Eve.

Aled was lying on the floor, waving his feet in the air, with his chin in both hands. He took no notice of them. Eve did not take her eyes off him; Nesta watched Eve.

She was there for an hour, until Aled finished watching television and went upstairs without saying anything.

'When can I see him again?' Eve asked, as they showed her through the uncles in the shop.

Politely, they all said 'Goodbye' and Nesta thanked her for coming.

After Eve had left, Nesta said to Delia, 'What other solution is there?'

The precious boy who needed to be closer to his mother and might, one day, bring her back to know them.

'Good afternoon,' said *Herald* Andrew, blithely, as if to say, '*I'm only doing my job.*'

Flash.

'One for the album,' smiled *Herald* Andrew. He followed them into the hospital reception. Lloyd trotted after him, hurriedly changing the film.

Bryn turned and stood in their way.

'Alright,' said *Herald* Andrew, holding up his hands. 'We'll wait outside.'

They went up the stairs and turned toward the wards.

'Aye, aye,' *Herald* Andrew said, half to himself, 'something in my water… what ward are they after then?'

Ellis Maynard was a fleshless cage of bones with his skin sagging over it like a yellowing canvas. Two fingers of his right hand, on the end of a stick-like wrist poking from a blue pyjama jacket, were livid with nicotine. His half-closed eyes, chafed red raw from rubbing, were watery slits at the bottom of deep sockets, darkened, like tiny calderas. His breathing rasped and his parched lips fluttered. His pupils turned slowly sideways to look at them. He did not see a vicar, a headmaster and a teacher: he saw demons.

'Oh,' said Mr Tanner.

Maynard tried to lift his poisoned fingers but they would not.

Reverend Elwiss was repelled but, somewhere deep within this living cadaver, was a soul not yet departed.

Bryn felt pity. 'Perhaps we shouldn't have come,' he whispered.

'Yes, we should, Bryn,' said Mr Tanner, 'he has no one else. This is not the boy I remember, whatever his faults. It is not what he could have been.'

Reverend Elwiss bent over and placed his hand on Maynard's forehead. 'Ellis, can you hear me? I am Reverend Elwiss.'

Maynard's throat clicked.

'Ellis? Can you hear me?'

He could hardly make out Reverend Elwiss' features, but his collar was white and he knew what it meant. He almost emptied with relief and his eyes drifted. Parading at the foot of his bed was everyone he had ever wronged. They crowded around. Maynard said, in a last voice, 'I hit him over the head with a bottle and pushed him into the river.'

Reverend Elwiss looked at Mr Tanner. 'Does he know what he's saying?'

'I don't know. Does he mean you, Bryn?'

'Bryn wasn't in the river,' said Reverend Elwiss. 'Ellis?' He clutched Maynard's hand a little tighter. 'Who, Ellis? Who did you hit over the head?'

'Jeffries.'

The parade faded away. Jeffries was the last to leave.

'Jeffries?' Reverend Elwiss looked at Mr Tanner.

Maynard closed his eyes. For a moment, they thought he had died but then his breathing came back.

'What should we do now?' asked Bryn.

'We should leave,' said Mr Tanner.

'I will come to see him again,' said the Reverend. 'I must.'

They departed from his bed in silence and it was not until they were in the fresh air that Bryn said, 'I would not have wished that on anyone.'

'Ellis Maynard or Detective Jeffries?' asked Reverend Elwiss.

'Either, both of them.'

'Neither would I,' said Mr Tanner, 'but we will have to take this to Sergeant Phillips. Detective Jeffries has a family and the circumstances of Maynard's confession will carry some weight in law.'

'Were we meant to hear it?' asked Reverend Elwiss. 'I have a dreadful feeling that we were guided here, but I do not feel God's hand in it.'

'God didn't tell you, Ernest, I did,' said Mr Tanner, unfairly singling out his representative because divine intervention was long overdue.

'Yes, you did' said the vicar, stung, 'but not what to expect. That you could not have known.' He paused. 'On the lips of dying men the truth.'

Herald Andrew and Lloyd were waiting.

'Try to ignore them, Bryn,' said Mr Tanner.

Herald Andrew told Lloyd, 'No more photos, there'll be plenty of time for that.'

'Will you come back to the vicarage?' asked Reverend Elwiss, who didn't want to walk on his own.

'I must go home to Laura,' said Bryn.

'I'll come back with you, Ernest,' said Mr Tanner, wanting to make amends, and needing company too.

'We'll finish the fruit cake,' said the Reverend. 'We can finish the fruit cake.'

'It's this way, Ernest.'

'Where am I going? I'm sorry, I don't seem to know where I'm going.'

'Do you have anything a bit stronger than tea?' asked Mr Tanner.

'What?' Reverend Elwiss frowned. 'Oh… yes, somewhere.'

4

PRIVATE ELGAN DAVIS 17
ERIC DRUCKER FELDWEBEL 25

'Here we are,' said Howell, 'I've found my old stamp book.' He put it on the bed.

Aled was underwhelmed. The book was dark green, old-fashioned looking with *The Model Postage Stamp Album* printed on the cover.

Howell opened it. There were black and white pictures of what stamps to collect. There were not many real stamps. In the section headed *Great Britain,* Howell pointed to a dirty brownish-red one and said, 'That's a Penny Red and, here, is a Two Penny Blue. They're rare and quite valuable.'

But they had none of the living colour of Idris' stamps, the scenes of faraway places.

Aled said, 'I like Uncle Idris' stamps better.'

Howell laughed. 'I told you, he's the real stamp collector, not me. I'll put it back then.'

'Who's that man?' asked Aled.

Gwen Evans caught the bus and then the train and then the bus again. It stopped outside Cardiff Prison and she got off, along with most of the other passengers.

She tried to imagine what a prison would be like, but she had nothing to compare it to, so she was terrified. He had refused to let her come to see him. If he had, she might have been used to it by now (if that was possible). He wrote: *Don't come and see me, Gwen. Not here, please.* But, now, he had no choice and, as Nesta had summoned Eve, it was about Aled.

Gwen waited outside with the other visitors from the bus. She hadn't realised who they were. She felt looked at and ashamed. She was ready to explain. She wasn't one of them. But they didn't speak; they didn't bat an eye. Wives, girlfriends, mothers, fathers, brothers, sisters, uncles, aunties, friends, fellow conspirators, petty miscreants and victims of absence and poverty. No children. Every story was unique, a special case. Except the tired ones who were beaten down. They were all caught in the mesh of blood, loyalty, plans and vengeance. Prison diaspora. What, who, could they blame? Circumstances, bad luck or the man waiting inside?

A bell rang and the doors opened. The faces of the guards, warders – whatever they were called – were impassive but watchful, not caring who or what she was or what her story might be.

Gwen would never forget the smell that met her, of noxious humanity, dirty water and wet mops, industrial polish and disinfectant, the tang of metal; the hard sounds and flat echoes, the sudden voices from long corridors, keys rattling on chains and the remote booms of cell doors closing.

A wan light came like sleet through barred windows high on the walls. The ceiling lights were on, their bulbs too weak to cast any shadows. The prisoners waited at regularly spaced tables with faces the colour of papier mâché.

He was thinner. He wore a dishonourable uniform that was not a soldier's. He had penal hallmarks stamped into him, *1966;* he had been placed beyond reach and transformed into its product, the man she had not seen for three years.

She sat down. 'Here I am, Alan,' she said.

He stared at her and began speaking, rocking slightly, pausing at the end of each sentence as if he was counting them off like beads with his fingers and would not stop until they were all said. Behind his eyes a tumult raged. 'Mr Tanner comes to see me, once a month or so. He brought Reverend Elwiss with him last time. Even Dewi Jones has been too, on the quiet, you mustn't say, will you? Jean's uncles have been. They tell me about Aled. He doesn't know I exist and I don't want him to know. There might come a time when he will have to. I hope so, when he's older and I don't suppose it will be long before he starts asking what's happened to his father and mother. Jean is the same as ever, I am told. Other than that, the days go by and the weeks and the months. That's my news.'

'What about me?'

He took a deep breath and let it go. 'I'm sorry. I know it was a mistake but I couldn't bear for you to see me like this. Please don't start blaming me, you, of all people.' The undemonstrative man she had known fought to contain himself. 'I was wrong, for me and for you.'

She smiled like a break in the clouds, a plot of sunshine on green fields. 'Of course, I don't blame you,' she said.

'Thank you.' He slid his hand across the table.

She closed her eyes when he touched her.

He pushed the cleft of his thumb into hers and stroked her wrist.

'You shouldn't be in here,' she said.

'But I am. I can't think about it, so I don't and you mustn't either.'

'It breaks my heart.'

'No, Gwen, please don't. It will make it worse.'

'There hasn't been anyone and, then, not since Geraint.'

'But there could have been. You don't have to tell me, I've got no claim on you. I never did.'

'We don't have to talk about that,' she said, 'just believe me when I say it.'

'Thank you,' he said, and turned away.

'It's true.'

'Well,' he said, quickly wiping his cheeks of recalcitrant tears. 'Well.'

She pretended not to notice. 'You've lost weight.'

'It's not difficult but, I can assure you, I haven't been trying to.'

'I won't say you look better for it, not dressed like that, anyway.'

'Thank you. I try to count my blessings.'

'It's about Aled, isn't it?'

'About you, too, Gwen, but, yes, it is. Jean's Auntie Nesta writes to me about him. I don't know whether I want her to or not, I think it makes it worse sometimes but, now, she has a proposal, if you can call it that. I understand what she's saying and they will decide what's best for him. I know they won't ignore me and I don't want to make it any more difficult for them than it already is. But he is still my son, Gwen.'

'What did she say?'

'They're getting old and they're worried about looking after him.'

'There was always going to come a time, Alan.'

'That time is upon us. Nesta has left it late, not intentionally, I think, but because I don't think she knew what to do. Aled's going to have to start school in September so, if they don't do something now, in two or three years' time, he might not have anywhere to go, other than I don't know where.'

'What do they want to do?'

'It's what Nesta wants to do. I'm not so sure the rest of them agree. She wants to ask Eve to take him. Nesta thinks she'd be willing, more than willing I would think.'

'*Eve*?' Gwen cried, in surprise.

'Nesta wants my permission, not that she needs it, but my blessing, yes, she wants that, and deserves it, I suppose, if I agree. She didn't put it that way, but that's what she's asking for. But there's something else, which is at the bottom of it. If he's with Eve, he'll be closer to his mother and, if she sees him, Nesta thinks it might bring Jean back to herself and he will come to know his real mother. They're all blind when it comes to Jean.'

'You know Eve won't want to bring that about, Alan, and Jean's reaction to Eve with Aled? I couldn't begin to imagine.'

'Nesta wasn't there to see to see Jean during the worst of it, was she? The only Jean she knows is the one she remembers before and the one she sees today. Whatever Eve did, Nesta thinks she only did it for him, which it's difficult to deny.'

'It's a lot more complicated than that, Alan.'

'I know it is.'

'I don't know what the solution is, Alan, but it's not Eve. She was my friend, she still is, but that was before it all happened. She was almost as badly affected as Jean in a way.'

'I don't want to lose what hope I have of him ever being a part of my life, and part of Jean's too, if that's ever going to be possible. But with Eve, I will be giving him up forever. She will disappear with him, I know she will. It will be as if he never existed. I have lost one son and I can't lose him as well. Is that selfish, Gwen?'

'None of this is your fault, Alan. Or Jean's, or Eve's.'

'No, it's not, but it's what we're faced with.'

'It will be put right, Alan.'

'How? Gwen, please understand, I must ask. I can't think of any other way. What about you? The little brother Huw never had; Jack and Huw in one little boy?'

All she had to do was catch the bus, then the train and then the bus to go home to Carmarthen and never write to him or answer another letter; and he, desperate not to believe that her silence was a refusal, would write another until, finally, he gave up and time erased her only visit to a prison to see someone she once knew, where he was left to rot from the inside out. And she would continue to live in the West Wales enclave, a quiet life of green fields, where the sounds of Cardiff Prison could not be heard, where the smell of it could never reach, a tidy woman whose son had been murdered, a golden-haired, six-year-old boy who would have laughed and made audiences laugh and cry with him, and her memories of Geraint whom the ground had called and broken her heart.

And Eve would have what she wanted.

When Gwen left the prison, she ignored the guards, warders, wardens, whatever they were called, and didn't notice the other visitors leaving at the same time. She carried with her a prisoner's troubles: to enact his wishes, to solve his problems, to make good what he had left behind. She didn't speak; she didn't bat an eye.

She caught the bus to Bridgend.

The three Welsh pillars of natural order, police, school, church, were being drawn together again by the unfortunate past, bound in harmony by the relentlessness of the law, its letter and spirit. Mr Tanner fervently believed it should be a haven for the wronged, a protector of the innocent and a fearless pursuer of the guilty. They must heed it. 'So why do I feel like this?' he asked himself. 'But what else can we do; where else can we go?'

Mr Tanner glanced at Reverend Elwiss who hadn't said a word since they met outside the school and walked into the town.

'We're here,' said Mr Tanner. He opened the door for Reverend Elwiss and they went in.

'We have important information concerning the disappearance of Detective Darren Jeffries,' Mr Tanner told the policeman behind the desk, 'and we would like to see Sergeant Phillips, if he is available?'

'Please take a seat,' said the policeman, 'and I will tell him you're here.'

They sat. Half an hour went by. 'I'm going to be late for assembly,' said Mr Tanner, looking at his watch. 'Bryn will have to take it.'

'Does Bryn know we're here?' asked Reverend Elwiss. His first words in an hour.

'Yes, he does.'

'Perhaps he should have come with us?'

'Assemblies, aside, Ernest, that would have been too much to ask. First the hospital to face the man who almost took his life and now here, where he was questioned about… where he was questioned.'

'Yes, I'm sorry. It was thoughtless of me.'

'I think you should tell Sergeant Phillips,' said Mr Tanner, 'the vicar administering to a dying man.'

'I know,' said Reverend Elwiss, 'that's what I've been thinking about.'

'I didn't mean that I thought you wouldn't. So long as we get the story straight, as it were, difficult as it is to believe.'

'If only it was a story? But it's not,' the Reverend sighed.

'No, it's not. How *long* have we been waiting?'

'When we are done here, I'm going back to the hospital.'

'Sergeant Phillips might want to come with you.'

'Will he? I hadn't thought of that. Ellis Maynard is beyond the reach of even Sergeant Phillips.'

'One would think.'

'I must see Ellis without a policeman present,' said Reverend Elwiss. 'Whatever he has done, it is forgiveness and consolation he needs now.'

'Mmm.'

It was Dewi Jones who appeared. 'Sergeant Phillips will see you,' he told them.

'Dewi,' exclaimed Mr Tanner, glad to see his former pupil, 'how are you?'

Dewi tried to smile, but his expression was strained, as if he wanted to say more but couldn't.

Mr Tanner frowned. 'Dewi?'

'Please this way.' Dewi held open the door and looked over their heads as they passed. He showed them into the interview room.

The chipped table, the rickety chairs, the big ashtray, the scuffed floor, the faded walls: Gwyn, Alan, Bryn, Roy, Eve, who had sat, in their turn, where they were sitting. Opposite, Detective Jeffries had pushed the chair back on two legs and waited for an answer.

Except for the muffled workings of the police station all around them, there was silence.

Then Sergeant Phillips was black in the doorway. He smoothed his moustache with his thumbs and pulled his tunic straight. He regarded them from beneath the peak of his cap, sharp as a guillotine.

Dewi stood in the corner with his hands behind his back. A muscle twitched in his cheek.

Mr Tanner could not make him meet his eye. 'I will catch you on your own when I have the chance,' he thought, and turned to Sergeant Phillips.

His peaked cap threatened them like a plague's beak.

He pulled his leather gloves tight over his knuckles as he sat down. He was as cold as a stone in winter. 'Darren Jeffries?' It was a question.

'Yesterday…' began Reverend Elwiss.

'Yesterday?'

'Yes, we would have come yesterday. We should have come yesterday, concerning a matter so serious.'

'If it was so serious, why not?'

'We had been to the hospital to visit a dying man.'

'Ellis Maynard,' said Sergeant Phillips.

'Yes, Ellis Maynard,' the Reverend said, uncertainly. 'Mr Tanner, Bryn Hughes and myself.'

'The teacher. Why isn't he here?'

'He is at school, taking assembly,' said Mr Tanner.

'Ellis Maynard is dying, Sergeant Phillips,' said Reverend Elwiss.

'He is not dead yet,' said Sergeant Phillips.

'You know?'

Sergeant Phillips didn't reply.

'Are you aware of his involvement in the death of Detective Darren Jeffries?'

'The disappearance of Darren Jeffries,' Sergeant Phillips corrected him.

'It is more than that,' said the vicar.

'Is it?'

'Ellis Maynard confessed to killing Detective Jeffries.'

'Darren Jeffries was not a detective at the time of his disappearance.'

'He confessed to killing Darren Jeffries during a fight when he hit him over the head with a bottle and pushed him into the river.'

'The river was searched and no body was found.'

'It is a deathbed confession, Sergeant Phillips, and possibly one of the man's last acts on this earth. There is no reason to doubt what he is saying is true.'

'The word of Ellis Maynard?'

'But he is *dying*, Sergeant Phillips. I will attest to his confession.'

'Does he know he's dying?'

'Yes,' said Reverend Elwiss. 'I do not believe he would have confessed if he did not think he was dying.'

'It might be too late to bring him to justice,' said Mr Tanner, 'but surely Detective Jeffries' family will want to know the truth? Do they hope he is still alive? Surely they have a right to know?'

'I have told you, he was not a detective when he disappeared. You have only Maynard's word that Jeffries is dead and there is nothing in Maynard's word that can be taken as real or true.' Sergeant Phillips stood up. 'I know his mind.' He ran his thumbs down his moustache and pulled his tunic straight. 'Jones,' he told Constable Dewi, 'please see these gentlemen out.'

'But Sergeant Phillips?' Reverend Elwiss protested. It was too late, he had gone.

'Dewi?' asked Mr Tanner.

Constable Dewi held open the door and showed them

into reception. 'Thank you Mr Tanner, Reverend Elwiss,' he said, and turned away.

'Dewi?' but the door had swung closed.

'I don't understand,' said Reverend Elwiss, appalled.

'We should talk outside,' said Mr Tanner.

'I don't understand,' said Reverend Elwiss, as they walked up Cardigan Street. 'Why must he behave like this? It was as if he didn't think it was important. A man's *life*?'

'It is possible he might have information of which we are not aware,' said Mr Tanner, searching for an explanation and failing.

'But he was not there to hear Ellis' confession. I am a Minister of the Church, a *Minister*.' He stopped on the pavement outside the ironmonger's and held out his hands. 'He can't just *dismiss* what I say. He has an obligation.'

'Does he?'

'Yes, he does, Raymond, I am telling you, he *does*.'

'I'm sure you're right, Ernest. But I don't think he dismissed what you told him.'

'What then? Why are you defending him? These are the ends of men's lives. I am their refuge, their interpreter. He cannot *choose* to ignore what I say.'

'I am not defending him, I'm only saying he must have other information. What else could it be?'

'But I am a Minister, a *Minister*. My office is not to be dismissed in this manner. It is not for me personally, it is for my office. These are men's lives.'

'I know, Ernest.'

They walked. The Reverend would not stop shaking his head. 'And the attack on Bryn? Is that of no consequence either? Why didn't we tell him that Ellis Maynard did that too?'

'I told Detective Jeffries and it's too late to prove it now.'

'Who didn't listen.'

'Calm down, Ernest. We must see what action Sergeant Phillips takes.'

'But, Raymond, he didn't acknowledge what we told him was of any value whatsoever.'

'Ernest?'

'Does my word carry no weight; does he not respect what I represent, my judgement, my training, my *Ministry*, the *Sacrament*?'

'Ernest?'

'But does he?'

'Ernest? I don't know why.'

Reverend Elwiss threw up his hands again.

'Ernest, calm down, please. There is always the possibility that, in his confusion, Ellis was mistaken. It would be understandable that, in the absence of any other evidence, Sergeant Phillips takes that view. It is possible, Ernest, that he may be reluctant to inform Darren Jeffries' family based on the word of a dying alcoholic.'

'If that is what he believes, Raymond, then he should have explained it to us, but he did *not* have any cause to disrespect my office. He *always* disrespects my office.'

'Ernest, I don't have an answer for you.'

'I am going to the hospital.'

'I should be in school.'

They parted without another word. After a few yards, Mr Tanner stopped and looked round, but Reverend Elwiss had already disappeared down Brynna Road toward the hospital. 'I should have agreed with him,' he thought. 'What was the point of arguing? He was right.'

It was morning break. Laura was on playground duty, her loose dress shaped around her bump in the breeze. 'Mrs Davies is waiting for you,' she told him.

Ellis Maynard was not conscious. He was more shrunken under the single sheet that covered him, as if it was ready to be drawn over his head. He had yellowed more. His stubble was like burnt gorse.

Reverend Elwiss quietly pulled up a chair and held Maynard's hand. He prayed over him in a low but audible voice, hoping his words would be heard and have some meaning: '*May his Soul and the Souls of the departed, through the mercy of God, rest in peace. Amen*.' He looked up and said, with feeling, 'I will be with you, Ellis,' as if he meant to defy Sergeant Phillips.

Maynard had slipped into a coma. If his mind was elsewhere, if the two could be separated, body and soul, before death, it remained a secret.

He watched Maynard's face.

A nurse came, saw, wrinkled her nose and left.

5

PRIVATE ALFRED EVANS 20
FREDERICK ENGEL UNTEROFFIZER 22

Salute: 'Good morning, Gerhard.'

'Good morning, Howell. I think you would like to leave the binoculars to the boy?'

'If you will let me, but not as they are.'

'They are yours, Howell, to do with them what you wish. But take off the lens caps and let what is in them drain away into the light. We must not let him see what is there.'

Howell took off the lens caps and laid the binoculars on their side.

'We will be able to watch over him.' Gerhard smiled. 'It is not strict military procedure, but which lens do you want, Howell? The left or the right?'

'The left, if I must choose, it's my better eye.'

'Then I will take the right. It doesn't matter which, the view is the same.'

‘I wish I could see him now.’

‘You will, when the binoculars are empty. We will be able to see him together.’

‘Prosser, come with me,’ Sergeant Phillips told him.

They got into his big, black car and it purred through the town, through Coychurch, and stopped next to a field in Pencoed. There was a small wood at the far end.

Sergeant Phillips pulled his gloves tight over his knuckles. He got out of the car, smoothed his moustache with his thumbs and yanked his tunic straight.

‘Prosser?’

‘Sir?’

‘I want this field and that wood searched. Every inch.’

‘What are we looking for?’

‘Search them and tell that reporter what you’re doing.’

‘But tell him what, Sir?’

‘To do as he is told.’ Sergeant Phillips got back into his big, black car and it floated away.

Prosser was left standing next to the farm gate. It was a big field. There were cows and cow pats. The wood was dark and solemn.

Vans of policemen began arriving, some of them with dogs. They had their instructions and began walking in a line, prodding the ground with sticks, toward the trees where the secret must be because nothing could hide in the expanse of cow-munched grass. Unless it was buried. The cows moved slowly out of the way and watched, dumbly, their jaws moving sideways and up and down.

'We're searching a field in Pencoed,' said Detective Prosser.

'What for?' asked *Herald* Andrew.

'I can't tell you. It's police business.'

'I need to know if we're going to come down there.'

'You need to know what I tell you,' said Prosser.

'He told you to tell us didn't he?'

'No. I'm doing you a favour.'

'Of course you are,' thought *Herald* Andrew, and put the phone down. 'Come on Lloydy-boy. We're being asked for.'

'It was the right thing to do?' Nesta told her sister.

'If you think so,' Delia replied.

'Howell thinks it is.'

'He hasn't said anything.'

'He doesn't have to. I know he does.'

Aled was curled up in the armchair in the back room under a rug, snug over his toes, still in his pyjamas. There was no fire in the grate, but the butter was where it always was, on the hearth.

Nesta and Delia watched him from the kitchen as they made breakfast. It was a cool but prescient July morning in the valley and the sky over the mountains was blue. The shadow of Nelson's Rock was slowly retreating and, soon, the sun would flood in.

'It breaks my heart,' said Nesta, 'I wish I was twenty

years younger.'

'Or thirty,' said Delia.

'Twenty, thank you,' said Nesta, her upper lip wrinkling. 'Long enough to see him off into the world as a young man. But if Jean could be herself again? He will be the best tonic she could ever have to bring her back to us. Then she could be his mother again.'

'If Eve gives him up,' said Delia, compressing her lips back at her.

Nesta stopped cutting the loaf. 'Why on earth wouldn't she want to see the boy with his mother again? She wants what is best for Aled.'

'Yes, I'm sure she does,' said Delia.

Howell came into the kitchen and went straight through without a word. The sun rose behind the outside toilet as he climbed the stone steps, straightening one leg at a time, pushing at them with his hands.

Sunlight stabbed like a magician's swords through the empty knotholes and skewered him as he sat. In his bedroom, it found its way, inching down the window, into the objective lenses of the binoculars and lit what it saw there for the first time in over fifty years. The cleansing began.

But Howell could not stay in the toilet all morning. Nesta was waiting.

'Was there anything from Alan in the post?' he asked her.

'No, nothing yet.'

'There can be no plans until we have, Nesta. You've rushed me and made up your mind before you listened, haven't you, as always?'

'There's no time, Howell. We have to find a solution before he starts school.'

He sighed. 'You see?'

'If it wasn't for me, Howell Morgan,' she snorted, 'nothing would get done.'

'I'll be in the shop,' he told her.

Herald Andrew had one foot on the bottom rung of the farm gate. Lloyd took some scene-setting photos of anything that could be considered a feature, but he couldn't find the right exposure to see into the trees.

Detective Prosser walked behind the line of advancing policemen and tried, unconvincingly, to be supervisory. He poked at the occasional clump of grass with his toe, avoiding the cow pats until, with one eye on Lloyd's camera, he slid straight through one and landed on his backside.

Flash.

Sergeant Philips' big, black car reappeared.

'Here we go,' said *Herald* Andrew.

Detective Prosser was trying to get the greenish sludge off his hands by rubbing them on the grass. It smeared up his sleeves. He looked up, with an expression of disgust and glutinously dripping fingers.

Sergeant Phillips put on his peaked cap, smoothed

his moustache and rested his gloved hands on the roof of the car. He said, 'I know his mind' and his eyes swept like a shadow over the field and far wood, over his men, bowed into their work, and the dogs straining at their leashes.

Flash. Tomorrow's front page.

Sergeant Phillips got back into his big, black car and left like velvet nap.

'I know what they're looking for,' said *Herald* Andrew. 'Things are looking up, Lloydy-boy. This'll keep us busy.'

Prosser held out his arms and shook his head.

Eve persuaded herself that events were imminent and her expectation became unbearable. She decorated his bedroom-to-be. She bought tins of beans which used to be his favourite. She went into town and looked for school clothes and found out the cost of new shoes. She stood outside the gates of the school and watched the children playing. She imagined meeting him there at going-home time and taking him to the park before tea. She caught the bus to Porthcawl and walked along the prom where she would bring him on Saturday afternoons to build sandcastles on the beach at Rest Bay. She had tea at Alphonsi's where Mario was reading the newspaper, drinking coffee from a tiny cup and smoking. When she brought Aled, they would see he was hers. She improved on the life his father and mother would have given him.

But she did not walk on the dunes over the buried city, past the remains of the castle to Kenfig Pool's clear waters where the luminous tresses of the girls swayed in the depths. It was where Jack might be. It would be impossible to explain and she could not face Jack. Aled was what was left and his name would be Guthrie, as it had been in Devon when he was eighteen months old. He was nearly five now. That was far enough; he would be nearly five in perpetuity.

She watched the clock in the front room as the days and nights went by, waiting for Nesta to ask her to come to take him away.

'Mrs Davies, welcome,' said Mr Tanner. His intention to be cordial but professional crumbled immediately. She was *luminous*.

'Thank you, Mr Tanner.' Her eyes shone and it could not be mistaken.

'Is she trying to bewitch me?' he thought.

'Mr Hughes has shown me around,' she said. 'It's a very nice school, a much bigger building than my old school in Maesteg, which was lovely but a bit cramped. I think children need space. Small spaces can oppress their young minds, or so I believe.'

'I couldn't agree more, Mrs Davies,' said Mr Tanner.

'I've been looking forward to starting, I must say.'

'Have you? There's plenty to do,' said Mr Tanner. 'All hands to the pump. Why don't you begin by reading to Form Two? They're not too boisterous.'

'Oh, I don't mind boisterous. It shows character.'

Intriguing. 'Do you think so?' he smiled, wondering how to keep her to himself for longer. He looked at his watch, hoping there was time. There wasn't. Form Two was waiting.

The children's wide eyes absorbed her. If they had been older, they might have noticed the way his hand played at the small of her back as he ushered her into the class, or the way she tilted her head slightly *so* when she looked at him through her lashes – quite frequently – or the way he continually glanced in her direction as he introduced her, beaming (which he never did). Who was this amiable headmaster they had never seen before?

They liked Mrs Davies straightaway because, with childish intuition, they knew she would not want to disappoint him by sending one of them to stand outside his office. They would be able to get away with a lot with Mrs Davies.

When Mr Tanner had finished his fulsome introduction, he dawdled at the door as she picked up a book and, with a parting flutter, opened it at page one.

In Form Three, Mr Hughes, deaf ear to the blackboard, brooked no nonsense in his measured way and, on the other side, in Form One, Mrs Hughes was teaching sums. They would have been astonished, amused, bemused (and a bit pleased) at what had just happened in Form Two.

But, as Mr Tanner walked down the corridor to his office, folding his hands behind his back, the worm began to gnaw again, a sharp pain of doubt, widening. He wanted to sit in the corner of the classroom, to offer unneeded moral support and breathe the sweeter air.

'Good evening, Mr Topliss,' he said to the caretaker, who was mending a window latch in the hall.

'Good evening, Headmaster?'

'Pardon? Oh, good morning, Mr Topliss.'

'Good morning, Headmaster.'

Mr Tanner remembered the boys playing British Bulldog, that one and only time he had allowed it, all afternoon and never calling them in until their mothers were waiting at the gates. Most of those boys, and the girls who had watched while they sat on the grass, had gone on to other schools (many to the Grammar School, of which he was proud). Most, but not all.

Later, when the school day was done, he sat alone in her empty classroom and watched the chalk dust waltz as his thoughts tilted back and fore: what they might do together, if he dare ask; to the debilitating suspicion that was inexorably rising. The closer its meaning came, the more he dreamed of confiding in her.

'I ought to go round and see Ernest,' he thought, but he couldn't face it, not today.

Laura was still resentful and he couldn't find the right moment to tell her. She went to bed and, in the morning, neither would speak first. Maynard's confession weighed on him all day.

But, as they walked home that evening, she blurted,

'Why *did* you go and see him?'

'I had to,' Bryn said. 'The Reverend thinks I went to forgive him, but I didn't. I wanted him to know that we had got on with our lives. I wanted him to see that.'

'Did he?'

'No, he was pitiful. I don't think he knew I was even there.'

She said, 'He wasn't worth the effort.'

The days she had waited at Bryn's bedside, listening to the machines, willing on each tantalising bleep as they delved like sonar pings for an echo of his continuance, and returning one by one by one, to confirm his life still was, but drifting in the deep, cold, deep.

Then *flash, flash,* the monstrous intrusion of that newspaper and that missing detective who had been so brave he had run away. Let Ellis Maynard die. *Alone.*

'Let the vicar think you went there to forgive him,' she said.

'I'm going to,' said Bryn. 'There's nothing else to say now.'

'It will make a good sermon.'

'That's not fair, Laura.'

'I know… I'm sorry.'

'A sermon but not much of an obituary.' He would not tell her about *The Herald* waiting outside. 'Two or three sentences, barely a paragraph. Not much at all for a life.'

'But more than he deserves. It wasn't worth you going, Bryn.'

'As it turned out, not for me, no.'

'Who else then? The vicar?'

'Yes, and for Maynard himself.'

'Why? I don't understand?'

Now he told her. 'He confessed to Reverend Elwiss that he killed Detective Jeffries by hitting him over the head with a bottle and pushing him into the river.'

'*What*… Is that *true*?'

'He's dying, Laura. I think it must be.'

'Bryn? He almost *killed* you too. Was he trying to kill you?'

'But he didn't.'

'But a murderer, Bryn? A murderer?'

'Mr Tanner didn't know what Maynard was going to say about Jeffries. He was only concerned for you and me. He was right, wasn't he? It puts an end to it. There can be no more wondering. Reverend Elwiss and Mr Tanner went to see Sergeant Phillips this morning.'

'Is that where he was?'

'And when Maynard dies that will close the book on it.'

'No it won't, Bryn. How can it? If Maynard attacked you and killed that detective, what else did he do? What about Gwyn Roberts and Alan Harris? What about those boys, what about them?' She had both hands spread over her belly.

He shook his head. 'Let's stop now, Laura, please. There's nothing we can do.'

They waited at the traffic lights to cross the road.

'Shall we get some chips to take home with us?'

'*Chips*?'

'It will save you cooking.'

'For *goodness* sake, Bryn.'

Outside the cinema, he said, 'Let's go and watch a film, then?'

'I don't want any chips and I don't want to watch a film. I just want to go home.'

They walked.

'I shouldn't have told you,' said Bryn.

'I'd have found out, wouldn't I? Something like this will be in that newspaper, won't it, and God knows what else about what he did. If you hadn't gone to see him, he wouldn't have had anyone to confess to, would he? He would have been left to die quietly and no one would have been any the wiser. Does anyone miss that detective? Do they?'

'He didn't confess to me, Laura. He confessed to the vicar. They were going to go see him without me, weren't they?'

'Why do men like him and Mr Tanner have to be so… *virtuous* all the time?'

'He is a vicar. That's his job. What else is he supposed to be? And Mr Tanner is Mr Tanner.'

'Why can't we move on with our lives, Bryn?'

'That's what I thought we were doing. That's why I went.'

'It was a mistake,' she said, adamantly.

Constable Dewi Jones was saved from being a miscreant by Mr Tanner who taught him that discipline without compassion was worthless and had no purpose. Before then, Dewi thought he was being picked on and his behaviour got worse. But, one day, in Mr Tanner's office, the boy forgot to scowl and Mr Tanner told him, 'Be fair Dewi and learn what it means to be fair.'

When he left school, Dewi joined the police. Mr Tanner watched his progress and Dewi knew he was being watched, even though they no longer talked, except to smile and say 'Hello' when they met when he was on his beat, until that day outside Alan Harris' house. Dewi needed Mr Tanner's approval. It was the battle to be his own man that was the hardest challenge.

Brenda was walking alongside him as they prodded at the ground with their long sticks. They were at the end of the line of policemen and a gap had opened between them and the others.

It was cooler when they reached the trees and went into the wood. They could hear the dogs yelping in the undergrowth.

He asked her, 'Is it me?'

She suddenly reached up and pulled his head close to hers. 'No, Dewi,' she whispered, 'it is not you.'

Quickly, they looked around, but they hadn't been seen.

Taken aback, but moved, he grasped her hand. 'But I'm angry all the time.'

'Don't be. You know who to be angry with.'

Under the gloom of the branches, he said, 'I hope we don't find anything.'

'You know we will, Dewi. That's why we're here.'

6

SERGEANT *GEORGE EDWARDS* 24
EWALD FRANK FELDWEBEL 30

In the middle of the day room, there was a war film playing on the old television's tiny screen. There was smoke and explosions, guns firing and soldiers frantically running about. The picture was grainy and the volume was turned off.

The chairs surrounded the war. Which war? A war. In each chair, there was a person. None of them were watching, although they could have, in the reflection of each other's eyes.

'Here she is,' said the nurse.

Gwen blanched when she saw her.

Jean had shrunk, or the chair was inhumanly large. She had gone so far beyond her age, the last three years might have been ten. Her limbs had drawn into her torso, like a bony foetus; but her expression had the hint of a smile, like the face of a saint beneath a shroud, a knowingness that could not possibly be there.

Gwen turned to the nurse and wanted to say, 'Is this how you're taking care of her, you should be ashamed of yourself,' but she was speechless.

'Talk to her,' said the nurse, abruptly, as if she alone was privileged to know what Jean wanted.

Gwen tried to gather herself.

'Go on,' said the nurse, and might have added, 'She won't bite,' as people do of their equivocal dogs.

'Jean? It's Gwen.'

Jean didn't move.

'She can hear you,' said the nurse. 'If you need me, I'll be through there.'

'How do you *know*?' Gwen snapped, but the nurse had gone.

Gwen took Jean's hand but it shrank back and her fingers bent slowly inwards again, like the straightened fronds of a plant.

'Alan sends his love,' Gwen said.

Jean's stillness was impossible to believe and her judgement was raining down. Now she would spring out of the chair and denounce her, 'I *knew* it, I knew all along.'

'Please understand, Jean. They found Huw's body in Porthcawl Harbour. Alan is in prison for Gwyn the Milk's murder, but everyone knows he's innocent. Aled went to live with your aunties and uncles at the shop, but they're getting too old, so Nesta wants to send him to live with Eve. The good thing is that he'll be able to come and see you. So, you do understand, don't you? We didn't mean it to happen. I'm sorry, but they never found Jack.'

But Jack was playing in the back garden. The window was open and Jean listened to them as she made tea. Aled was in his highchair, banging on the little plastic table with his fists. Alan wasn't home from work.

Eve looked over the fence and smiled.

The boys ran out into the back alley and into Gwyn the Milk's field.

Jean leaned through the window and called, 'Don't go far, tea's nearly ready.'

The boys stopped and turned. They looked at each other and then they ran up the slope toward the milking shed, laughing.

'You too, Huw,' Jean heard Gwen calling. She wiped her hands and began to lay the table.

'Happy, happy,' she hummed a little song to herself.

But all Gwen could say was, 'I've gone back to live in Carmarthen, that's why I haven't been to see you sooner,' and no more.

The day room was too hot but Gwen stayed long enough to be polite. 'Goodbye, Jean,' she said, as she got up to leave. 'I'll come and see you again.'

The nurse said, 'She enjoys company,' as Gwen passed her desk and hurried outside into the warm July day to breathe.

On the train, the guard leant over for her ticket and asked, 'Are you alright? Is there anything I can do to help?' as Gwen cried, with her forehead resting against the window and Swansea passing by.

'No, I'll be fine,' Gwen said. 'You're asking too much of me, Alan,' she thought, 'too much.' Whatever she did, how could Aled be the prize?

Delia took Aled down to Porth on the bus. She had a big handbag with sweets at the bottom and his arm disappeared up to the elbow as he rummaged for them. There was a man on the bus who had long blond hair and was called Mostyn. Auntie Delia knew him. He was probably one of his cousins.

After Delia had been to the optician's, where he waited, swinging his legs on the chair outside the little room as she had her eyes tested, they went to the toy shop as a treat. But the spiteful woman kept saying, 'And that one's over the pound mark too,' at every toy Aled liked. She preferred to be nasty than sell toys to well behaved little boys.

When they came out of the shop, without any toys, the river had turned black because the coal wash had been opened higher up the valley. The bus back up to Trebanog took longer than the one on the way down.

When they got home, Aled played with his friends on the mountain behind the Beinon. They slid down on pieces of cardboard.

After lunch, Idris took him to the very top of the mountain, much further than he was allowed on his own (too far for Howell, now). They walked along the ridge. The view was corrugated with valleys, all pointing south to the sea, each with a river of its own. When they reached the pit, Wales' cavitary agony, with the winding gear driven into its centre like a nail, Idris held Aled's hand as they looked down at the men and machines moving like shadows in the dust that bellied to its lips. This was why the river ran black.

In the morning, Reverend Elwiss was at his desk in the study. It looked out on the garden, in shade now, as it only caught the sun in the afternoons and then it slanted into the room – his favourite time and place – and edged up the back wall until it grew dark and he went into the lounge to do the crossword.

There had been no rain, the lawn was straw-coloured but the apple trees were leafy, like old men in bad wigs, but still surprisingly fruitful later in the year.

He didn't want to leave, but he meant to keep his promise.

'I'm going to the hospital,' he told Deborah, in the hall.

'Will it be much longer?' she asked.

'I don't expect it will be long, but I must go. It will be a merciful release and better for him if it comes quickly. There's no hope, none whatsoever, so praying for any continuance wouldn't be… well, no.'

'Will you be home for lunch?' she asked.

'Who knows, Deborah, it's in God's hands.'

'It usually is, dear. I'll wait until you get back, then, shall I?'

'That might be best.'

Reverend Elwiss was fulfilled by the last moments of strangers. It gave him purpose without involvement. If Mr Tanner had not revealed his secret, Maynard would have remained a stranger (although he had seen him meandering up Cardigan Street occasionally, but that didn't count) and, then, if he had been called on in a professional capacity to see to his dying moments, he might have chatted to Deborah about it over tea and been quietly satisfied at a job well done.

'But I do know what this man has done,' he thought, as he left the vicarage. 'My duty is clear.'

'When can we go back to the farmhouse, Auntie Nesta?' Aled asked.

'When it's holiday time again,' she replied.

'When's that?'

'It's a little time to wait.'

'A little time? How long is that?'

'After Christmas has come and gone.'

'After Christmas has come and gone?' He repeated, with a frown. 'That's not a little time, that's a long time.'

'Why don't you go and help your uncles in the shop, there's a good boy.'

Aled narrowed his eyes as if he was only pretending to be a child and about to accuse her of not telling him the truth.

'Go on, there's a good boy,' Nesta told him.

Whatever he had decided, the moment passed, his face brightened and he skipped away down the passage, a little boy again.

Aled could only just see over the counter.

There was a steady stream of customers. Emlyn's commentary, when he saw them coming through the shop window, made Howell and Idris laugh and Aled was beginning to understand enough to repeat what he shouldn't.

(Idris said, 'We're going to have to be careful what we say in front of him now, especially you, Em.'

Howell thought, 'Be thankful for him as he is now.')

Emlyn said, 'Here she is.' Mrs James never bought a full bag of sugar. The uncles dolled it out with a teacup and she only paid for it when the bag was empty. It wasn't only sugar: a bit of bacon, a bit of cheese, milk, 'only half a bottle, mind,' which she brought with her. She lived across the road.

'She treats this place like her own bloody pantry.' Idris kept a tally on a separate page of his book, entitled, *Mrs Sugar,* underlined.

'Here he is,' Tommy Two Fags, who lived three doors down, at least five times a day, except on Saturdays when he would appear from the Beinon Arms and get through a packet of twenty, two at time, and asked for a light before he left the shop, to go back to his unfinished pint.

'Mrs Whistle, give us a song, love,' who couldn't help whistling through a gap in her front teeth when she spoke. Sausages, of which she and her husband were fond, sent the uncles into giggles.

'I *c…*can *ss…see* you,' said Dai Airlock, who coped with a dreadful stammer and puffed out his cheeks as he limbered up for the next sentence. 'He's *sh…shooting* up isn't he?' He was a funny man who would never be a lightning wit. He ruffled Aled's hair which said more than words.

Mrs Lewis said that too. She was always surprised by how much he'd grown since yesterday.

At 4.30, when the last of his afternoon customers had been shown out of the Beinon, Glan, the landlord came in. He pinched Idris' stool from behind the counter (making Idris stand) and shared the gossip. He hauled Aled up onto his lap to listen to them swapping tales. Aled could smell the beer and cigarette smoke on Glan's waistcoat as he played with his watch and chain. One day, Aled wanted one of his own, and a waistcoat pocket to keep it in.

In the evening, he played draughts with Howell. Sometimes he won. Emlyn had carved some chess pieces and they taught him to play but he never won at that. It made the uncles think of Jack, but they could not tell him.

Aled always had bubble bath in the big cast-iron bath with legs. He never wanted to get out until the water went cold.

He shared a bed with one of his aunties (he didn't mind which and they usually took it in turns). Soon, he would need a bedroom of his own or they would have to put another bed in with one of his uncles, but not with Howell.

The binoculars' efflux hung like a mist during the night.

Maynard was still alive when Reverend Elwiss drew the curtain around the bed and pulled up a chair. He laid his hand on Maynard's and said a short prayer. It was a sham privacy because every sound could be heard throughout the ward, including the Reverend's whispers, so if the other patients could not see Maynard die, they could hear him, and there was nothing to delay it, no tubes or machines, and he was unencumbered by anyone's best wishes for a speedy recovery. No one, nothing, was trying to preserve him. It wouldn't be long.

The Reverend crossed his legs and folded his arms and settled down to wait, concentrating on Maynard's face.

Half an hour went by.

He composed the beginnings of a sermon but his mind wandered and Maynard's features swam. He jarred them back into focus. But he was soon drifting away again.

An hour.

'So many symmetries,' he thought, one of his lately favourite words. 'How long has it been since Bryn was lying here, although not here exactly – no, was it? Is it the same ward? It might be.' He clutched his knees and rocked. A man was coughing in a bed nearby. 'There are others who might benefit from my being here too.' He bent down to tie a loose shoelace and tied the other one as well and wetted a finger to polish a scuff away. His eyes bulged and he sat back up too quickly and felt faint. He rubbed the tops of his thighs slowly.

'This is the essence of vigil, isn't it? Vigil: from the Latin meaning wakefulness.' He felt smug at knowing that. 'I am wakeful as I wait; I must be wakeful so that the dying are not alone.'

Another hour.

'I'm not going to be home for lunch, am I?' He stuck his head round the curtain, like a tortoise wearing a ruff. 'Excuse me?' he asked the nurse, in a loud whisper. 'Is there somewhere I can get something to eat?'

'Yes, Vicar,' she answered, in a normal voice, 'in the cafeteria downstairs. Just follow the signs.'

'Thank you.' He struggled with it for a few minutes, then he touched Maynard's wrist and told him, 'I won't be long, Ellis.'

The people in the cafeteria nodded at him and some of them smiled. There was only one reason for a vicar in a hospital: 'How does he do it, day after day? It must take its toll. Vicars are men like you and me, they must be, mustn't they?' The queue parted to let him be served first.

He thanked them and went to the front.

When he got back, Maynard breathed. Reverend

Elwiss sat down more heavily than he meant to.

Into the afternoon.

He had other parishioners who might have need of him. Maynard was not, strictly, one of them – or was he? Reverend Elwiss didn't know where he lived.

The nurse could call him at the vicarage should there be any change. Change? What change could there be? There were no more stages left between what he was and dead. She would, therefore, be calling to tell him that Maynard had died. Reverend Elwiss looked at his watch and fidgeted. 'I'll wait until teatime – early evening, then, and come back first thing in the morning – or I might call in later during my walk.'

Maynard was looking at him. *Caught*. 'You're awake,' the Reverend exclaimed, startled.

'Yes,' said Maynard, through his cracked lips. He waved his coloured fingers at the plastic beaker on the bedside cabinet.

'Would you like a drink of water?'

'Yes.'

Reverend Elwiss held it to his lips.

Maynard let his head sink back onto the pillow.

'I'll fetch the nurse.'

She took his pulse and felt his forehead. 'You've returned to us, Ellis,' she said, trying not to sound disappointed. 'I'll be back shortly. Will you be staying with him, Vicar?'

'For a while.'

'Let me know if he needs anything, will you? Well, Ellis… *Maynard*, well,' and she stepped through the curtain and pulled it closed behind her.

Here he was, alive and conscious: no longer the curiosity, the exhibit, the Reverend's project, the lingering soul, the stranger: the man himself, body and soul intact.

'How are you feeling, Ellis?'

'Alright.'

'That's good. How long have you been awake?'

'Long enough to see you.'

'I've been here since this morning, Ellis.'

'What for?'

'I came because you have been very ill.'

'Why? I didn't ask you to.' He tried to raise himself on his elbow but flopped down.

'You're weak, Ellis. You must recover your strength.'

'Where's that nurse?'

She put her hands on her hips. 'Ellis,' she told him, 'you've only just woken up.'

'Give me something. I'm not staying here.'

'Now you can stop that, right now, Ellis. I'm not putting up with any of your games. Do you hear me?'

'I'll do what I want. It's got *fuck all* to do with you.' His eyes began to glitter. 'So *fuck* off.'

'You obnoxious man,' thought Reverend Elwiss.

'You can stop that, right *now*, Ellis.' She looked at Reverend Elwiss and shook her head to apologise. 'I don't want you in here a minute longer than you have to be but, this time, you should count yourself very lucky. It's more of a miracle. Perhaps you could start by thanking the vicar.'

'Why?' Maynard turned his head to one side and ignored her.

'I will leave you, then,' said Reverend Elwiss, 'I wish you a speedy recovery.'

Outside the ward, the nurse told him, 'He's been in and out of here more times than I can count. But, this time, Vicar, I thought that would be an end to it. Nobody would miss him. I shouldn't be saying it, especially not to you, but it's a fact.'

As he returned to the vicarage, he told himself, 'I have done my duty and now it is for the police. He must face the judgement of the law.' His heart sank. 'No, it is beyond my jurisdiction, what more can I do? Anyway, they don't want my help.' He was tired. 'Let it wait until morning. I'm sure Raymond will agree.' He reached in his pocket for his front door key. 'Deborah?' he called, 'sorry I missed lunch… he didn't die. He didn't bloody die,' he said, again, angrily.

He sat in the hall chair. 'I want to be who I want to be all the way through. I want to be who people think I am.' He climbed the stairs slowly, as if his disappointment was a knapsack of bricks.

'Why must we Nesta?' Howell asked her. 'Why can't we wait to hear from Alan?'

'We will.'

'Good.'

'I will take him to Eve's for a visit, that's all, and possibly stay overnight. She won't mind. There's no harm in that. We don't have to decide anything for final.'

'Nesta, you're only storing up trouble, you know that, don't you?'

'It will be familiar to him, in the event, well, in the event that he goes there.'

Howell shook his head. 'Why can't we just wait?'

'Because there's no time,' she replied, with that familiar, stubborn set of the jaw when she wasn't going to listen. 'We can't just ship him off one day to a new home and to start school for the first time.'

'Nesta, we don't know if Alan will even agree to what you're proposing.'

'What *we're* proposing. Howell, time is against us and what other course of action do we have?'

'It's against my better judgement, it really is.'

'It's only for a visit to begin with.'

'Have you considered what Eve will do if Alan doesn't give his consent?'

'Eve wants what is best for him,' said Nesta, 'as we all do.'

'You're building up her hopes.'

Nesta's jaw set tighter. 'Aled comes first.'

'You're always more certain when you're uncertain, Nesta, and you've always been the same.'

'I'm going to bed,' she said, where Aled was already asleep.

7

PRIVATE DAVID FLINT 19
GEORG HOFFMANN GEFREITER 20

Salute: 'Good morning, Gerhard.'

'Good morning, Howell, and how did you sleep?'

'My sister is determined to send him away.'

'So you have said.'

'I know we cannot keep him for ourselves much longer.'

'For ourselves, Howell?'

'For his sake, Gerhard, but, I must admit, for ours too. It's two ends that won't meet.'

'Unfortunately, that is one of the eternal questions.'

'It's just that I'm not sure what she's proposing is the right way forward.'

'She has the best of intentions for him, I am sure.'

'She does, I would never question that, but she is so determined to find a solution, I don't think she's seeing things clearly.'

'Do you have a solution, Howell?'

'I wish I did, but that doesn't mean any solution is the right one.'

'What about all his relatives here?'

'I've been thinking about that, and Nesta has, but they either have mouths to feed of their own or they're old like us. It wouldn't be right or fair and what if he had no choice but to go underground when he's older? What else would there be for him here?'

'What about the shop?'

'There is that. But what do we do until then? I think we might have to give it up in a few years, before he's old enough to look after it. And I want more for him than the colliery or the shop.'

'That's understandable, Howell.'

'Then there's his mother.'

'Yes.'

'Nesta thinks it will help to revive her. Perhaps it will. I'd give anything for Jean to be well again, but I don't know. Yes, I do,' he said, quietly. 'I'm afraid she will never be the same.'

'The answer will present itself, Howell, perhaps from an unexpected place.'

'Will it? I hope so. Nesta's taking him to visit Eve.'

'She has a history with him, does she not?'

'One that he was too young to remember. I'm driving them down there. It's all happening too quickly. But that's Nesta all over.'

Rose Davies took more time than usual with her hair and make-up, more time choosing a blouse and then dithered over the choice of skirt to go with it and even longer over her shoes, of which she had four pairs. She looked at the ensemble in the mirror and changed her blouse. And changed it back again. 'Just so? Demure but with a hint of... *something*.' It wasn't easy, but too easy to be '... provocative? No, attractive', but without looking like she'd made an effort. 'Is that about right?' It was a bright morning, warm later, so she put on the lightest of jackets and was nearly out of the door when she changed her mind about her handbag. 'Ready now?'

She set out for school briskly, catching up and passing groups of children and mothers gossiping. 'Good morning,' she said.

'Good morning, Miss.'

Doug Protheroe was on his way to the office when he saw her crossing the road at the top end of Cardigan Street. He growled deep in this throat before he could control himself.

She glowed like an opal. Her figure was full but well-proportioned and her bottom swayed, but didn't sashay, like a pendulous fruit in a tropical breeze. Downwind, he smelled her, a girlishly delicate scent but musky, especially ripe this morning for an aged buck, curling back his nostrils. She could be the model for an old master, a fleshy Ruben's nude... He had as much chance of having her as the painting itself. He shook his grizzled self and went on his way.

'Good morning, Mrs Hughes,' Rose said to Laura who was on playground duty, trying to counterbalance the weight of her growing child by pressing her hands into the small of her back. 'Would you like a rest?'

'Would you mind?' replied Laura, gratefully.

'Not at all, if I can borrow your whistle?'

Laura handed it over and Rose put the lanyard over her head.

Laura waddled inside, no longer self-conscious as she puffed and sweated. It amused the children, many of whom only had a vague understanding of what was wrong with her, and the mothers smiled knowingly from beyond the gates.

'Good morning, Mr Topliss,' Rose greeted the caretaker who was bustling in overalls and wellington boots holding a spanner and a toilet plunger, frowning, as he headed toward the boys' toilet block at the top of the playground.

'Good morning, Mrs Davies,' he muttered, his mind on visions of little toilets overflowing like drunken sherry glasses and rude boys flushing them over and over to make the mess go away. They were. He shooed them out of the toilets and they scattered like mice. He splashed through the puddles with a grimace.

She walked slowly around the playground, coyly parading, turning her flank this way and that to let her feathers catch the light.

Mr Tanner did not appear.

She looked at the clock over the main doors and reluctantly fetched the brass handbell and rang it. The children lined up. For the first time (but many times before in her old school in Maesteg) she announced, 'Registration, in you go.'

Rose didn't have a class to register so she went to look in at Mr Tanner's office to say hello. He wasn't there. Neither was he in the hall getting ready for assembly. Disappointed, she sat down behind the table at the end of the hall where all the teachers sat.

Mr Hughes came in first. 'I think Mr Tanner has been delayed again.'

'There's nothing wrong, is there?' she asked.

'At least the holidays are nearly upon us,' he replied.

The children began to come into the hall.

Howell reversed the van out of the garage. It rattled and squealed: these mountains had always been too much. In its dreams, it had been made for wide, flat roads and gently sweeping bends with the wind in its grille but, much like a pony banished from sunlit fields to the mine, it had been consigned to the Rhondda Valley. After many years of unnatural service, it was close to giving out completely. Pembroke had almost been the last straw and, yet, its complaining springs and oil-dry heart were being pressed into duty once more. There was no certainty that it would get to Bridgend and back, twice.

Howell loaded the small suitcases into the back of the van and told Aled, 'Jump in.'

Nesta got into the passenger seat with Aled on his knees behind her and his arms over her shoulders, watching the road ahead. She felt his soft warmth against her cheek and reached back to tickle his chin.

If Eve took Aled, he would never come back except to visit (and how often? Not often, she knew – more at the beginning, and then not at all). It was the end to an unexpected part of her life she had come to cherish more than any other.

If she had to, how many more years could she stretch this out? Three, five? She tried to work out the number of days but her maths wasn't good enough (a question for book-keeper Idris). She almost told Howell, 'Stop,' as he turned out onto the road. But it wasn't possible and, even if by providence she lasted that long, she wouldn't be able to cope long before the end.

The van's tappets complained bitterly.

They didn't speak on the way and Aled's head nuzzled against her neck.

Mr Tanner said, firmly, 'No, we must tell them, Ernest. They must be made to listen and, even if they do not, they will not be able to say they didn't know or that we didn't make every effort.'

'Haven't we already done that?' asked Reverend Elwiss, sulkily.

'Then we must do it again.'

'I'm sorry, but what good would it do?'

Mr Tanner looked at him. 'Have faith,' he said.

'It's not a question of *faith*, Raymond,' bridled the vicar, taken aback that his friend would say such a thing.

'No, I didn't mean… no, faith in the police and what they're there for.'

The vicar stopped ruffling. 'Then I think I would prefer to observe their methods from a distance. We are not policemen, as has been made very clear.'

'No, we are not. They have a job to do, but so do we; one is of no use without the other. They are as accountable to us as we are to them.'

'In a perfect world.'

'Ernest, please?' said Mr Tanner, exasperated, as much with himself as the police and his friend. 'I'm not trying to defend him.'

'I'm sorry. Yes, they are.'

'Let me speak to him this time?'

'I wish you would, Raymond, because I'm not sure I would be able to contain myself. You must understand that I am duty bound to consider the reputation of the Church.'

'We must try to remember that he is only one policeman, he is not the police.'

'He is in Bridgend, it would seem,' said Reverend Elwiss.

Mr Tanner blew out his cheeks. 'Well, be that as it

may.' They were outside the police station. 'Here we are,' said Mr Tanner.

'Here we are indeed,' said the vicar.

Eve saw them through the bay window. She came out to stand in the porch with her hands clutched against her throat, dressed in her best.

Nesta put on her hat, a kind of red, silk turban, and adjusted it before she got out of the van.

'Hello, cariad,' Eve said.

Aled hid behind Nesta's legs and shyly peeped. 'Her again,' he thought.

Howell brought the suitcases. 'Hello, Eve,' he said, 'you're looking well.'

Eve only saw Aled and didn't reply. She bent down and held out her hands to him, 'Come in.'

'I'm going to get away,' said Howell.

Eve said, 'You must come in for a cup of tea after your journey, surely?'

The van was flaking rust at the kerb and made a silent plea, 'Oh *please* go in.'

'Thank you,' Howell said, 'but I want to call in to see Jean and then I must get back to the shop.'

'Oh,' said Eve, 'give her my love, won't you?'

'Can't you tell her yourself?' Howell thought. 'I'll see you tomorrow, young man,' he told Aled.

Aled looked at Nesta with a puzzled expression.

'We're going to be staying with Auntie Eve tonight.

Won't that be a treat?' said Nesta.

'*Auntie* Eve?' asked his eyes.

'We're going to have lots of fun,' said Eve. 'Shall we go to the beach at Porthcawl?' She looked at Nesta.

'Won't that be fun?' Nesta told Aled, now almost incidental, as the two women, dressed to the nines, bargained over him.

'And then we can take a walk down to the school?'

'Perhaps,' said Nesta. 'Shall we do that, Aled?'

Aled looked from one auntie's face to the other and suspected designs on himself.

'Let's go and have some tea, shall we? Lemon squash, Aled? It's your favourite.'

'Is it?' he asked, slowly, feeling that this new auntie presumed too much.

''I'll be off, then,' said Howell.

'Can I come with you, Uncle Howell?'

The two women laughed nervously and tried to press Aled inside. He held back.

Howell stroked Aled's hair. 'You be a good boy, now, and I'll be back tomorrow to pick you and Auntie Nesta up to take you home.'

'*Home*,' stabbed at Eve's heart. She almost pulled Aled inside by his arm.

Howell looked at Nesta, who ignored him with a fixed smile.

Mr Tanner asked, 'Could we speak to Sergeant Phillips?'

Then they sat down to wait, expecting to be made to.

But, within minutes, Dewi appeared. He hesitated before he shook their hands, as if he was afraid to be seen to be familiar. The policeman behind the desk watched.

'We're here to see Sergeant Phillips, Constable Jones.'

'He's not here, Mr Tanner.'

'Will he be back soon?'

'I don't think so.'

'Then we must speak to you instead.'

'Couldn't it wait until Sergeant Phillips gets back?'

'I'm afraid not' said Mr Tanner. 'It's important.'

Dewi led them through to the interview room.

'What's the matter, Dewi?' Mr Tanner asked, immediately the door was closed.

'Nothing's the matter.'

'Yes, there is. I know you too well, Dewi,' said Mr Tanner, 'but this won't wait.'

When he was still in school, Dewi remembered Mr Tanner asking him over and over as he stood before him in his office, 'Did you break that window, Dewi Jones? Answer me. You won't be going anywhere until you do. Did you break that window?'

'No, Sir.'

'Did you break that window?'

Until Dewi answered in a whisper, with downcast eyes, 'Yes, Sir.'

'There, you see? That wasn't difficult was it?'

Broken windows.

'You heard what we said about Ellis Maynard.'

Dewi pulled himself up straight. 'Yes, I did.'

'Ellis thought he was dying when he told us.'

'That's why we're here,' said Reverend Elwiss, more hopeful of progress and respect. 'He's made a recovery. He's awake so Sergeant Phillips can question him properly. The law can take its course. He was also responsible for the attack on Bryn Hughes.'

'I told Detective Jeffries at the time,' said Mr Tanner, 'and he ignored me.'

But Dewi retreated. 'I will tell Sergeant Phillips when he returns,' he said, stiffly.

'Dewi, what's the matter? Tell me won't you? It will go no further.'

'There is nothing the matter,' Dewi repeated, the furrows between his eyes straining.

They passed Brenda Colcannon in the corridor on their way out. She shook her head.

Dewi did not say goodbye. He disappeared as if every second was too long.

'Hello, my beautiful girl,' Howell said to Jean.

Her lopped smile did not reach her bleak eyes. The television mutely offered more wars, news, game shows, romance, musicals, Peyton Place.

'It's more than I can bear to see you like this,' he said. The truth, as she was, before him, he was begging her to come back to the unbearable truth. Three years and she did not know; and Alan, counting the same years, who did.

He kissed her forehead as he said goodbye.

Jean kissed Jack goodnight, 'Sleep tight my lovely boy,' she whispered.

'Please tell me that was worthwhile, Raymond?'

'I don't know. I wish I knew what was troubling Dewi.'

'Maybe he can't tell us,' said Reverend Elwiss. 'You were right, they think we are interfering with their investigations.'

'And what should they investigate if not the confession of a dying man to a terrible crime?'

'As you said, perhaps they are.'

'Yes, I know I did.'

'I don't think there's much more we can do,' said Reverend Elwiss.

'I will *not* let it rest, Ernest,' said Mr Tanner, angrily. 'And nor should you.'

'I meant as far as the police are concerned, Raymond,' replied Reverend Elwiss, grimly smug, as if to say, 'now you know how it feels.'

'Who else are we supposed to go to? We're not detectives, are we? We can't go around behaving like vigilantes, can we? You're a vicar and I'm a teacher, for goodness sake.'

'I'm as upset as you are, Raymond. But I am at a loss.'

Mr Tanner didn't hear him.

Weaving towards them up Cardigan Street, feeling along the walls and shop windows, was Ellis Maynard. He had no flesh to keep him upright; his limbs abraded, bone on bone, as if he was clawing from the grave but, still, he came on.

The headmaster and the vicar stood, speechless, in the middle of the pavement. Behind them, The Red Lion had yet to open. Shoppers stared and walked in the road.

It was all Maynard could do to lift a cigarette to his lips.

'Ellis, what are you doing out of hospital?' demanded Mr Tanner.

Maynard pointed with the trembling cigarette.

'It's not open yet,' said Mr Tanner.

'I'll wait,' Maynard croaked.

A big, black car drove slowly past and turned left at the traffic lights.

Mr Tanner had an overwhelming desire for Rose and, afterwards, he would close his eyes and sleep.

They watched Aled making sandcastles and the sea liquefying them. Nesta took off her shoes and went for a paddle. The foam tickled her ankles and she scrunched her toes. The wind came fresh and uncontained from other lands; the sky was milky and vast. Very bright. The sound of the sea: there was no need to talk. She closed her eyes to listen and feel. It was wonderful to be here, so different to how the mountains crowded.

But we are the same Wales.

Mr Alphonsi was drinking from his tiny cup and smoking as he read the paper. Nesta and Eve had coffee and biscuits, Aled had a Knickerbocker Glory with a gobstopper bleeding into the ice cream at the bottom of the tall glass. He inched it out with a spoon as long as a sword. It pressed against his front teeth and he had to breathe around it.

They walked to the end of the prom. Then they caught the bus back to Bridgend.

'Shall we go down to the school?' Eve asked.

'Why not?' said Nesta, soothed by the sea.

'The children will have gone home so perhaps we can have a look around.' But Mr Topliss had already locked the gates and they couldn't see anyone inside. 'That's a pity,' said Eve. 'Aled, what do you think of the school?'

A big, black car drew up. Sergeant Phillips got out. He smoothed his moustache with his thumbs, pulled his tunic straight and put on his peaked cap.

The two women were silent. Aled craned his neck.

'Mrs Brown,' he said.

'Guthrie,' she protested, feebly.

'You are Eve Brown and Nesta Morgan and this is Aled Harris.'

'Morgan,' said Nesta, 'Aled Morgan.'

'Aled Harris,' said Sergeant Phillips. 'Do you mean to take custody of this boy, Mrs Brown? Are you entitled to?

Are you fit to care for him?'

'I love him,' said Eve, trembling.

'You abducted him. And you, Mrs Morgan?'

'I'm not married.'

'He was placed in your care and now you mean to give him up?'

Aled looked at Nesta.

'I would never – please, not in front of the boy. The nice policeman's joking, Aled.'

'Am I? His father is in prison for murder, his mother is in an institution and you mean to surrender him to the woman who abducted him and whose husband was convicted… convicted of *what*, Mrs Brown? Tell me; tell Mrs Morgan.'

Eve shrank back; Nesta pulled Aled into her hip and tried to block his ears.

'Are either of you fit to care for the boy? I see everything,' he said, 'all and everything. I know your minds.' And he took off his peaked cap, got back into his big, black car and left them outside the empty school.

It was nearly three hours from Carmarthen to Trebanog by bus, train and bus. Half the day had already gone when she arrived at the shop.

'Who's this?' exclaimed Emlyn, seeing Gwen through the window. 'It's Gwen Evans.'

She came in.

'Gwen,' said Idris, 'have you come to see us, all the

way from down west? *Delia*,' he called, 'look who's here.'

Delia came through from the back wearing her flower-patterned housecoat. 'I was about to go up to wash and change. Gwen? What a nice surprise,' was all she could think to say.

'I've been to see Alan,' Gwen said.

'In the prison?' asked Delia, shocked. 'Come in,' and she hurried Gwen out before customers could hear. Idris and Emlyn followed leaving the shop to look after itself.

'Nesta's not here,' Delia told Gwen, 'she's gone with Aled to visit Eve in Bridgend. Howell's taken them. He should be on his way back now, but Nesta and Aled are staying until tomorrow.'

Gwen sank into a chair without being asked. 'That's why I'm here. Nesta wrote to Alan about Aled going to live with Eve.'

'Yes,' said Delia, 'she did.'

'Alan doesn't think it's the right thing for Aled.'

Emlyn and Idris looked at each other.

'Why didn't Alan write back?' asked Delia.

'He wanted to talk to me first, so that's why I've come to see you myself.'

'Oh,' Delia said. 'Oh. You must speak to Nesta, Gwen. Or you could wait for Howell?'

Gwen lifted up her hands and let them fall onto the arms of the chair. 'If you don't mind, I'll wait for Howell?'

Child's Body Found

There was a photograph of Sergeant Phillips with his gloved hands on the roof of his big, black car surveying all before him.

A child's body, believed to be that of Rhodri Mitchell, 7, has been found in Dowglais Wood near Pencoed.

Rhodri went missing in October 1966 along with two other boys, Huw Evans, 6, and Jack Harris, 6.

Huw's body was uncovered by the tide in Porthcawl Harbour not long after he disappeared. It is believed that Jack may lie buried somewhere in the dunes near Kenfig Pool. But, even after extensive searches, nothing has been found.

The latest discovery comes as a result of the painstaking efforts of Sergeant Phillips who has always maintained a steely determination to find the missing boys. He told The Herald, *'Jack Harris will be found and I will bring to justice whoever did this. Time will not protect him.'* The Herald *continues to give Sergeant Phillips and his officers any support within its power to bring to a close a tragedy that haunts the town to this day.*

8

corporal *IANTO GRIFFITHS* *21*
FREDERIK KELLER *oberleutnant* *30*

Mrs Wright, the church warden, organist and antique fusspot was arranging flowers in the tall brass vases on either side of the aisle.

He was disappointed to see her there but, before he could slip away, she spotted him.

'Hello, Vicar,' she said.

'Hello, Mrs Wright, have you much more to do?

'Not much more and then I'm done.'

He sat down in the front pew and looked at the altar. Christ looked back with a wooden expression meaning whatever the beholder wanted it to.

Mrs Wright adjusted a wayward rose to get it to stand upright alongside the others. She stood back with her head to one side. 'Another little job done,' she told herself, and headed for the organ.

She busied in the corner of Reverend Elwiss' eye,

humming, as she poked the duster between the pipes. She never read the newspaper and gossip was sinful. This was her whole world and had been for over half her life.

In the lesser holiness of his study, Reverend Elwiss tried again. His wife came in. 'Deborah, *please*?' he protested.

She ignored him.

'Deborah, I'm trying to think.'

She sat down and crossed her legs. 'Are you? Tell me what you're thinking and I'll leave you alone.'

'I don't know what to think, that's why I'm trying to think.'

'It's not surprising the newspaper has upset you,' she said.

'It's more than that. Please Deborah?'

'I can wait here or you can come and find me.' She knew he would, searching her out wherever she was, usually in the garden or the kitchen. Occasionally she made herself more difficult to find and, sometimes, he needed prompting. This was one of those times. Then he would present his conclusions and have them altered.

'I was in the church,' he said.

'Mrs Wright's there at this time of day.'

'Yes, she was. I forgot. Which was why I came in here.' He rested his head against the back of the chair.

Deborah waited, knowing it would come and, after some minutes of silent, but relentless inquiry, he began to explain himself to the white stucco that ran around the edges of the ceiling.

'I felt it in church just now, and before. It came to me when I was leaving the hospital with Raymond and Bryn. I told them, although I'm not sure they were listening after what we'd just witnessed. I can't put my finger on it. If Mrs Wright hadn't been there, I think I would have understood.'

'I'm listening, Ernest, go on.'

He looked at her, 'Why was Ellis Maynard brought back? I have never seen a man closer to death. We thought he had died at one point. And where is he now?' Reverend Elwiss looked at his watch. 'In The Red Lion, I would imagine.' He sighed and pushed himself upright and watched the apple trees swaying heavily in the warm breeze with their crop still green and hard. 'And the police, what have they done? He confessed to a murder and he is free to go to the pub.'

'Because Sergeant Phillips didn't react in the way you wanted him to?'

'I didn't *want* him to react… you mean he wasn't grateful? No, he was rude.'

'Was he, Ernest? Rude?'

'Yes, he was. He was rude to me *and* he insulted the Church.'

She pursed her lips.

'And, yes, I was upset at the time, but that passed. And, no, that's not it; that's not it at all.'

'What then?'

'And this latest discovery, if that's what it is? At last, Rhodri Mitchell's family can lay him to rest and we must give thanks for it, if only for that. They can mourn him, certain in the knowledge of where he will lie. But terrible memories will be raked over. They have found the poor child's body but they cannot find who did it? How can there be one without the other? And how did they know where to look, Deborah?

'Doesn't he deserve credit for finding him?'

'Yes, I will admit that. We didn't know he was looking for Rhodri Mitchell or that he may already have found him.'

'Well, there you are! Doesn't that prove Sergeant Phillips knows more than he is prepared to tell you?'

'We were trying to help. Raymond and I had some cross words about it, well, not cross exactly, but it certainly upset us both. I think I ought to apologise to him.'

'Raymond will understand, I'm sure,' she said.

Reverend Elwiss rubbed his forehead. 'Why haven't they found Jack Harris? Where is his lonely grave? I don't know what it is, Deborah. It won't lend itself to any words I can find, but I have a foreboding that worse is to come.'

'You don't know that, Ernest.'

He took a deep breath and closed his eyes. 'Deborah, why do I believe in God?'

'It is your faith, Ernest.'

'Have faith,' he murmured.

'But you do.'

'This is the opposite of what my faith stands for but it is of the same realm.'

The shaded swirls of the stucco began to writhe as the light changed.

Nesta put Aled to bed. In her own home, Eve was excluded. Nesta and Eve didn't speak during the whole evening. Nesta went to bed early. Eve, alone again in her front room, relived the times and knew her hopes had slipped away.

In the morning, Nesta was packed and ready in her silk turban before breakfast. Eve went into the garden. Weeds had grown through the smashed frames of the greenhouse, untouched for so long. Now, she mowed the lawn between the overgrown borders and the once vegetable patch, pitted where the policemen had searched. As she pushed the mower up and down, Eve was full of exhaustion and defeat. Every thirty seconds or so, she passed the window where Nesta was sitting with Aled on her lap.

Howell didn't arrive until midday. Nesta was on her feet as he pulled up outside.

Eve knelt before Aled. 'Cariad, cariad.'

He was bewildered as to why he was there, what it had been for, who she was. She frightened him with her emotions, crying as she grasped his hands, releasing them only when Nesta led him away by the shoulder.

Howell came in and took the cases out to the van.

Nesta came back. 'I'm sorry, Eve,' she said, 'I shouldn't

have brought him.'

'Can I come and see him?' Eve asked, plaintively.

'Perhaps,' Nesta replied, which meant 'no'. They had not discussed any plans; it was unsaid and did not have to be withdrawn. It was a visit and that was all.

Nesta held Aled tight all the way to Trebanog. She said, it was all she said, until they reached the shop, 'That was a mistake. Now I don't know what to do.' She took Aled inside.

Howell breathed a sigh of relief as he put the van away, but he didn't know what Nesta would say when he told her about Gwen. She might even think he'd gone round her back.

'I shouldn't have told you about Ellis Maynard, Bryn. I am sorry for it now.'

'He wasn't expected to live, Mr Tanner. You weren't wrong to tell us.'

'But that's no comfort to Laura, now she knows who he is and what he did to you both. If we hadn't gone to see him, it wouldn't have mattered whether he had lived or died. It's my fault.'

'No, that isn't true,' said Bryn.

If Mr Tanner was fallible, who was left? For the first time, they stood together on the high place and only Bryn's unwillingness to believe it stopped Mr Tanner from slipping. There was no set time to be grown-up: some too young, some never, some at exactly Bryn's age.

'We would sooner know it was him,' said Bryn, 'because now we're not left wondering who it was.'

'And Jack Harris has still not been found,' Mr Tanner nodded toward *The Herald* on his desk, folded crisply below the headline. 'The injustice is tangible to me.'

Bryn was the first to see the pain the headmaster had endured, so plainly, privately, rising into words that he could no longer hold back. Bryn would see the diminishment of other good men, as one day, so would his own son, not yet fully formed in Laura, who would try to resist the weight of inheritance, passed onto him by the failing capacities of the father he was to love and never believe he could doubt.

Bryn would not allow Mr Tanner to be an ordinary man. He stood up. 'I have my class.'

'Take care, Bryn, and take care of Laura.'

'I will.'

Rose came in as Bryn left and Mr Tanner made a determined effort to be headmaster again. She uplifted him and he brightened. 'Thank you, Mr Hughes,' he said, as if their meeting had been about hymns for tomorrow's assembly.

'Am I with Form Two again today?' she asked.

'You are, Mrs Davies.' She didn't want to leave and he didn't want her to. He said the first thing that came to him. 'What sort of books do you like to read, for yourself that is, not the children?' He smiled, clumsily. 'You said you like to read?'

'Anything historical, I love history.'

'Ah,' said Mr Tanner, 'historical novels or the classics?'

'Both.'

'I do too. In fact, if you will allow me,' he dared, to his surprise, 'I have one or two favourites that you might like to read. You might already have read them, of course, but I could dig them out?'

'I'd love to, Mr Tanner.'

'Would you? Then I will as soon as I get home this evening.'

'That's so kind of you.'

Should he ask her to call him Raymond? A bit too soon? After she'd read one of the books would be the right time, and only outside school, where they could meet to discuss it. He tried to think of a book she wouldn't have read. Nothing obscure, but something that would begin to reveal an intriguing side to his character. He wondered how much of a risk to take. He did have one or two famously raunchy novels (for their time).

'Not at all, Mrs Davies. I will do my best to find something that will divert you.'

She smiled effortlessly. 'I look forward to what books you think I would like.' Should it be Rose? Not quite yet. He was the headmaster who was lending her some books: a man with educational motives.

After she had gone, Mr Tanner imagined her. He regretted not being more open about his intentions (which were?). 'Why didn't I just say it, even if I made a fool of myself? *Carpe diem*. What if I don't get another chance?'

Doug Protheroe rubbed his hands together but it generated more heat than enthusiasm and it was too hot for exertions. 'There's mileage in this one, Andrew,' he said, with a forced lilt in his voice and stale eyes.

'Right you are, boss.'

'So, what have you got?'

'Lloyd's got some shots of where he was found, good close-ups too.'

'That's a start, but you can do better than that.'

Herald Andrew laughed. 'And we're off down to see where he lived and his school and I'll try and interview the parents, of course.'

'Sensitively, Andrew.'

'*Boss*.'

'No, really.' Protheroe looked at *Herald* Andrew over his reading glasses. 'Sensitively.'

'Yes, boss,' said *Herald* Andrew, sceptically, expecting a wink.

'What else, come on. What about Prosser? What does he know?'

'Not much, I expect,' said *Herald* Andrew.

'Ask him anyway,' said Protheroe. 'Find out if there are any new suspects.'

'I was going to do that, boss. Lloyd and me are meeting him at The Red Lion later. It's worth a try, anyhow.'

'Good.'

'What about getting an interview with the man himself?'

Protheroe snorted.

'Just a thought.'

'Off you go then. Scoot.'

'Lloydy-boy?' called *Herald* Andrew.

'There we are,' said Protheroe, when *Herald* Andrew had left. He laced his fingers and swivelled his chair to face the window, feeling tired after his little act. The river was lower still. Submerged logs and tree roots were beginning to appear. The water was gasping like a banked fish. No rain was forecast. He didn't feel the thrill of the hunt. 'Vacant,' he thought, because it was almost the right description and it was all he could summon: no wife, no children and no friends, only the newspaper and his protégé to spread the word when he was done.

When Aled was safely watching television, Nesta told Howell about Sergeant Phillips. 'He must have been watching us. But why would he do that?'

'Perhaps he was watching Eve.'

'Eve? After all this time?'

'I don't know why, Nesta.'

'He frightened Aled. How dare he?' Vulnerable Nesta, flinging up barricades of umbrage. 'It was totally uncalled for.'

'Sit down,' said Howell, gently.

'I don't think Aled understood,' she said. 'He hasn't

said anything, but who knows what he's thinking. You know what he comes out with sometimes. Can't Sergeant Phillips see that we just want what is best for him? I'm afraid to go to Bridgend now. And Jean? What about Jean?'

'He has an unfortunate manner about him,' Howell told her, gently. 'He is that sort of policeman. But you can see how he might interpret things. They've found the body of that other boy, haven't they? Right or wrong, perhaps he has to see it that way?'

'But that's nothing to do with us. We must keep Aled close by, now.'

'He means no harm to him, Nesta.'

'The law can harm him if it's used in the wrong way. It's done enough harm to this family.'

'I didn't say I thought he was right,' said Howell. 'None of this is right but we have to try and make sense of it or we won't know what to do.'

'What then, Howell?'

'Gwen Evans came to see you.'

'Gwen Evans? All the way up here? What for?'

'She has been to see Alan.'

'In the *prison*?'

'He wanted to talk to her about Aled.'

'Why her? Couldn't he have written to me? He could have answered my letter.'

'It was your letter that stirred things up. He told Gwen that he doesn't want Aled to go to Eve.'

'Did he say that? Why?'

'Nesta, I can think of lots of reasons and that policeman told you some of them.'

Nesta's eyes searched to and fro. 'Do you think we could look after Jean here? That might be the answer.'

'How could we *possibly* look after her, Nesta, when we don't think we can care for Aled much longer?'

'Then you think of something. Why is it always me?'

'Alan has asked Gwen if she would look after Aled.'

'What? But she lives in West Wales, somewhere. How far is that from his mother? It's further from Bridgend than here. That's not the answer. How can it be?'

'Alan knows it's not his decision. He knows he can't force us to do anything and he's not trying to. But he has a right to make his wishes known. We're going to have to think about it.'

'Does she want to have him; why did Alan think of her? That can't be right.'

'Because you wrote to him about Eve; because of Huw. Because of Jack, Nesta. Aren't they good enough reasons as any?'

Nesta shook her head. 'He's a little boy, a child and we're talking about him as if it's a game of pass the parcel. I think he's going to have to start school here. I don't see how we have any other choice. Perhaps it's not such a bad thing, after all? Where are you going? I'm talking to you.'

'I'm going to take Aled for a walk up the mountain,' said Howell. 'They're not too busy in the shop.'

'Why do you always run away?' she demanded with

her hands on her hips. 'Go on then, *go*.'

There was no reasoning with her until she calmed down. Howell didn't reply.

Nesta heard him talking to Aled and then the front door closing. She went into the kitchen and cried until she felt better.

'Jones,' growled Sergeant Phillips from the end of the corridor, 'Jones,' as Constable Dewi came closer. 'Jones.' Sergeant Phillips smoothed his moustache with the outsides of his thumbs and edged his face closer. 'Harris' son.' Sergeant Phillips sliced the peak of his hat slowly across Dewi's forehead. 'Do it, Jones. *Do* it,' and the '*oo*' went deep into Dewi's heart and coiled in his lungs.

Constable Dewi Jones and Policewoman Brenda Colcannon sat in the car outside Eve's house.

'Let's get it over with,' said Brenda.

'Hello, Eve,' said Brenda, when she answered the door.

'What do you want?' Eve asked. Her face was pinched and stained.

'Is Aled Harris here?'

Eve shook her head. 'No,' she said, in a tiny voice, 'no, he's gone back to Trebanog with his Auntie Nesta.'

'We're sorry to have bothered you, Eve,' said Brenda.

On their way back to the police station, Dewi pulled off the main road and into a lane. He stopped the car in a lay-by and Brenda rested her head against his shoulder.

'Uncle Howell,' asked Aled, when they were sitting high enough up the mountain to see over the rooftops, 'when can we go back to the farmhouse again?'

'Well,' said Howell, 'I'd go tomorrow if I could.'

'So we don't have to wait until after Christmas?'

Howell looked at the little boy. 'Christmas? Why Christmas?'

'Because Auntie Nesta said we did.'

'Did she?'

'Yes. But if you say we can go tomorrow then we won't have to, will we?'

'When I said tomorrow, I didn't mean tomorrow, I meant soon.'

'So why did you say tomorrow if you didn't mean it?'

'It's just a way of saying soon.'

'Will you tell Auntie Nesta and work something out then?'

Howell could not have loved Aled more deeply. His voice cracked. 'I will do that, young man. I most certainly will do that.'

It was the best of the day, warm but fresh, cloudless, a day like it was before they began mining coal in the valley, before anyone but farmers had a reason to live there, when the river was sparkling clean, when the slag heaps were not like men. Howell was always remembering. He had seen too much and lost too much to agree to have this little boy sent from him to an uncertain future.

9

PRIVATE MARC HARRIES 19
HERSCHEL LANGE UNTEROFFIZZER 28

Salute: 'Good morning, Gerhard.'

'Good morning, Howell.'

Howell rubbed his eyes. 'They're not empty yet, are they?'

'You haven't looked through them, have you, Howell?'

'No, and I wasn't going to.' Howell put the binoculars back on the windowsill, lying on their sides.

'Have you decided anything about the boy?' Gerhard asked.

'No. Whatever we do will break our hearts, but they were always going to be broken.'

The Red Lion was gloomy and still, warmer and softer than a church, seductive, but no less truthful. It was only one step away from the street, as are churches. Shoppers passed the door and didn't try to look in. Reverend Elwiss stepped from one to the other, a missionary entering the den to save a wayward soul, both irritated and relieved he had thought of coming, because this was the only way he would know.

A look of surprise came over the landlord's face. He stopped polishing a hand pump. 'Vicar? Can I help you?'

'Thank you, but I am here to see Ellis Maynard.'

'Ellis?' The landlord's eyebrows disappeared up his forehead.

Maynard was on his stool at the bar. He was the only customer. It was a few minutes past 11.00 and the door had just been unbolted. Maynard turned and beheld the priest. He shook his head, as if to say, 'Not you again,' and demanded, surlily, 'What do *you* want?'

'Keep a civil tongue, Ellis,' the landlord snapped, 'or that will be the last drink you have in here today.'

'Could we sit at one of the tables, Ellis?' asked the vicar. 'I'd like to talk to you privately, if I may?'

'What for...?' but the landlord was glaring and Maynard slid off the stool. He picked up his pint and tottered toward the corner of the bar, too sober, too weak, too ill, and desperate to dull the pain.

'Can I get you anything, Vicar?' asked the landlord.

'No, thank you,' Reverend Elwiss replied.

Maynard's hands were shaking. It took four or five pints to stop them. This was only his first and he had to hold the glass in both hands to lift it to his mouth. He gulped the beer down but didn't take his bloodshot eyes off the vicar.

'Would you like another one?' asked Reverend Elwiss.

'Yes.'

The landlord brought a pint and banged it down. It spilt over the table. 'Sorry, Vicar,' he said. He turned to Maynard, 'And don't expect table service when the vicar's not here, Ellis.'

Maynard clutched it and began sucking it into himself. He was like an emaciated, quivering monkey.

Reverend Elwiss did his best to hide his disgust.

Maynard didn't notice and wouldn't have cared if he had.

Reverend Elwiss waited. 'I wanted to speak to you, Ellis,' he began.

Maynard took another noisy slurp, then another. Beer dribbled down his chin.

'Because what you told us in the hospital, when you believed you were dying, was the mark of a man with a conscience.'

Maynard ran the back of his hand across his mouth and sniffed phlegm deep into his throat, hacked it back up and rolled it around his mouth. Then he washed it down and finished his beer.

'You were delivered from death almost miraculously after you made your confession. I don't know if you have any faith but I do not believe you would want to carry your secret beyond this life. You have been given a rare opportunity, Ellis.'

Maynard peered into the empty depths of his pint and looked at the vicar enquiringly.

'I'll buy you another pint in a moment, Ellis, but then I want you to come with me to the police station and repeat your confession to them. Make it right. Listen to your conscience as you did on your hospital bed. I will be there to support you.'

'I didn't die,' said Maynard.

'No, you didn't. You have been reprieved for a reason.'

'I didn't confess to anything.'

'Yes, Ellis, you did. You spoke the truth when you were near to death. Doesn't that mean something?'

'No. Why should it? What did I confess to?'

'You know what, Ellis. It is not something anyone could forget.'

'Try me. If you won't tell me, I'm going to get another drink. Or will you get me one?' Maynard rattled his glass on the tabletop.

'Do you really want me to repeat it? Here?'

'Up to you.'

The vicar took a deep breath, leaned closer, and told him.

'No I didn't,' said Maynard. He levered himself slowly to his feet, meandered to his stool at the bar and lit a cigarette.

'Was he rude to you, Vicar?' asked the landlord. 'Were you, Ellis? Because if you were, you can get out right now.'

'No, he wasn't rude.' As he passed Maynard on his

way out, Reverend Elwiss said, 'Remember, Ellis, my door is always open and so is the church.'

Maynard twirled the ash off the end of his cigarette on the lip of the ashtray and took a deep drag with his eyes distant and half closed. The day was beginning to take care of itself.

When Reverend Elwiss had gone, the landlord asked, 'What did the vicar want, Ellis?'

Maynard shrugged. 'Dunno.'

The landlord shook his head. 'Good men offer to help you but you're not worth it,' and he went back to stacking shelves.

Outside, in the bustle of the street, Reverend Elwiss looked back at the frosted windows and thought, 'Maynard is not the heart of this matter. There's nothing I can do for him. Deborah is wrong and I am right, but I wish I knew what it was. I should speak to Raymond. I've already left it too long.'

In the church, Reverend Elwiss asked again, but the moment of telling had gone, interrupted by Mrs Wright.

Eve, angry and pale, appeared with the mothers at the school gates. She had seen them through the bay window, a fruitful morning tide, and gone out to be caught up and carried along with children's voices all around and the mothers talking, prohibited from becoming one of them by what she had done, Sergeant Phillips and the absent seed.

Mr Tanner saw her there, with her arms hanging by her sides, watching the mothers letting their charges into his care and leaving.

'Eve?' he said. 'Come with me.' Meekly, she did. They stood behind the big tree at the grassy end of the playground where they could not be seen from the school. The children were not allowed to climb it (but they did, and fell out and broke arms and collar bones).

'You have suffered enough,' he said, and told her all he knew and suspected as it came to him, simultaneously, fluently and with horrific clarity.

Her eyes widened as she listened and turned her head to stare into his face.

'There,' he said. 'There.' He left her under the tree, as shocked at what he had just said as she was. As he walked back to the school building across the empty playground, he asked himself, 'What have I done? I should have told Ernest, not Eve.'

He had two books for Rose. He put them in the drawer of his desk where they couldn't be seen.

'You take assembly, please, Mr Hughes. Whatever hymns you decide.'

Bryn stood up, '*Morning Has Broken.*' They sang. Then the children sat cross-legged. 'Mr Tanner, would you?'

Mr Tanner shook his head. 'Not this morning.'

'Aren't you feeling well?' Bryn whispered.

'Please continue, Mr Hughes.'

'This is the last week for those of you who will be leaving us for new schools next term.' Bryn glanced at Mr Tanner and felt like a usurper. These were not his words to say. He caught Laura's eye and frowned.

'*The Lord's Prayer.*' In Welsh. '*Amen.*'

'Rose?' asked Mr Tanner as the children filed out. 'Could I see you for a moment?'

'Yes, of course.'

He took the books from his drawer. 'I thought you might like these.'

'Oh, thank you, Mr Tanner.'

'Please call me Raymond, when we're not in school.' He managed a smile.

'When we're not in school, Mr Tanner?'

'Would you like to meet me for tea on Saturday afternoon? We can discuss the books. I hope you haven't already read them?'

'No, they're new to me. I look forward to reading them and discussing them over tea.'

'I will look forward to it too. May I call you Rose, Mrs Davies, when we're not in school?'

'Of course, Mr Tanner.'

'Form Two again, Mrs Davies.'

'Form Two, it is, Mr Tanner,' and she tucked the books under her arm.

Mr Tanner tapped on the glass porthole of Bryn's classroom door. 'I have an errand to run,' he told him. 'I shouldn't be long.'

Bryn stepped into the corridor and closed the door. 'Is something wrong, Mr Tanner, can I help?'

'No, but thank you for asking.'

His footsteps became heavier as he passed The Red Lion. He became a spectator of himself, curious about the errand that could make the headmaster leave his school, so stony-faced, at this time of day.

'Nesta?' asked Howell. She was still cross with him, as sometimes she could be for days. 'Now we know he can't go to Eve. I know you wanted him to be closer to Jean, but it was never going to work. They won't allow it because of what she did, no matter how much she says she loves him. I don't mean to be harsh but I think it's got more to do with what she wants than what he needs. That's not to place any blame on her. I'm not sure she's aware of it, to be honest. And his father is against it and that matters. It's not your fault, Nesta.'

Nesta refused to look at him.

'He can't stay here, you know that and it's wrong to start him in school when he'll have to come out of it and start somewhere else just when he's settling in. That wouldn't be right, would it?'

She clutched the draining board.

'If we're not careful he could end up in care in two or three years' time. Let's not fool ourselves that it couldn't happen. How will the council see it? His father's in prison, his mother can't look after him and we know we can't.

Think about it Nesta.'

'That will *never* happen,' she said, slowly.

'No? Now, before you say anything, hear me out. We have a possible solution, don't we? It might even be the answer we're looking for. The only objection, as far as I can see, is the distance and even that's not impossible. Carmarthen's not the other side of the world. We can get the train from Cardiff. Gwen can drive, I think, so we could even give her the van. We won't need it much longer.'

Nesta didn't answer.

'Or we can sell it and get a car for her. Why not? And we can provide some money to help with his upbringing. We can go down there every couple of weeks and he can come here in the school holiday. They both can. We can even go back to that farmhouse in Pembroke.'

'No,' she said, 'no,' and walked out of the room.

'Duw, Duw,' Howell said, under his breath, and went through to the shop.

'Prosser,' said Sergeant Phillips, 'go and see Harris. Tell him I've found the Mitchell boy. Tell him prison will not keep me from him. Tell him I know he did it. Tell him I have seen his son with Eve Brown. Repeat it, Prosser.' Sergeant Phillips grew taller.

'I've got to...' Prosser stammered.

'*Tell...*'

'Tell him he's not safe in prison, from you, Sergeant Phillips. That you know he did it. Tell him that you've found Mitchell.'

'Tell him I know his mind.'

'You know his mind and you've seen his son with Eve Brown.'

'Do it Prosser, and tell that reporter.'

Herald Andrew and Lloyd found Detective Prosser coming out of the police station. 'I'm busy,' he said.

'Not too busy, I hope, to talk to two old mates,' said *Herald* Andrew. 'We can go down The Red Lion if you like?'

Detective Prosser wished. 'I can't. I've got an interview to do.'

'So how did he find the body, then, Gordon?' asked *Herald* Andrew. 'He's got to have a new suspect, hasn't he?'

'You don't expect me to tell you that,' said Prosser.

'Tell us who you're going to interview then? It's got to have something to do with this, hasn't it?'

'I told you, I can't tell you anything about it.'

'We'll see you get some credit for it, Gordon.'

'I don't do this job for medals.'

'Alright, then, if you can't say, we'll leave you alone, won't we Lloyd?'

'You know I shouldn't tell you, don't you?'

'We know, Gordon, but you're in tight with him, aren't you? We rely on you. You know that?'

'Alan Harris,' said Prosser.

'Aye, aye? In the prison. Well, well. Get a shot of the detective, Lloydy-boy, in anticipation.'

Flash.

'And another one.'

Flash.

'I've got to go,' said Prosser.

'Of course you do,' said *Herald* Andrew. 'You've got important work to do.'

Prosser swaggered unconvincingly to his car.

Flash.

Herald Andrew watched him go. 'A pound to a penny Sergeant Phillips told him to tell us. How shall we play this one, then? You didn't use all those photos of Harris, did you? It's a shame we can't get some of him in the nick. I wonder will they bring him to Bridgend for questioning. Now, there's a possibility. We'd better keep a sharp eye or… *or…* we could get Prosser down The Red Lion and get some beer down him. He'll tell us if they are going to bring him back here, no problem at all. Is that a plan Lloydy-boy? I think it is.'

It was a summer's day in a village just outside Carmarthen. Gwen's small, stone cottage was at the end of a rough track. It had a large garden with an orchard and raspberry bushes overlooking rolling countryside. The primary school was less than a mile away in the middle of the village. There were other children in nearby farms.

It was where Gwen grew up, where she had met Geraint when he had come there to stay with his uncle on holiday and help with the baling. The following year he started underground but, by that time, they were writing to each other and she had been to Bridgend to meet his parents.

She took out Huw's *Big Book of Theatre and Film*.

All these women clamouring for Aled. But history would unfold and no one could stop it. When it did, he must feel loved and safe. This was a better place for him than Bridgend, where he would always be the boy who was, until he became the man who was and knew the past he could not escape, his story told and retold behind his back and every look telling him.

On the inside cover of *The Big Book*, Gwen had written, *To Huw, all my love, Mummy, Christmas 1965.*

Would it become *To Aled, all my love, Gwen, Auntie Gwen, Mummy? Christmas, birthday*?

Her second son, her second chance? Did she have the right to supplant the first? Would it dim his memory; would she tarnish it by loving another little boy and laughing with him? Where could she tell the village he came from? The stork?

'How could Mummy forget you, Huw?' asked Geraint. 'We won't let her, will we?'

'No, we won't,' said Huw, 'of course we won't. How could she forget me?'

'You will always be with me, Huw,' Gwen said to herself, closing *The Big Book* and putting it back on the shelf in what might become Aled's bedroom.

10

SERGEANT RHYS ISSACS *24*
MAX LEITZ *GEFREITER 19*

This was the dangerous time because she would have to reveal more of who she was, and so would he, and there was a chance something could be misinterpreted. But she let herself imagine two silhouettes walking slowly into a mellow sunset, arm in arm, one of them the headmaster, to everyone's amazement. Her late husband would not begrudge her this happiness. He would have liked Mr Tanner, he had always looked up to important men and she had been his defence against any belittlement.

Their marriage would be a discreet ceremony, presided over by his friend Reverend Elwiss, followed by an intimate reception (she was already thinking about venues) and their picture in *The Herald*.

It was to be. He would surrender and be happy to do it, glad to be bossed about and only pretend to complain: someone to care whether he was eating properly, whether he should wear a coat because, 'It's not as warm as you think,' who would make him take her to places he would never bother to go on his own, who would smile at his foibles and be comfortable with his silences. She could put away her wiles, so tiring, and be content to please him in all ways for the rest of their lives.

She read the two novels he had given her and tried to smile at the parts which she thought were supposed to be amusing and shed a tear where they were sad. She had to persevere because they were long and the Victorian language was quite difficult – she had known he wouldn't choose anything modern – and the print was small and condensed, but she was determined not to be caught out when he asked her if she had enjoyed them ('Very much, Raymond,' she would reply, radiantly, as if they – he – had opened new vistas for her). He would be reading them carefully again, too, which was good, because he was making a real effort to impress her.

After their tea on Saturday afternoon, what next? She couldn't leave that up to him; she couldn't let him embarrass himself with a lame suggestion. So, it was going to be a whole day out, with lunch and a glass of wine (or two). Cardiff, possibly, the museum, the bookshops in the arcades around The Hayes? After that, they could begin to see each other out of school regularly and, soon, he would be calling around unannounced and, by then, it would no longer be a secret.

Rose Davies and Raymond Tanner; Rose Tanner;

Mr and Mrs Raymond Tanner. Raymond, never Ray, and her way of saying his name, 'Raymond,' softly, with an indulgent smile and a hint of the bedroom whenever no one was looking. She wanted to make him happy; she was *going* to make him happy.

Dear Roy

This is the last and only letter you will ever receive from me so do not write back.

Our life together is over. Do not try to get in touch with me when you're released from that place, if you ever are. I have tried to think of our years together as happy, but they weren't, were they? They were a waste. That was my life, Roy.

I don't know what I was to you from the beginning. We grew up together. I don't know how you could do this to me. I haven't tried to forgive you. I know I can't and when I think about you all I get is more angry. I have to live with that.

I haven't got a future because of you. Every hope I had has been stolen from me. You have destroyed my past and my future. If you said sorry I wouldn't believe you. I don't know how I ever believed a word you said.

Prison is where you belong, Roy Brown, now and forever.

Eve Guthrie

Rose arrived at the school eager to see him. Now, every glance would have a different meaning.

Bryn was on playground duty. 'Good morning, Mr Hughes,' she said.

At assembly, the children and teachers were gathered, waiting for Mr Tanner. He didn't appear.

'*Quiet*,' Bryn told the children, and went to look for him.

He wasn't in his office.

Bryn took assembly in a hurry. He sent them back to their classes without *The Lord's Prayer* in any language.

'Mr Rees, would you take my class for the first lesson; Mrs Davies, would you take over for Mr Rees?'

'Is there something wrong?' Rose asked. 'Is Mr Tanner unwell?'

'I don't know. I'm going to his house to find out. I don't think I'll be long. I'll be back by morning break at the latest.'

Bryn knocked at the front door but there was no answer. The curtains were open and he could see through the front room to the back garden. He went down the side passage and tried the back door. It was locked. He threw stones at the bedroom window and shouted. He looked under the mat for a key. There wasn't one.

He ran to the police station and came back with Dewi. 'You'll have to kick the door in,' he told him. 'Something's very wrong.'

'I know,' said Dewi. He shattered the lock with his boot.

The house was empty.

'*Where* is he? He's not been himself lately.'

'I was rude to him,' said Dewi.

'Rude? Why?' asked Bryn, puzzled. But there was no time.

'I'll ring the hospital from the station,' said Dewi.

'The vicar might know where he is,' said Bryn. He called the vicarage from a phone box but no one answered.

'Hello, Jean,' said Eve.

'She's had lots of visitors this week,' said the nurse.

Something exciting was happening in black and white: there was smoke, galleons and swordplay from someone leaping about the rigging who was probably Errol Flynn.

Jean's mysterious smile.

'Go and ask your dad to get more coal in, Jack,' she told him.

He jumped up and ran outside to tell his father who was talking to Uncle Roy. 'Mum says she wants you to bring more coal in.'

'Oh, does she?'

'Yes.'

'You better had then,' said Roy, smiling and putting out his cigarette on top of the fence they had creosoted during the summer.

'Where's Huw?' asked Jack.

'I don't know,' said his father. 'Why don't you go and find him?'

Jack ran into the alley, past Roy and Eve's house and into Huw's garden where Gwen was hanging out the washing. 'Where's Huw, Auntie Gwen?'

She took a clothes peg from between her teeth. 'Up in his room.'

He was, poring over *The Big Book*.

'Are you bringing that coal in?' Jean asked, through the kitchen window.

'I'm doing it,' said Alan.

'Where's Jack gone?'

'Gwen's,' Alan replied, heaving the bucket of coal over the step.

'Aled's asleep upstairs, so careful you don't bang that bucket.'

'I won't,' said Alan.

'It's been a long time, Jean,' said Eve. 'I'm sorry. I know I should have come to see you but things have been difficult. But I'm here now.' She touched Jean's hand but drew back. 'I only took Aled because I was afraid for him and because you were ill and couldn't look after him. I know it was the wrong thing to do. I would have brought him back when it was safe, I would. You do believe me, don't you?

'I think, if we hadn't been found, we might have had a happy life together… but I knew it wasn't to be.

'I can't help loving him. I loved Jack too. I loved them both as if they were my own. I always wanted children but, now, I never will. I can't tell you how sorry I am that all this has happened. I'm sorry for us all.' She looked into Jean's face. 'But don't come back until all this is over, will you?

'Goodbye, Jean,' Eve said, for the last time.

Deborah was tying back plants and plucking out stray weeds.

'Leave the gardener something to do,' Reverend Elwiss told her. He had come out to sit on the bench under his study window.

'He's not thorough enough,' she said, holding back some prickly stems in her gardening gloves to snip a flowerless head. 'There, you see? Have you finished your sermon?'

'No. It will be fine once I make a start.'

'You haven't started it yet?'

'Not yet. But I will.'

'What is it, Ernest? I need to see to that big rose bush which is falling over.'

'Do you think I should try again with Ellis Maynard?'

'Why, dear? To what end? Can you stop him drinking himself to death?'

'No.'

'Can you make him repeat his confession to the police?'

'No.'

'Then you have your answer, Ernest.'

'Partly. I just keep thinking, have I done enough?'

'You've done all that you can, Ernest, more than you should.'

'This is about a man's life, Deborah, two men's lives.'

'Yes, I know.' She tilted her head and looked down the flowerbed. 'Two lost souls. You thought Ellis Maynard had something to do with the missing boys, too, didn't you?'

'I thought it was possible.'

She sat down next to him and pulled off her gardening gloves. 'But you don't think that now?'

'No. The answer to what happened to them is not with him. I'm sure of that.' He sighed. 'Deborah, I am only a parish priest and you should be organising the church fete and I should be worrying about the church roof, not this.'

'I am organising the fete and you should finish your sermon.'

'I will finish it.'

'Then after you have, worry about the church roof.'

Bryn came round the corner of the house, out of breath. 'I thought I heard you. I've been knocking at the front door.'

They looked up. 'Bryn? Shouldn't you be in school? The holidays haven't started yet, have they?'

'He's not here, is he?'

'Who?'

'Mr Tanner. He didn't come in this morning and we can't find him. He's not at home, we looked. I had to fetch Dewi and he kicked the back door in.'

'What?' said Reverend Elwiss, standing up. 'He kicked the door in?'

'Dewi's phoning the hospital from the police station.'

'Ernest,' said Deborah, taking charge, 'telephone the police station from here to see if Dewi has any news. Then call the school to see if he's turned up there.'

They went inside.

But when Reverend Elwiss put down the receiver, he said, 'No, he's not in hospital and he isn't at the school. Think now, Bryn, is there any reason why he might not have come in today?'

'I *have* been thinking,' Bryn said. 'He's not been himself lately.'

Reverend Elwiss looked at his wife. 'Nor have any of us, Bryn.'

'Not like this, Vicar. He always puts the school first. He was so weighed down. He seems to have got old suddenly.'

'I was quite short with him,' said Reverend Elwiss, 'I'm sorry to say. I didn't stop to think how it might have affected him but one doesn't, not with him. We all expect him to be a tower of strength. Perhaps this has affected him more deeply than we know.'

'He was upset about telling Laura and me about Maynard. He thought he shouldn't have and he was talking about finding Jack Harris.'

'Ernest went to see Ellis Maynard in the pub,' said Deborah.

'It wasn't any use,' said Reverend Elwiss. 'I don't know

why I thought it would be.'

'Would this have anything to do with him?' asked Bryn.

'We mustn't jump to any conclusions,' said Deborah. 'He hasn't been missing long.'

'Missing?' said Reverend Elwiss. 'Let's not say that. I *hate* that word.'

Prosser sat behind the prison chaplain's desk, loaned to him for his visit, and felt important. There was a metal cross on the wall above his head made of two nails.

Alan came in with a warder, who waited at the door with his hands clasped behind his back.

Prosser pretended to study some papers he had found on the desk. 'Sit,' he said, without looking up. 'I'm Detective Prosser.'

Alan sat.

Prosser leaned back. He tapped the desk with his finger. 'I've got something to tell you, Harris. I've had my eye on you.'

'Can you see through walls, Detective Prosser?'

'I didn't say you could speak, did I? And I'm here to tell you what I've seen. Do you want to know what it is? Well, I'm going to tell you, Harris.' Prosser rested his hands on his chin with his elbows on the table and his mouth twitched. 'Do you want to know? Do you?'

Alan didn't reply.

'I've found the boy.' The twitching became a taunting

smile and his eyes cruel and weak.

'Jack?'

'Not him. Rhodri Mitchell.'

'I read the paper,' Alan said.

'Your other boy is with Eve Brown. Did you know that? You think you're safe in here, don't you, but I'm going to get you for it because I know every thought you have. What do you think of that, Harris?'

'Can I speak now, Detective Prosser?'

'Go on then.'

'You haven't got it quite right have you? What Sergeant Phillips told you to tell me was: tell him I've found Rhodri Mitchell, tell him I know he did it, tell him prison will not keep me from him, tell him I know his mind.'

'Don't you tell me what he told me to tell you,' Prosser spluttered.

'Tell Sergeant Phillips I know *his* mind, Prosser. But you won't.'

'I'll tell him anything I like.'

'I don't think so,' said Alan. 'You're just his latest whipping boy. You even look like Jeffries, and look what happened to him? And, after you, there'll be another one.'

'I'm nothing like Jeffries.'

'Aren't you?' Alan turned to the warder. 'Would you take me back to my cell, please?'

'You'll go when I tell you to,' said Prosser.

'Go back to Bridgend, Detective Prosser.' Alan stood up.

The warder looked disdainfully at Prosser and said, 'I'll tell the chaplain he can have his desk back.'

As Alan made his way back to his cell, he thought, 'Please, Gwen. Don't delay.'

'Nesta,' said Howell, finally running out of patience with his sister, 'you moping about the house isn't helping, is it?'

'I'm not moping.'

'Whatever you're doing, then, stop it. Now, you listen to me for a change.'

'Don't you lecture me, Howell Morgan.'

He stood in the doorway so she couldn't pass.

'Let me by, Howell.'

'No. You're going to listen.'

She took a theatrical breath and shoved her hands into the pockets of her housecoat. 'I haven't swept the pavement yet,' she pouted.

'Let Delia do it,' he told her. 'Now, we're going to take Aled to visit Gwen so we can see where she lives and have a proper talk with her.'

'It's too far.'

'No it's not. We don't have to rush, we can take our time. We'll take the train from Cardiff.'

In its tin garage behind the shop, the van breathed a sigh of relief.

'Now, don't argue, Nesta, because, if you don't want to, I'll take him on my own.'

A tear ran down her cheek. 'But he's all we've got left,

Howell.'

He put his arm around her. 'Come on, now, it will all work out for the best in the end. Eve was never the answer, was she?'

'No,' Nesta shook her head. 'No.'

'There we are, then.'

'Aled Harris is no longer with Eve Brown, Sergeant Phillips.'

'Where is he, Jones?'

'Gone back to the Rhondda with Nesta Morgan.'

'Go and see her, Jones. Take Colcannon with you. Tell her I am watching.'

Prosser was waiting in the corridor. He went in.

'Prosser,' said Sergeant Phillips, 'you didn't tell him, did you?'

'I did, Sir.'

'No, you did not. He told you. I know your mind, Prosser. Get out.'

When Prosser came out of the police station, *Herald* Andrew and Lloyd were waiting. 'How did you get on, then, Gordon?'

'Good,' said Prosser, who was white.

'Can we buy you a pint?' asked *Herald* Andrew.

'Yes,' said Prosser, weakly, 'yes.'

Howell held up the binoculars. Two points of brilliant light almost burnt into the carpet. 'They're empty,' he said, 'they're healed.'

‘Look through them, Howell.’

To the top of the mountains and the sky, to the wispy clouds just appearing.

‘What can you see?’

‘A long way,’ said Howell.

‘Good,’ said Gerhard, ‘we will share the view together.’

Howell looked through the left lens. He felt the presence of his friend at his side: two eyes, one view.

11

PRIVATE *MORGAN JENKINS* 20
JOST MEYER GEFREITER 21

The fiery eyes were wreathed in white steam rising from the steelworks. They looked down the length of Sker Beach, where the surf stretched a long way out, to where the waves crashed over rocks at the far end. Behind was the buried city with its broken tower rising out of the sand. The box-car's doors were partly open, the rain had obscured the slew of tyre tracks and new grass had grown between them. The search had failed but, beneath the clear waters of Kenfig Pool, the beautiful girls held Jack in their arms and wrapped their long weeds of hair around him. To Pink Bay, then Rest Bay; to Porthcawl, to the fair at Trecco; to Nottage and across the estuary to Ogmore and, there, the dunes ended.

'Did you find him?' asked Laura.

'No,' said Bryn. 'I fetched Dewi. We searched his

house but he wasn't there.'

One hand rose to her mouth and the other stayed with her restless child. 'Do you think something's happened to him?'

'Yes, I do.'

'Oh, Bryn, do you really think so?'

'Who's on playground duty?'

'Paul.'

'Where's Mrs Davies?'

'Still in Form Two when I last saw her.'

'The police will be asking questions but we must still take lessons as usual. The children mustn't know anything is wrong.'

'How will we do that, Bryn?'

'As best as we can.'

Sergeant Phillips' big, black car pulled up outside the school. He got out, smoothed his moustache with the outside of his thumbs and yanked his tunic straight. The children's piping voices died away and they watched in silence. Detective Prosser got out of the passenger side and came round the car. Sergeant Phillips didn't look at him. He swept over the playground like a harbinger crossing a dark plain and went in through the main doors.

Bryn waited at the end of the corridor, hating and fearing the necessity of his presence.

'Prosser,' said Sergeant Phillips, looking directly at Bryn, 'speak to Mrs Hughes and I will speak to *him*.'

Prosser disappeared into a classroom and came back

out again. He went into another where Laura was waiting behind her desk, with the register before her, closed: inside were the names of the lost boys. 'Here,' she had whispered for them, every morning for three years.

'Lunch break is nearly over,' said Bryn. 'I don't want to alarm the children.'

'The break will be as long as it needs to be, *Mr* Hughes.'

Bryn had not heard that voice since the interview room, interspersing Jeffries' accusations with deep, rumbling demands that made his ears bleed and his vision shiver.

Jeffries had kept repeating, over and over again, 'Say you did it, because we know you did... say you did it because we know you did.'

And Bryn had answered, 'I didn't, I didn't, I didn't.'

'Tell me, *Mr* Hughes.'

Only in his nightmares, when he sweated and clutched for Laura.

'Where is he, *Mr* Hughes?'

'I don't know. That's why I went for Constable Jones.'

'*Mr* Hughes, you *know* where he is.'

'No, how could I?'

'Because you knew what he was going to do when he left the school.'

'No, I didn't.'

'Yes, *Mr* Hughes, you did.'

'No,' Bryn shook his head, 'I didn't. He said he had an errand to run, but he didn't tell me what it was.'

'Tell me, *Mr* Hughes.' Sergeant Phillips pouted his moustache.

'He was thinking about Jack Harris, after the discovery of Rhodri Mitchell's body.'

'*My* discovery. Then you know more than you are telling me and I will know.' Sergeant Phillips walked back up the corridor to the main doors. 'Prosser.'

The classroom door opened and Prosser came scuttling out. He looked at Bryn and showed his teeth.

Laura rubbed her belly. 'What did he ask you, Bryn? He wasn't here long.' She remembered what Jeffries had called her in the interview room and, again, in the hospital, when she thought Bryn was dying.

'He said I knew more than I was telling him. He said I know where Mr Tanner is.' Bryn ran his fingers through his hair. 'I didn't know what to say.'

'I told that detective that Mr Tanner hadn't been himself lately,' said Laura.

'I'm not sure you should have said that.'

'But why not, Bryn, that might be why he's gone missing.'

'Because they will use it against us like they did last time.'

They went out to the playground. Sergeant Phillips' big, black car had gone.

'Did they speak to you or Mrs Davies, Paul?' Bryn asked him.

'No, why would they?' yodelled Paul Rees, for whom

Sergeant Phillips held a boyhood terror.

'Get the children into class, Mr Rees. Break should have finished ten minutes ago.'

Mrs Davies read to Form Two, but she didn't remember the story or hear the words she spoke.

It was a long afternoon.

The mothers gathered outside the gates.

Mr Topliss appeared from the boiler room or some other place of inner workings. He was wiping his hands on a rag. 'Where's Mr Tanner, then?' he asked Laura.

'We don't know,' she told him.

'He's usually in one of the classrooms having a think about this time, when you lot have all gone. That's what he does. I have to make sure I don't lock him in.' He laughed.

'You haven't heard, have you, Mr Topliss?'

'Heard what?'

But Laura went into every classroom, hoping to find him, as if he had been hiding for some unfathomable reason. Lastly, she went into his office. It smelt faintly of Rose's perfume. A copy of *The Herald* was still in the wastepaper bin next to his desk. She came out, hot with the baby and an aching back. She sat down on one of the children's chairs and tried to stretch out her legs.

'This…' he waited for the pips. 'This is Douglas Protheroe… hello? Yes?'

'This is Eve Guthrie. I was Eve Brown, but I'm not anymore.'

'Eve Brown – Guthrie?'

She was disappointed he didn't sound surprised.

'Yes, I know who you are, Mrs Guthrie.'

'Miss Guthrie. *Miss*.'

'*Miss* Guthrie. How can I help you, Eve?' He searched amongst the papers on his desk for an unbroken stub of pencil and pulled his notebook out of his jacket pocket. 'Now.'

'I haven't got much change,' she said.

'Would you like me to call you back?' He could hear her breathing. 'What is it, Eve?'

'I read the paper.'

There were always letters, mostly from cranks, which he stuffed into the filing cabinet in no particular order, and anonymous phone calls which he noted. But he couldn't ignore her – he wanted to, but he couldn't.

'They've found one of the boys, haven't they?' said Eve.

'Yes, they have.'

'I've got information about all the missing boys.' She said their names: 'Jack Harris, Huw Evans and Rhodri Mitchell. And about Gwyn Roberts.'

For a moment, Protheroe let the receiver dangle away from his ear as he tried to make up his mind. 'What information, Eve? Where are you?'

'In a phone box.'

'Yes, I know. Would you like someone to come and see you at your house?'

'No, not there. I'll come and see you.'

The pips.

'Eve Brown,' he thought. 'Poor Eve Brown. Gone but not forgotten. Guthrie? Poor bloody woman.' Protheroe banged his desk. '*Fuck it,*' he shouted. He stood up and looked out of the top pane of the sash window. The river was steaming, suffocating in the sun.

'*Andrew!*' he yelled. 'Up here, *now!*' He heard *Herald* Andrew's feet on the stairs and slumped into his chair. 'We all come running,' he thought, 'like good little newspapermen.' He ran his hands over his face.

'Right,' he said, when *Herald* Andrew appeared. He wearily pulled himself upright and threw his reading glasses onto the pile of papers on his desk. 'Guess who I've been talking to?'

'Who, boss?'

'You've got all this to look forward to,' Protheroe thought. 'Lick your lips, Andrew.'

Herald Andrew licked his lips.

'We have another angle,' he said, with a sardonic little laugh.

'Boss?'

He knew the story *Herald* Andrew would write if he left him to get on with it. 'We'll see her together,' Protheroe told him.

'We're taking Aled to Carmarthen to see Gwen Evans tomorrow,' said Nesta.

'All that way?' asked Delia. 'Tomorrow?'

'It's not far by train from Cardiff. I was going to write, but there's no time to wait.'

'She might not be in,' said Delia. 'What will you do if she's not there?'

'We'll have to come back.'

'What does Howell think?'

'He agrees with me,' said Nesta.

'But you said… is it the right thing to do?'

'Then *what* is the right thing to do? It's always me who has to decide, isn't it?'

'But what about Jean, Nesta? Don't you want Eve to have him now? Why, Nesta?' Delia's bottom lip was beginning to quiver.

Nesta didn't reply. She went up the passage and into the shop.

Mrs James was there, buying two cupcakes from a packet of six.

Idris was sitting on his stool behind the counter. He made a note under *Mrs Sugar* in his tally book.

Emlyn watched Mrs James crossing the road with a cupcake in each hand. 'She'll be back in a bit,' he said. 'What do you think? She hasn't had any bread since yesterday. An egg? Or bacon? No, it won't be bacon. She'll be in for that in the morning. Nothing like planning ahead is there, love?'

Nesta waited in the shop for a while, watching her brothers in their brown shop coats not doing very much because there weren't enough customers for three of them (ever). Howell didn't pay her any attention. The matter was settled and he would not let her reopen it. She had forced him to make up his mind and got the answer she didn't want. Nesta went out and stood next to the shelves of stock in the passage. Her heel nudged a mousetrap.

After a while, she relented and went back to the kitchen to make up with her timorous sister, but Delia wasn't there. Nesta looked through the door and saw her sitting in the armchair crying. She could hear Aled pattering across the landing and coming down the stairs. 'Delia?'

Delia heard him too. She pulled a hankie from her sleeve and wiped her eyes. She came into the kitchen and bent over the cooker. It wasn't time for lunch so she pretended with a saucepan and gathered herself.

Aled asked, 'When can we go to the farmhouse again? Uncle Howell says we don't have to wait until after Christmas.'

'We're going on a day out tomorrow,' said Nesta. 'You, me and Uncle Howell.'

Delia looked at her sideways with weepy eyes.

'To the farmhouse?' Aled asked. 'Can I go in the sea?'

'To a different house, this time.'

'What sort of house?'

Nesta didn't know. 'It's almost the same, but different.'

'How?' asked Aled. 'Is it on a farm?'

'It's in the countryside close to a farm.'

'How long will it take to get there?'

'Quite long, but not long.'

'Is it further than Porth?'

'Yes,' said Nesta, 'quite a bit further, an hour or two on the train.'

'Are we going by train? Are we, are we?' He jumped up and down. Then he stopped and frowned. 'When we get there, will I be seeing that new auntie again?'

'No, not this time.'

'Good.'

'*Aled*.'

'How did she know what my favourite squash was? I didn't know it was my favourite.'

'She guessed. Go and see how they're getting on in the shop. They might need your help. Go on, go and see.'

'I will,' and Aled skipped down the passage, happy that they were going back to the farmhouse by the sea and oblivious to her quandary.

Delia asked, 'Can I come too, please, Nesta?'

'No, it's best it's just Howell and me. You can come next time.'

Delia went up to her north-facing bedroom and its granite view.

The downstairs office was empty. Eve went quietly up the stairs. It was hot and stuffy and she felt lightheaded. Protheroe's door was open but she couldn't see inside. She hesitated and her shadow fell across the doorway.

'Come in, Eve, please.'

Protheroe was behind his desk, *Herald* Andrew sat on one of the old chairs and Lloyd was standing in the corner. He focused his camera on her.

'Thank you for coming, Eve,' said Protheroe. 'Please, sit down.'

She looked at *Herald* Andrew and remembered fending him off with an umbrella outside the police station.

'Would you mind if Lloyd takes some photos?' *Herald* Andrew asked.

Protheroe frowned at him.

Herald Andrew shrugged.

Flash.

'Oh,' Eve flinched and turned away. 'Take as many as you like,' she said, blinking.

Flash.

Lloyd's camera lens was prehensile.

'There's only us here,' Protheroe told her, 'so there's no rush.'

Herald Andrew had his notebook balanced on his knee and his pencil cocked between his fingers. He had a carnivorous look, as if he was watching a lost fawn from the long grass. 'It's been a long time, Eve,' he said, as if they had parted on friendly terms.

'The other boy has been found,' she said, 'and Huw.' Her hands searched across her lap for somewhere to rest. 'But not Jack.' She hunched her shoulders as if they hurt.

'Yes, he has, Rhodri Mitchell. Poor boy,' said Protheroe,

slowly, watching her closely. 'Are you quite well, Eve?'

'I want the world to know who did it,' she said, and began to tip to one side.

Herald Andrew leaned forward.

She sat up straight.

Lloyd's camera protruded into her face.

Flash.

Protheroe put his hands over the lens.

Lloyd stepped back and pointed his camera at the window to adjust the light settings. He crouched.

Flash.

'Lloyd,' Protheroe half-turned to him. He paused to moderate himself. 'Who, Eve?' he asked, as gently as he could.

'Roy *Brown*,' she spat his name, her eyes blazed. '*He* took the boys and he killed Gwyn Roberts.' She dwindled suddenly, exhausted by her outburst, spent.

'Oh,' Protheroe started.

'Roy Brown, Roy Brown,' she murmured.

'I shouldn't have let her come here,' Protheroe thought. 'I should have seen her on my own.'

Herald Andrew's pencil scratched at his notebook.

Eve pushed her hands between her thighs and squeezed them. Her dress rode up above her knees.

Lloyd hurried to change his film.

'Why have you waited so long to say anything, Eve?' Protheroe asked her.

'He is a mon-ster,' she said, pronouncing the two

syllables as if it was an indisputable medical term she had just been told but didn't understand, a diagnosis for which this was the treatment.

'But why wait until now? Did he tell you he did it?'

'No, he didn't tell me. He didn't have to *tell* me. I knew. Of course I did.'

'How did you know, Eve?'

'Boss?' said *Herald* Andrew, in a hissy whisper, 'she's told you.'

Protheroe ignored him.

'He was always out when the boys disappeared and I saw him going up to Gwyn Roberts' farm on the night he died. I watched him go. He knew Gwyn had seen him.'

'I could be wrong,' Protheroe said, gently, 'but I don't believe Gwyn told the police that.'

Herald Andrew was shaking his head vigorously behind Eve's back.

'He did tell them, but they didn't believe him,' said Eve.

Lloyd stood outside the door to get a different angle.

Flash.

'They thought Alan did it. But he didn't,' said Eve.

'Then why didn't you tell the police straightaway? Alan Harris has been in prison for three years. You were his neighbour.'

'Roy Brown was my husband,' she said, as if it was a terrible revelation, the indisputable conclusion to her argument. 'And now I want the world to know what he did.'

'The world will know, Eve, but you will have to tell Sergeant Phillips.'

'No,' she said, quickly, her face filling with alarm. 'That's why I'm here. It can be in the paper. He mustn't know it was me. He's taken my life away.'

Flash.

'Who, Eve, Sergeant Phillips?'

'He'll never come out of prison now. He deserves it. And there's nothing he can do to give it back. The boys are gone.' She pulled her hands out from between her thighs and wrapped her arms around herself. 'I would have been a wonderful mother.' She was rocking. 'Aled's life is ruined too. His mother is gone and she won't come back. Why would she want to? And his aunties are too old. There's only me and he won't let me have him.'

'Roy won't?'

'That's what Roy said when he saw Nesta and me outside the school with Aled. It's because of *him*. I'd be the best mother he could have. She can't look after him and she's never going to be able to and his father's in prison.'

'Thank you, Eve,' Protheroe said. 'It was very brave of you to tell us.'

'When will it be in the paper?' she asked.

'Soon.'

Eve's nostrils flared as she breathed. Her cheeks were clammy. 'This is how Jean was,' she said. 'You see? I can be a mother too.'

Protheroe picked up his reading glasses, folded them and slid them into his shirt pocket. But when he looked at her, a splurge of misery on the other side of his desk, he couldn't hide his pity. 'Let me walk you home?' he said.

'I'd like to walk on my own.'

'I don't think you should, Eve.'

'I will walk on my own,' she said, firmly.

'Then I'll see you out.'

When Protheroe came back up, *Herald* Andrew was gabbling excitedly.

'What a splash this is going to make. *Boom.*'

Protheroe lowered himself into his chair. 'No, Andrew, we're going to hold off on this for a while.'

'*Boss*? We can't. It's one of the best stories we've ever had.'

'Did you believe her, Andrew?'

'I don't know. Does it matter?'

'Yes, I think it does.'

'Boss, what's the *matter* with you?'

'That's enough, Andrew. That's the way it's going to be.'

Eve watched the children through the bay window on their way home from school with their mothers. 'He did it and that's the end of it.' What Mr Tanner had told her had been a dream, it had never happened because Roy did it, *Roy*.

Reverend Elwiss came out of the vicarage.

'Is there any news?' Deborah asked.

'No, none,' he replied. 'I couldn't speak to Dewi, he wasn't there and all they would say is that they're looking.'

'Did they say where?'

'No.' Reverend Elwiss walked down the garden to the apple trees. He stood with his hands at his groin as if in preparation to lift them to his face. 'This is the test,' he said, telling himself.

She was next to him. 'What do you mean, the test?'

'Nothing.'

'Please, Ernest, don't try to make this into something else.'

'I'm not trying to.'

'Yes, you are, so stop.'

'I am not.'

'There's nothing any of us can do but wait for news.'

'Please, Deborah.'

'Then stop seeing great designs in everything.'

'I'm not.'

'Just be worried, will you?'

He turned and she saw the hurt and fervour wrestling there.

'I'm sorry, Ernest, I know it's your way of seeing things... I'm going inside.' She left him in the garden.

'She feels it too,' he thought. He went through the garden gate into the graveyard and into the church. He sat in the front pew.

He looked up at the small, wooden figurine. 'Tell

me?' he asked.

'*Jack Harris.*'

Reverend Elwiss spun round in fright. 'Deborah?' But he was alone.

12

SERGEANT SELWYN KIMBER 29
GERWIN NEUMANN OBERSTLEUTNANT 34

Salute: 'Good morning, Gerhard.'

'Good morning, Howell. So, an important day?'

'Yes, it is.'

'I am sure it will go well.'

'I have never wanted something so much, Gerhard, that I did not want.'

'If we could live forever, there would be no need for such difficult choices.'

'But we don't live forever.'

'Or if only you were a few years younger?'

'If we all were. That's what Nesta says, as if it would make the years go away.'

'You can watch through the binoculars,' said Gerhard.

'I will be able to see all the way down to Porth and up to the top of the mountain.'

'I think you will be surprised. Believe, Howell.'

Howell picked up the binoculars and put them to his eyes. 'Porth…' he swung them round, 'mountains.'

Gerhard laughed. 'And when you were away during the war, what did you think of?'

'Home.'

'Which was?'

'The valley, the shop, everyone I knew.'

'And?'

'The mountains.'

'You see, Howell? Do you see?'

Howell put the binoculars to his eyes again.

Gerhard said, 'You are seeing what you thought about when you were far from home.'

'I am,' said Howell, quietly.

'And Aled too. All your days until you can no longer see. The binoculars are an instrument of sight and memory and you can see whatever you want to see. We both can, with a lens each.'

'And fill them back up?'

'Exactly, Howell, and fill them back up with life.'

Howell placed the binoculars on the windowsill. 'I must be going, or we will miss the bus to Cardiff.'

Headmaster Goes Missing

Raymond Tanner, headmaster of Bridgend Primary School, has not been seen since Tuesday when he left the school early telling staff he had an 'errand' to perform.

The alarm was raised when he did not show up at the school on Wednesday morning. Police had to break down the door of his home to get in, but there was no sign that he had returned there on the previous evening. Police are conducting door-to-door enquiries and have widened their search around Bridgend.

A teacher at the school told the police, 'He hasn't been himself lately,' and there have been growing concerns about his state of mind. He is said to have never fully recovered following the disappearance of two of his pupils, Jack Harris, 6, and Huw Evans, 6, nearly three years ago in October 1966. Huw Evan's body was found in Porthcawl Harbour soon after but what happened to Jack Harris is still unknown. It is thought that the recent discovery in Pencoed of the remains of a third boy, Rhodri Mitchell, 7, who went missing at the same time, could have triggered a breakdown and Mr Tanner may have become confused and possibly lost.

Sergeant Phillips told The Herald, *'We are doing all we can to find Mr Tanner and appeal to anyone who saw him on Tuesday afternoon or evening to come forward as a matter of urgency.'*

Raymond Tanner has been headmaster for over twenty years and has dedicated his life to the school.

The search continues.

The rolling hills of Carmarthen were gentle, so different to their muscular cousins to the east where lay her bituminous David who had risen, glistening black from the pit at the end of each day, to be washed clean before he came home to her waiting arms, and Huw, as yet unnamed, awaiting his term. She thought of him, searching for her in the sightless night.

'We won't have to wait long,' said Geraint.

'What are we waiting for?' asked Huw.

His father smiled. 'You'll see.'

Sergeant Phillips' big, black car came slowly down the prom in Porthcawl. It stopped near the harbour. The tide was in and the boats pulled tight on their anchors, rigging thrummed and gulls wheeled and cried. He rolled his gloved fingers over the steering wheel as if he was waiting for someone. He pouted his moustache and smoothed it with the outside of his thumbs. Walkers bent to see inside. He ignored them and they went quickly on their way, glancing back, herding their children. Drinkers in the pub on the opposite side of the road stepped away from the windows; the queue at the ice cream van grew less until there was no one and it left for Rest Bay. The rising swell thumped into the seawall. The sun was bright on the Somerset coast, Devon and Cornwall across the Bristol Channel. The fiery eyes. When the prom was deserted, Sergeant Phillips' big, black car moved away from the kerb.

Gwen thought, 'I don't know how to make it come about; I

don't know if I want it to.' She pictured a little boy playing in the garden, nearly Huw's age. She would have to watch him and never let him out of her sight, not for a minute: the joy and the burden, a child in her life again. 'It is too much, Alan. He will make me love him and I will be afraid to lose him. You have left it all to me and I don't know what to do.'

What did Alan imagine? Farms, subtle hills, the sky and the river, seeing what he had not and would never see? She could send him photographs so they would have real places to talk about when they visited… when they visited? *They… we.* Already, it was unfolding. 'Should I tell Aled so that he grows up with it? How old must he be before I do?' What about Jean? In Aled's past, his father and mother could not be separated. And Jack? I will have to tell him he once had a brother. 'It is too much to ask, Alan, even for you.'

She put down her mug. Through the window, she saw a man and a woman coming up the road. The woman was wearing some kind of turban affair. Between them, holding their hands and skipping, was a boy.

Dewi drove. The road got steeper as they neared Trebanog. 'I'm not going to do it,' he said. 'It's wrong and I won't. They've done nothing to deserve this.'

'Then let's tell them we were passing,' said Brenda.

'Passing? Trebanog?'

'I'll think of something,' she said. 'We don't have to

say he sent us.'

But, when they reached the top of the precipitous hill, Nesta and Howell were already on a bus with Aled that was pointing into the valley, nearly at the river, on its way to Cardiff.

Dewi parked the car next to the Beinon Arms.

Emlyn saw them as they waited to cross the road. 'Id?'

Idris looked up from his tally book. 'What's this, then?'

'That's Dewi and Brenda, isn't it? What can they want?'

'We were passing,' said Brenda, when they came into the shop.

'Passing?' asked Emlyn, frowning. 'Up here?'

'There was a witness to a case we had to see in Porth,' said Brenda, 'and we thought we'd come back this way and call in and ask after Aled.'

'That's very kind of you,' said Idris. 'But Aled's not here. He's gone with Howell and Nesta to see Gwen Evans in Carmarthen.'

'Oh, have they?' said Brenda. 'That's a shame.'

They didn't stay long; there was nothing to say.

'Thank God,' said Dewi, when they were on their way back to Bridgend. 'Now we don't have to lie.'

'We can tell him they'd taken Aled out for the day,' said Brenda. 'We don't have to say where.'

'I'll be surprised if he doesn't ask,' said Dewi.

'Then we don't know, do we?'

The road suddenly came out into a bowl-like valley, arrestingly fertile, with a wood and bright fields as if it was a haven from the black, necrotic flows inching down the mountains on either side.

'Would you mind if we didn't go straight back?' Dewi asked.

'No, not if you don't want to. What do you want to do?'

Dewi pulled over. 'Shall we get out?'

They climbed over a stile into a field. The bracken reached up almost to their waists. There was a stream at the bottom of the valley, sparkling and clean but rushing to join the Taff only a few miles away that would foul its purity, steal its oxygen and pour it, lifeless, into Tiger Bay.

'It's nice here,' he said.

Brenda reached up and ran the outsides of her fingers down his cheek.

Dewi didn't move.

She reached up and gently pinched the point of his chin between her thumb and forefinger and turned his face toward her and kissed him. 'No, we don't have to go straight back.' She smiled. 'Is this what you wanted to do?'

They looked around. There were no cars on the road. They knelt and took off their uniforms and, naked, pressed flat the bed of ferns and sweated and writhed in the mottling sun.

Then they lay side by side and listened to the birds and the gurgling water. It was hot and still and the bracken had a bitter-sweet smell.

'Thank you,' said Dewi.

She didn't answer for a while. 'You're not going to ask me to marry you, are you?'

He laughed. 'I think we've broken some rules.'

'Why? We weren't wearing our uniforms and that's the first time I've heard you laugh in a long time.'

'Is it?' He put his hands behind his head, but it was not in repose. 'I went to see Alan Harris in prison.'

She rolled onto her side, making the bracken rustle. 'Oh, Dewi. Did you?'

'I told him I would do what I could to help and spying on Aled or Eve and his relatives is not helping him is it?'

She placed her hand on his chest.

'I think I might leave the police,' he said.

'Don't, Dewi. You were meant for it. Remember what you were like in school?'

'Before Mr Tanner put me straight?'

'There had to be something in you to put straight.'

'Mr Tanner never gave up on anyone, did he?' said Dewi. 'Not even Maynard.'

'What good would it do if you left the police? You'd never be able to help him then, would you?' She sat up.

He stroked her back. 'I was right though, wasn't I? I know you agree, Brenda.'

'Come on, we have to go.'

'Do we? Why don't we stay here forever instead?'

'That would be nice, Dewi, but what happens when it rains?'

They poked their heads above the bracken. A sheep was watching. 'Baa,' it said, and resumed chewing.

'We weren't seen, I hope,' said Brenda.

'It's too late now,' said Dewi, 'and we might as well be hung for a sheep as a lamb.'

They shuffled awkwardly into their clothes sitting down.

'I've got green stains on the elbow of my blouse,' said Brenda.

'How are you going to explain that?'

'I'll tell him we were shagging in the bushes.'

When they were back in the car, Dewi asked her, 'Shall we do that again, soon?'

'If the sun's still out,' she replied, winding down the window. 'It's like an oven in here.'

'There's no rain forecast,' he said, 'but what if there was?'

Brenda laughed. 'Then we'd have to think of somewhere else where we wouldn't get wet.'

'What is this?' said Bryn, holding up the newspaper.

'Let me see, Bryn.' Reverend Elwiss read it carefully.

'Laura told that policeman, Prosser, that Mr Tanner hadn't been himself but she didn't mean it like this. He must have told the paper. But they've twisted it all out of shape. I told her they would.'

'Could there be some truth in it, Bryn? Could he be wandering about somewhere, confused? It is a possible explanation.'

'No,' said Bryn, 'not like they've made out. The discovery of Rhodri Mitchell's body upset him, but he wasn't confused.'

'An errand is a strange word to use as an excuse for leaving during school hours, isn't it? It's as if he was trying to make light of something serious.'

'Yes, I thought that,' said Bryn. 'But I didn't think to ask him, it wasn't my place to. I should have done.'

'He wouldn't have told you, Bryn, not if he didn't want to.' Reverend Elwiss looked around Mr Tanner's office. 'Have you looked in his desk?'

'No,' said Bryn, offended that the vicar would think he had.

'We should. Come on.'

They looked in the drawers. There were sediments of chalk as hard as limestone and white dust covered everything: pencils, a stapler, a confiscated penknife, a catapult and lots of old elastic bands with perished rubber.

'There's nothing here,' said Bryn, still feeling uncomfortable. 'But I wouldn't know what to look for.'

'Anything,' said Reverend Elwiss. 'Anything at all.' He sat in Mr Tanner's chair.

Bryn stared. 'Um,' he began.

'It's better to do something than nothing.' Reverend Elwiss placed his fingers together with his elbows on the desk and pushed at the tip of his nose.

Bryn forced himself to sit down in the chair opposite.

The vicar looked at the wall above his head; Bryn looked at the vicar and, slowly, the man beneath, whom Raymond called Ernest, began to emerge. 'Break's nearly over,' Bryn said, before he saw too much. 'I'm going to have to go back to my class in a minute.'

But the vicar wasn't finished. 'Ever since we went to see Ellis Maynard in the hospital,' he said, without taking his eyes off the same spot on the wall, 'I have had a growing sense of disquiet. It's difficult to describe, but a feeling – God *forbid* – that someone is waiting and watching; that events are…' he shook his head, 'beyond our control or our reason. I'm not explaining myself very well, am I?'

'Waiting for what, Vicar?' Bryn asked. 'For this?'

'I don't know. I'm not sure I should be telling you.'

'Shouldn't you?' asked Bryn.

'Vicars are fallible but they're not supposed to be foolish.'

'Is it foolish, Vicar?'

Reverend Elwiss stopped looking at the wall. 'Deborah calls them my premonitions, not that I have them all the time. But she can't dissuade me from this one. I wish she could.'

Bryn should have been honoured, in an ambivalent way, that another bared soul was intent on confessing in this sanctum of initiations, as if to say, 'It's time you knew. There are no certainties, only the pretence of them for a while.'

In the wastepaper bin Bryn read the old headline upside down.

Child's Body Found

'Sergeant Phillips said I knew where Mr Tanner was.'

'I don't know why he would say that, Bryn. But I am not a policeman.'

'When I was in the police station and he accused me of having something to do with the boys' disappearances, he didn't ever tell me why. Then it was in the paper and Maynard saw it.'

'I know, Bryn,' said Reverend Elwiss. 'Raymond and I were on the receiving end of *The Herald's* version of news, not that it can ever compare with your dreadful experience.'

'Who told the paper, Vicar?'

'Well,' said Reverend Elwiss, sliding his fingers tight together, 'it is unlikely that Detective Prosser would have said anything to *The Herald* without asking Sergeant Phillips first.'

'Or Sergeant Philips told him to.'

'As I said, Bryn, I am not a policeman. Perhaps they think it will help to find him.'

'Will we find him, Vicar?'

Reverend Elwiss shook his head. 'God willing, we will, but I don't know. I fear for him, truly I do. Go and see to your class. I am going to sit here for a while.'

The gift.

'Is this another new auntie?' asked Aled.

Nesta looked at Howell. 'Yes,' she said, 'this is Auntie Gwen.'

'Hello, Aled,' said Gwen, 'you've grown.'

Aled frowned. How did these new aunties know so much about him?

'The last time I saw you, you were a baby.'

'Oh,' he thought, 'that's not fair. How am I supposed to remember that?' He looked up at Nesta, 'Why are you wearing the tea cosy again, Auntie Nesta. It's not cold.'

Gwen and Howell burst into laughter. Nesta was flustered.

'I didn't like to tell you,' gasped Howell.

'What's wrong with it?' Nesta demanded, crossly. 'What do you think of it, Gwen?'

Gwen had tears running down her face and couldn't speak.

'Well, I'm not taking it off. It's not a tea cosy, you *cheeky* boy.'

'Yes, it is,' said Aled, not understanding why Howell and the new auntie were laughing. 'It should be in the cupboard in the kitchen.'

Howell and Gwen laughed even harder. Howell was doubled up and clinging to the gatepost.

'I'll never be able to wear it again,' said Nesta and then she started laughing too. She pulled out the hat pin and snatched the turban from her head. 'It was expensive.'

'For a tea cosy,' spluttered Howell.

Even as she laughed, Gwen watched Aled, now with

his arms folded, annoyed at being excluded from the incomprehensible joke, and her heart melted. Alan had not given her a burden: it was an act of kindness. He was healing her.

Eve tore open *The Herald* until she reached the rugby reports of Wales' tour to Australia at the back. Then she screwed the pages up.

A strengthening wind moaned through the dunes and blew sand into a yellow haze over Kenfig Pool: the colour of sulphur. The fiery eyes burned. They saw Sergeant Phillips in his big, black car. They saw Mr Tanner but would tell no one. They knew where Jack was. They knew what had happened to Huw Evans and Rhodri Mitchell. Gwyn the Milk too. They had seen Ellis Maynard and foretold the death of Darren Jeffries. Through the walls, they saw Alan in his cell and Roy Brown in his. They saw Jean in the armchair next to the old television, but they could not see what she saw because it wasn't real: it was the past as it should have been and could not be remade. They saw Eve and knew what was next. They saw Aled, puissant child, the remaining. They saw the ageing aunties and uncles. They saw Gwen. They could see Geraint's body deep underground and they saw him now, with Huw. They watched Dewi and Brenda in the bracken. They saw, but would not reveal if they were guiding or guided.

13

PRIVATE *GEOFFREY LLEWELLYN* *20*
JOSEPH NAGEL *GEFREITER* *22*

She could feel her colours dimming and her feathers growing dull, her juices drying and her skin beginning to craze. He was meant to be the last; she had given her all and succeeded, relieved to know she could still interest a man and make him pursue her. Many men had, in those carefree days when they came running.

'Because you think something has happened,' she told herself, 'it doesn't mean it has.' But she imagined him lying in a ditch, collapsed in a field, drowned in the sea. What would he be to her if he wasn't found? A moment of optimism snatched away. The unleavened memory would fade and become a dull regret, a permanent reminder of age, like lumbago, when once her limbs had been supple. What then? Days of dreariness and widowhood? Would she be able to rouse herself for one more try? Would it work if she did?

A new headmaster would be appointed to whom, there was a possibility, she could present herself. If he was of a similar mould. If he wasn't married. Grasping at straws, it would be easy to succumb and offer sex as the prize. What then? She might still be lonely – lonelier.

But what else could she do except wait? There was no one she could tell and trust to keep it secret. What if the police found out and questioned her and it got into the paper (with her picture. That put her in two minds) and made it appear unseemly, a bit grubby even, as if she was belatedly staking a claim. He was a proud man, not in a vain or brittle way, but in his way, privately, circumspectly wrapped up in himself. This behaviour was so out of character, she couldn't imagine what had made him do it. Something must have happened. It must have. A special man. 'Yes, a special man and now I might have lost him.'

She was becoming tearful and went to stand under the big tree at the grassy end of the playground away from the children. But, when she looked up, there was a face like a pale fruit in the foliage. 'Come down,' she called, quickly trying to be teacher-like. 'I can see you. Oh, it's you – again. Come down, Timothy. Straightaway, please. You know you shouldn't be up there.'

Timothy swung on a branch, wrapped his arms around the trunk and began to shimmy down.

'Is Martyn up there with you?' The inseparable duo.

Another face appeared.

'Come down, both of you. Is there anyone else?'

'No, Miss,' said Martyn, following Timothy down the trunk. They dropped to the ground.

'Go and play,' she told them. 'Go on.'

They ran off, relieved and surprised not to be sent to stand outside Mr Tanner's office.

He could come through the school gates at any minute and ask, 'What's all the fuss about?' and she would burst into tears and he would know, and he mustn't, not before they had reached an understanding which could only be when *she* was ready. '*Ohhh*.' She was planning the next stages of her campaign to snare him before she knew he was safe.

Gregory was keeping very still, lying flat on a wide branch. He watched her through the leaves.

She shivered. 'There must be a simple explanation... but people don't just go off like this, unless something has happened to them. Especially not him.' How she wished he would come through the gates. It would be worth some tears. She could hide behind the tree.

Who would tell her when they found him? Bryn, Laura, Paul, Mr Topliss even? Would she have to read about it in the paper? Tomorrow or the day after? How could she grieve? Would she grieve? 'I've still got his books.'

She heard the bell and took a deep breath. Break was over. She tried to compose herself but her poise was all aflap.

Gregory jumped out of the tree and rolled on the grass. He ran round to the back of the boys' toilets from whence he emerged, sauntering, to follow the other children into class to tell them what he'd seen.

'Another pint, Gordon?' asked *Herald* Andrew.

'Go on then,' Prosser replied, feigning reluctance as if they were being forced on him. He had a hunted look, much like Jeffries before Sergeant Phillips cast him aside. Whatever information he had - not much now - *Herald* Andrew was adept at wringing out of him with barely concealed disdain as Prosser went through the motions. It was a tedious exercise.

Sergeant Phillips would be on the lookout for a replacement: pliable and eager but not bright enough to make his own way and desperate to please. One or two of the younger detectives at the station looked promising.

But *Herald* Andrew had one last thing he wanted Prosser to do and, after that, he didn't care what happened to him. 'So, what's the news, Gordon? What have you got for us?'

At the bar, precarious and skeletal, Ellis Maynard watched through one screwed-up eye, itching to interrupt and being pointedly ignored.

After three or four pints, Detective Prosser was reasonably lucid but garrulous, the sweet spot before he started rambling. After five or six, Sergeant Phillips was, '*Brilliant*. Tough, mind, but *brilliant*.'

'Any progress on finding the headmaster?'

'We'll find him,' said Prosser, 'there's no doubt about

that.'

'You've got some leads, then?'

Prosser's attention wandered.

'That would be no,' thought *Herald* Andrew, 'or you don't know.'

'We'll find him, no doubt about it,' said Prosser, again.

Herald Andrew looked at Lloyd who, not much of a drinker, was nursing an untouched pint. Every evening he attended these tiresome meetings and didn't say a word. *Herald* Andrew was not sure he listened to what was being said or why he came. No photography was required.

'I know where he is,' slurred Maynard, waiting for the chorus of, '*Do* you?' which didn't come.

Herald Andrew looked up irritably.

'I do,' said Maynard. 'Do you want to know?'

'Not really,' said *Herald* Andrew. He turned back to Prosser who was beginning to sway over the table. 'Well met,' he thought.

Maynard held up a finger and slowly wagged it. 'In the duuunes,' he dribbled, pitching forward and grabbing at the bar to stop himself falling. 'Oooh, but I bet you never thought of that.' He wiped his mouth with the back of his hand. 'I think that deserves a pint.'

'I don't think so,' said *Herald* Andrew. 'Are you alright for a beer, Gordon, because me and Lloyd have to go and see someone? Don't we Lloydy-boy?'

'Yes,' said Lloyd.

'You'll still be here when we get back though, won't

you? We won't be long.'

Prosser blearily jerked his head in Maynard's direction. 'I'm going to see what Maynard knows,' he tried to whisper. 'I'll buy him a pint and get him to spill the beans.' He cackled, as if he wasn't sure if he'd made a joke, and got to his feet and lurched toward the bar where Maynard was leaning on both elbows, staring at a pile of loose change, trying to work out if he had enough to pay for his next drink.

Prosser slapped him on the back. 'Ellis, my old mucker, what do you know?'

Herald Andrew shrugged at the landlord who shook his head. 'Come on, Lloydy-boy, we better be quick or Prosser will be out of it. This might be our last chance, so let's make the most of it.'

'Yes,' said Lloyd, 'that's obvious. He'll be in the Raven.'

Herald Andrew looked at him in surprise. 'You see more than you let on, don't you?'

'I do,' said Lloyd.

In the Raven Arms at the other end of Cardigan Street. Protheroe was wedged at a corner table, alone and brooding over a whisky. He didn't see them come in.

'Hello boss,' said *Herald* Andrew. 'I wondered if you might be in here.'

Protheroe looked up. 'Andrew? I am indeed here, as you can see.'

'Can I get you another one of those?'

'You can, thank you, but let me pay.'

'That's alright boss. My treat for once. Go and get a couple of pints and a whisky,' *Herald* Andrew told Lloyd.

'I'm going to have a whisky too,' said Lloyd.

Herald Andrew pulled a stool from under the table.

'I know what you're going to ask me, Andrew,' said Protheroe.

'I've just popped in for a pint with Lloyd.'

'Come off it, Andrew. You never come in here.'

'But look, boss, she came to us, didn't she? It's new information.'

'That's just it, Andrew, as well you know. She needs to go to the police first and then we'll run with it, but after and *only* after, we've been given the nod.'

'Prosser's in The Red Lion,' said *Herald* Andrew.

'Oh yes.'

'I can tell him and he'll tell you-know-who and we'll be running with it tomorrow. Guaranteed.'

Lloyd came back with the drinks.

'You said Prosser was going the same way as Jeffries,' said Protheroe.

'He is, isn't he, Lloydy-boy?'

'Yes,' said Lloyd, holding his whisky up to the light as if he was inspecting a negative.

'You've got it all planned, haven't you?' said Protheroe.

'Boss? I can't leave it too long or Prosser will be so pissed he won't understand what I'm saying.'

Protheroe tipped his new whisky in with the old and ran his tongue inside his upper lip where stickiness was beginning to coat his teeth.

'Boss? Prosser won't keep.'

'Go, Andrew,' said Protheroe, quietly. 'Just go.'

'Come on Lloydy-boy. Neck it.'

'What?' asked Lloyd. 'I've only just got it.'

'Then knock it back.'

Lloyd managed it in two gulps and a grimace and they hurried out.

Protheroe thought, 'I'm getting too old for this,' as he watched them leave. 'I should have said no.' But he knew, if he had, *Herald* Andrew would have done it anyway. 'The changing of the guard,' he sighed. 'And he's welcome to it. I never thought I would think that. Ah well,' and he finished half his drink. 'I think I'll have another one of those,' and he finished the other half.

She recognised the handwriting on the envelope and didn't want to open it. But she did, and read it twice, growing hot with anger.

Dear Eve,

I got your letter. I know you told me not to write back, but I had to. I am still your husband. I can understand you not coming to visit because it's a long way but one letter in three years, Eve? And a letter like that too?

What I did was wrong but I didn't mean to ruin your life. That isn't a fair thing to say.

I am paying for what I did now. Justice is being done so I'm not going to complain about it. But what's worse is that

I have nothing to come home to. How can I ever set foot in Bridgend again if you won't have me? I've only got a couple of years to go so what am I supposed to do when I'm let out? Then I will have paid, won't I?

I hoped we'd be able to carry on our lives in some way but, after what you said in your letter, it seems you're dead set against it. I don't understand why?

I wish we'd had children. It would have been different then.

I'm not going to ask you to forgive me because you said you won't. That's the hardest part.

With love, Roy

With love? That was Roy. The man who always thought he could wheedle his way in, to bring her round, with lies and threats if he had to. She could hear his voice as she read and see the glimmer in his eyes as he studied her face for weakness.

Children? That was Roy. He was suggesting they might if she allowed him home: children to love him in their innocence, to use and hold over her, to corrupt them to his ways and send them out into the world to search out more Eves.

His words fell on barren ground. All his power over her had gone. She despised him.

She tore the letter up into tiny pieces and burnt them in one of his ashtrays, expunging in small, violet flames the phantasms of his broken promises.

They sat in the garden and watched Aled as he played, climbing on the dry stone wall and jumping off.

'Careful,' said Gwen, 'those stones are not very steady.' But Aled was too caught up in his game to take any notice.

'It's lovely here,' said Nesta.

'Yes, it is,' said Howell, 'beautiful and not far from the sea too.'

'He loves the beach,' said Nesta.

'Boys do,' said Gwen. 'I could never get Huw out of the sea. Huw and Jack.'

'He can't go to Eve,' said Howell.

Gwen shaded her eyes to look at him.

'We do not know what will become of Jean.'

'But we're not giving up hope,' said Nesta.

'Hope of what, Nesta?' asked Howell, in a final voice. 'Even if she recovers we don't know to what extent. And when she finds out about Jack? And Alan? What will that do to her? Can you imagine that? After all she went through? I don't think she would survive the shock. I wish it was otherwise, but we must face it, Nesta.'

'I will not stop hoping,' said Nesta. 'I refuse to.'

'It's not a question of hope,' said Howell. 'We all hope, but that's not why we've come to see Gwen, is it?'

Nesta stroked her embarrassed hat and folded it irrevocably. 'Aled is so precious to us, Gwen,' she said.

'I know he is.'

'Are you doing this because Alan asked you to, Gwen?' Howell asked her. 'Or because you want to?'

Gwen took a moment to answer. 'Because I want to and not to replace Huw, I can never do that, but because Aled needs a mother and I need a son and, I promise you, I will love him as my own.'

Howell leaned over and clasped her hand 'Thank you,' he said. He cleared his throat. 'Now, then, to practical matters. You can drive, can't you, Gwen?'

'Not the van, Howell Morgan?'

'No, Nesta' said Howell, patiently. 'Gwen, you must allow us to help you in any way, including financially. These things are important. They won't go away because we don't like to talk about them.'

'It's really not necessary,' said Gwen.

'Which is what I expected you to say,' he said, and smiled. 'No buts. We want to help. It's important to us, it means a lot and because we should. A car, you see,' he said, looking at Nesta, 'not the old van. Gwen will be able to visit without having to catch buses and trains and she can take Aled to the beach whenever she wants.'

'Howell Morgan,' said Nesta, shaking her head.

'Are we going to the beach, Uncle Howell?' asked Aled, excitedly, who had finished jumping off the wall and was now standing behind Nesta.

'Not to take my eyes off him for a minute?' thought Gwen, who hadn't seen where he'd come from (or might have gone to).

'Why not?' said Howell. 'We've got all afternoon.'

'Let's then,' said Gwen. 'What a good idea.'

‘Yes, Aled,’ said Howell, ‘we’re all going to the beach for the rest of the day.’

‘That’s Aled,’ said Huw. ‘Why is he here?’

‘He’s coming to live with your mum,’ said Geraint. ‘So you will have to help look after him. Like a big brother.’

Aled ran down the garden, shouting, ‘We’re going to the beach, we’re going to the beach.’ He stopped in front of Huw. ‘Do you want to come too?’

Huw looked up at his father.

‘Yes, of course we do,’ said Geraint.

Dewi and Brenda sat together over coffee in the canteen and pretended to talk about what they should, forgetting themselves and leaning close with smiles and eyes, because nothing was a secret. ‘What can he do?’ Dewi asked, feeling almost free of him because of her.

Sergeant Phillips stood in the doorway. He ran the outsides of his thumbs down his moustache and yanked his tunic straight. ‘Tell Nesta Morgan. Tell Gwen Evans. Go and do not stop on the way to Carmarthen. Find them and tell them I know the boy is there. Then I am going to move you both to other duties.’ He left.

‘That’s your answer,’ said Brenda.

Dewi shook his head. ‘He can’t know.’

14

CORPORAL *GARETH LEWIS* 22
HORST OBERMANN GEFREITER 19

Salute: 'Good morning, Gerhard.'

'Good morning, Howell. You were late home last night. Did it go well?'

'It did.'

'And Aled?'

'He's going to live with Gwen. Nesta's going to stay for a week or two, at least until he starts school. We spent most of the day at the beach.'

Gerhard smiled. 'So everyone enjoyed themselves?'

'Yes. A load has been taken off my mind, but I am going to miss him.'

'A solution has presented itself.'

'It has, Gerhard. As you said it would.'

'I'm glad for you and for Aled, for all of you.'

One day soon, a car? But, for now, a bus, a train and then

another bus to Cardiff Prison.

As Gwen waited outside for visiting time to start, she recognised some of the faces and thought some of them recognised her. They were becoming familiar and it would only be a matter of time before she was asked, 'What's he in for?'

And she would have to say, 'Murder – but he didn't do it.' Would she say that?

The doors opened and they filed in.

That smell, the purposelessness; comfortless pillows ground out like pestles.

Alan was waiting for her at the same table, barely lit by the light coming from between the bars in the high windows, although it was another hot and cloudless day outside.

This time, they held hands without hesitating.

'Well?' he asked.

She smiled. 'Aled's with Nesta in Carmarthen. Howell brought them down. They didn't tell me they were coming and it was a big surprise. But it's agreed, Alan. He's coming to live with me.'

His shoulders gave way and his head bent to the table. He sobbed in full view of the other inmates and their visitors with small, stuttering explosions, jolting her arms. His only privacy was not to look at them. If he had fallen to the floor and died, a blanket would have been placed over him.

She watched helplessly: her strongest man.

'Thank you, Gwen,' he said, at last.

A haze of weak sunlight drifted in as if it didn't belong and melted away.

'No,' she said, 'he is the link to you, and Jack and Huw, and Jean too.'

'Yes, he is. But to think of it that way?' He grasped her hands tighter. 'We know what my future is, but Aled's is before him. He is all our futures, he mustn't carry the past with him.'

'He didn't make the past, Alan. It's not his fault, but he mustn't find out on his own, and he's bound to, so I'm going to tell him as soon as he's old enough.'

He shook his head. 'I dread it.'

'He'd never forgive us if we didn't.'

'How you will explain it, Gwen?'

'With the truth. What else is there? And I think I should tell Jean, even if she doesn't understand.'

'But supposing she does? No, please don't.'

'But I feel like I'm usurping her.'

'You're not. He needs you. Don't tell her, Gwen, please? It's best she doesn't know, not like she is now.'

'That's what Howell said to Nesta.'

Alan nodded. 'Howell was very close to Jean, closer than the others, I think. But he sees things as they are. He always has. You won't tell her, will you?'

'It's like hoping she doesn't get better.'

'This started before she became unwell, Gwen. There's nothing we can do about that.'

'Then I won't tell her,' Gwen sighed.

'Good.'

She felt his reprove: her strongest man. 'Nesta's going to stay until he starts school. But he seems to have settled in already. We've been to the beach every day.'

'He always loved the beach,' Alan said, thinking of Rest Bay, which he would never see again. 'Sometimes, I wish I could forget everything that ever happened before I came here.'

In the depths, someone began to pound a radiator. It grew louder as another joined in, then another and another and feet began to stamp to the resonating, primitive memory of fires under star-filled nights; every pipe, bar and door jumped to its metallic pulse. Suddenly, there was a shriek, distant but piercing, and the pounding stopped. For a moment, everyone continued to move to its beat before they realised it was no longer there. If some poor other had to be sacrificed to make it start again, then give him up.

On the table next to them, a couple started to argue. It began with venomous whispers but, soon, they were shouting. The warder near the door watched.

'*No*,' the man shouted. 'No, you will *not*. Who do you think you are? I'm *telling* you, right.'

She thrust her head forward and said, with a sneer, 'And what can you do about it?'

Dumbed by rage, his mouth opened and closed and no words came out.

'There's nothing you *can* do about it,' she jeered. '*Nothing*.'

The warder came over and stood next to them.

'I'm going,' she said, and left.

The man stayed for a few moments, shaking with anger, his hands clenching and unclenching, then he got up and shuffled out.

'And that,' said Alan, 'is why a man murders his wife. If he could, he would wring her neck, wouldn't he? She knows it but it'll be a long time before he gets out and I don't think she'll be waiting for him when he does. He robbed a post office and someone got badly hurt but, other than that, he's a decent man. It's too easy to judge, Gwen, but it helps not to get too close to people. But, there we are.'

When it was time to leave, Gwen said, 'It won't be long and I'll be bringing Aled to see you.'

Alan looked around at everyone saying goodbye. Some sadly, others who couldn't wait to get away. 'You don't often see children,' he said, 'except babies. Perhaps they're ashamed to bring them. I can understand why.'

'No, Alan.'

'And I'm nothing like them, Gwen? None of us are any different. One mistake can make us all the same. There are some truly bad men in here, but not as many as you'd think.'

'But you've done nothing wrong and Aled will know it. This place isn't you; it can't make you into what you're not.'

'It already has.'

'No, Alan. Huw didn't know his father but, I promise, Aled is going to be proud of his.'

A big, black car pulled up outside the gates. Bryn felt him enter the school, engulfing the sunlight window after window as he passed down the corridor on his way to the playground at the far end.

At the boys' toilet block, he looked over the wall into the tiny cubicles.

Mr Topliss came out of the storeroom. He saw Sergeant Phillips and halted.

'Mr Topliss.'

'Yes, Sir?'

'You have seen men die.'

'Yes, Sir, I have. But I wish I had not.'

'In war, but not in peace?'

'Yes.'

Sergeant Phillips looked Mr Topliss up and down, the old soldier who had served and was proud. 'Come here,' he said.

Mr Topliss stepped from the ranks.

Sergeant Phillips towered over him. 'Everyone is a suspect,' he said.

'A suspect?' stammered Mr Topliss, who remembered a cruel Sergeant Major of similar dap who had been bayoneted during a sandstorm.

Small faces appeared, standing on chairs to peer out

over the windowsills.

Sergeant Phillips walked slowly around the edge of the playground until he arrived back at the school gates. He leaned against his big, black car and folded his arms. He looked down the length of the building and dust began to fall from between the bricks. He pushed himself upright and went to stand under the big tree, staking its trunk of ages like a matt, black rod. The branches bent, and filigrees of light played through the leaves and went out on him.

'Get away from the windows,' Bryn told his class. 'Read on your own until I come back.'

'What does he want, Bryn? Has he found Mr Tanner?' asked Laura, coming to stand next to him under the door arch.

'I don't know,' Bryn replied.

She trellised her fingers over her belly that was taut enough to split like a turtle's egg and tried to push the baby deeper inside her, but its tiny hands were pressed against its face, and its feet were crossed under its thighs, ready to squeeze out of her. She was overcome with a sudden wave of giddiness and swayed.

Sergeant Phillips' hand delved into her groin and pushed between her legs and waited for the head to fill his palm: a boy.

The baby twitched and stretched, trying to straighten itself.

Laura felt a stabbing pain and her waters broke and ran down her legs and over her shoes. 'Bryn,' she gasped, and reached to steady herself. 'The baby's coming.' Her knees gave way and she sank onto Sergeant Phillips' gloved fingers, feeling them uncoil to stretch her further apart. He held her up.

'No, let me lie, please.'

His fingers corkscrewed into her like the mouthparts of a lamprey and grazed the bloodied fontanelles. 'I feel your mind, child.'

'But it's not due. It's too soon,' said Bryn. He stuck his head inside the door. '*Mr Rees!*' he yelled, whose classroom was the closest.

Sergeant Phillips withdrew his fingers and smelt them. He pulled off his gloves and threw them into the grass next to the tree, where they crisped like old leaves and were quickly buried in the mulch.

Bryn lowered her to the ground.

'I think I fainted,' said Laura.

Sergeant Phillips' big, black car slid away toward Cardigan Street and disappeared.

Paul Rees came running. Children tumbled out of their classrooms and crowded around the door to see.

Rose appeared.

Bryn cradled Laura's head in his lap. 'I told you,' he said, 'I told you to stay at home. Why won't you ever listen?' His voice quavered. 'Would you get the children back into class please, Mrs Davies?'

She gathered them, shooing them before her with outstretched arms. They were transfixed and wouldn't move.

'*Inside*, back into your classes,' he barked. 'Paul, call an ambulance. Use the phone in Mr Tanner's office.'

'Is he still watching?' asked Laura.

The tree was moving in the breeze again. 'No,' said Bryn, 'he's gone.'

Mr Topliss hurried over. 'Is there anything I can do?' he asked.

'You're going to have to help watch the children,' Bryn told him.

'I can do that,' said Mr Topliss. 'I'll keep an eye on them for you. Don't you worry.'

The ambulance came. Bryn looked at Paul Rees. 'You're in charge,' he said.

Prosser was at the bar of The Red Lion with Maynard.

'I'm the Grim Reaper, me,' said Maynard. 'This is where coppers come to die.' He laughed. 'They send them to me and I take care of it. Did you know that, then?'

'You should be careful what you say,' said Prosser.

'Why's that? What are you going to do about it because, whatever it is, it's too late now.'

Prosser didn't reply. He had gone straight to Sergeant Phillips. 'I should have waited,' he kept telling himself. 'Roy Brown, Sir, he did it, all of them, the boys, Gwyn Roberts. Eve Brown told me.'

'You've been drinking, Prosser.'

'Eve Brown has admitted it was him.'

'To that reporter, Prosser, not to you.'

'No, Sir.'

'Get out. You are no use to me when you're sober.'

'But, Sir?'

'Are we having another pint?' Maynard asked. 'Or don't you want to drink with the Reaper?'

'Why do you always talk out of your arse, Maynard?'

'Because it talks more sense than you,' said Maynard, looking at him with another man's knowing smile. 'You went running to him, didn't you?'

'What? Do you know something you're not telling me, Maynard?'

'Do I?' asked Maynard.

'Did you take care of Jeffries? You can tell me, I won't say.'

'Naah,' said Maynard, drunk again. 'Just talking out of my arse.'

'The house seems very empty,' said Howell. He was in the shop with Idris and Emlyn.

'Yes, it does,' said Emlyn. 'It was the right thing to do. It's for the best. And here she comes.'

Idris opened his tally book.

'Nesta thinks that too, now,' said Howell, 'but you know what she's like.'

Delia watched the unlit fire: no Aled to love and no sister to have to agree with. Lunch was done and the afternoon stretched before her. The sun made it emptier.

In the morning, breakfast was made and cleared away; the shop was opened and the pavement was swept and more jobs were done and then it was lunch. Lunch was made and cleared away. The shop reopened. Then Delia washed and changed. Tea. The evening. To bed. And again. Except on Wednesday afternoons and Sundays when the shop was closed. This had been her life until Aled came to live with them.

She went into the other room to watch television. The test card. She switched it off.

'I'll make a cake. It will always get eaten and I can take it down to Gwen's when we go.' That set her off planning a visit. 'I don't mind going on my own.' A long way for Delia. 'I can stay for a few days.' Then, unpredictably, wildly, an insurrection began. 'How much longer will we have the shop? We could sell it and move down there.' Gwen's cottage became the farmhouse in Pembrokeshire overlooking the sea. No mountains: 'I don't think I'd miss them, not when everything's been uphill. What a lovely place to live.'

Jean's name tolled like a bell. Delia was ashamed. 'But we are neither here nor there,' she protested, bravely. 'Unless she could be moved to Carmarthen?' Delia went into the shop.

Mrs James was on her way out with an egg.

Delia said, 'Why can't we sell up and move to Carmarthen and Jean can come with us?'

Emlyn and Idris looked at her and then at each other

in amazement. 'The shop,' said Emlyn.

'We can sell the shop,' said Delia.

'Sell the shop?' said Idris.

'It has crossed my mind,' said Howell.

'Has it?' asked Emlyn.

'Yes,' said Howell. 'I was thinking about it on the train on the way back, because at some point we're going to have to, aren't we?'

'I don't know what Nesta will say,' said Emlyn.

'It will all depend on Jean,' said Howell. 'Nesta will say that Carmarthen is too far, but there may be a way round it.'

'Will you tell Nesta, Howell?' Delia asked.

He smiled. 'We'll have to make enquiries about Jean. We're going to have to find her somewhere where she can be looked after and I've no idea how these things work.'

Nesta went back to the rest of the afternoon. She took the cake out of the oven and put it on the table. 'This is still home, though, isn't it?' As if to leave would be to betray the whole Rhondda Valley which would never welcome her back. Delia Morgan, tiny in the kitchen beneath the mountains, was so precious to its well-being she might not be allowed to go. And, in a way, she was, and all the other women like her.

Jean, if anything, was tinier in the great chair that held her, but her curious smile was unchanged and her blank eyes were serene. There could have been a whole world behind them or nothing at all.

Gwyn the Milk's cows regarded Jack and Huw with bovine stares that might have been mistaken for wisdom. Gwyn walked them up the slope to the milking shed with the two boys alongside him, each carrying small sticks of their own.

'Why is Penguin always last?' asked Huw, of the black and white cow who was yards behind the rest.

'It's her way,' Gwyn replied. 'They've all got their little ways. You won't make her go any faster.'

As they neared the gate, the cows formed a line and went through one by one. Queen Penguin held back so they knew, cows, man and boys, that it was her choice.

'She's getting on a bit,' said Gwyn. 'But she mustn't hear you say that or there'll be ructions.'

Jean watched from the back garden. 'They do love helping Gwyn, don't they? At least, Jack does. Huw's never going to be a farmer, is he?'

'No, he won't,' said Alan. 'But they've got their whole lives ahead of them so who knows?'

Gwen said, 'Goodbye, Jean, take care of yourself.'

'I can't just sit here and do nothing,' said Reverend Elwiss to his wife, who was holding her knitting, with needles crossed.

'What else can you do, dear? Except get in the way?'

'I don't know. I've been trying to rack my brains to remember something he might have told me, any clue to where he might be, but I can't think of anything.'

'*Oh*, I can't do this,' said Deborah, and she thrust the knitting into her sewing basket. 'I haven't made a single stitch.'

'I'm going to sit in the church for a while,' said Reverend Elwiss, 'and then I'm going for a walk. Perhaps something will jog my memory.'

The sun was coming through the stained glass window and the altar flowed with colours. It severed Christ in two: his head and torso were in shadow and his legs were brightly lit in yellow, red and blue. 'I cannot see his face,' thought Reverend Elwiss. 'But, then, dawn would have to be sunset, the world would have to be remade upside down, the universe rearranged and time itself altered. It could be done, if only for a moment… I'm not imagining it, am I?' he asked, out loud. 'Tell me, please, Lord?' Reverend Elwiss waited until only Christ's bent feet were in the light and he left before the silence became a refusal and Deborah was right.

On the way to the playing fields by the river, he passed The Red Lion where Detective Prosser and Maynard were being incomprehensible to each other at the bar, and the Raven Arms where *Herald* Andrew and Doug Protheroe were coming to their one-sided decision and Lloyd was admiring his whisky.

He followed the path along the riverbank until

he reached the spot where Bryn had been attacked and stopped.

He rubbed his forehead with the heel of his hand and bunched the skin into his hair. 'I cannot see what is in front of me. It's right before me and I can't see it. This… *malignity* challenges me. It's not my imagination; I have a purpose in this. Why must she disparage me?'

The sound of the river came from beneath the steep bank. Gulls reminded him of how close they were to the estuary, with the dunes to the west. He heard the wind in the trees and felt it, cool on his cheek, a whispering breath. 'You're here.'

15

LIEUTENANT GUTO MORRIS 25
EMIL ORTMANN VIZEFELDWEBEL 28

Bryn called his father from the hospital. 'Laura's gone into labour,' he said.

'*Luv*,' he heard his father call, 'Laura's having the baby.'

Bryn heard his mother in the background, growing louder as she came rushing. 'She's early.'

'But that's not unusual, is it?' asked his father, sounding panicky. 'It'll be alright, won't it?'

'Give me the phone and let me talk to him,' his mother said, taking charge. There was the sound of rustling and then her voice. 'When did she start?'

'This afternoon, when we were in school.'

'She shouldn't still be in school.'

'I told her that,' said Bryn.

'Then why didn't you put your foot down?'

'She wouldn't listen. You know what she's like.'

'I know what you're like,' said his mother. 'How is

she?'

'Fine, I think. She was when I saw her before they took her in.'

'Where are you now?'

'Waiting outside with the other fathers.'

'Useless, the lot of you,' said his mother. 'You tell us as soon as you know. What did Mr Williams say?'

'I'm going to call him next.'

'Bryn, now, you listen to me. You should have called him first. She's his daughter. That was quite wrong of you.'

'Mum?'

'So, you call him first before you call us. Is that clear. I don't know. What will he think?'

The nurses came and went and, each time, the men looked up expectantly. One by one they became fathers and were led away.

The delivery rooms rang with the cries of woman and language. 'He's never bloody coming near me again.' The cries were indistinguishable. He didn't think it was Laura. She wouldn't say something like that – but she hadn't given birth before.

Bryn began to pace up and down. He had laughed when his father had told him he would. 'No, I won't. Of course I won't. That's silly.'

'Wait and see. I did.'

Another would-be father was doing the same. They crossed in the middle of the waiting room like guards on sentry duty. The other man chain-smoked, lighting cigarettes with the butt of the one before. The smoke was soon thick. Bryn went out into the corridor to pace. The women's cries were louder there.

When he returned, the man had gone, presumably summoned (at last), but the smoke still hung about the lights. The nurses came and went and ignored him. Bryn was alone.

If the choice was between his wife and the child, which would he choose? Laura. Which would she choose, herself or the child? The child. If the choice was between him or the child?

It was too much to ask for both and all. It might be given or it might not. There was bound to be a price. He paced. Maynard should have died, but he had been delivered back to The Red Lion free of charge. That wasn't fair.

Next door, his son or daughter, part way between his wife and the world was almost ready to reveal if it had two arms and legs, ten fingers and toes, if it could see and hear.

'A perfect child, please; please, a perfect child?' As Laura had bargained as she waited at his bedside. What could he promise, what would be enough?

A nurse appeared leading a big, a *huge* woman, who was puffing, with a rolling walk like a ship in a heavy sea with the waves swamping its decks. The words 'distended abdomen' were too polite: somewhere in there, beneath a marquee-like smock, was a baby hippo.

Bryn felt a bit better and stopped pacing. Someone

was worse off.

Her weedy husband followed, pathetically solicitous and ineffectual, and she, puce as an aubergine, ignored him. How on earth, how unlikely? Their original mating must have been a bizarre event, as he clambered up, risking suffocation if he slipped or she rolled over, unaware of what he was trying to do. Against the odds, he had succeeded and escaped without being eaten.

'Wait here,' said the nurse to the weedy man, who perched on the edge of a chair and glanced about nervously, unable to keep his eyes still. Next door, in the delivery room, they secured his wife and she began to bellow. The poor man jumped up and hopped about like a sparrow.

'Mr Hughes?' asked the matron, set back from a frontage of bosoms.

Laura had bags under her eyes and her hair was stringy and wet.

Bryn counted.

He kissed her. 'Well done,' he said, unable to take his eyes off his new son.

'Things are never going to be the same,' she said.

'I don't want them to be. He's all I could have hoped for.'

The baby slept against her neck. 'Yes, he is,' she said, kissing the top of his head.

'I'd better spread the news. 'I'll call your father first, then my mum and dad.'

The telephone was answered almost before it had

time to ring. 'You have a grandson,' Bryn told him. 'We're going to call him Raymond.'

'How is she?' asked Laura's father.

'Tired, but that's to be expected.'

He rang his parents and told them, 'A boy… we haven't thought of a name yet.'

Reverend Elwiss knocked on Bryn and Laura's door and waited agitatedly on their doorstep. He knocked again and tried to peer through the window. 'Where can they be?' he asked himself.

He gave up and hurried back to the vicarage.

As expected, his wife was in the garden, watering the flowers in the relative cool of the evening. There were shadows under the apple trees. The grass was scorched after days of heat. In the long light, it appeared white. She saw him coming round the side of the house, walking quickly and out of breath. She put down the watering can and took off her gardening gloves.

'I have to find him,' he told her, with his eyes wide and bright. 'I must.'

'Calm down, Ernest.'

'No, I have to go.'

'Where?'

'To find Raymond. I think I know where he is.'

'Where?'

'I can't say. I'm not exactly certain. Please don't ask.'

'Sit down,' she told him, and led him to the bench.

He sat down and stood up again.

'Calm down.'

'No.' He walked to the flower border and back. 'Do I need a coat, do you think?'

She followed him through the door into the kitchen and into the hall.

'Where are my car keys?'

'In the drawer where they always are.'

He opened the drawer and took them out. 'I can't remember if I've got any petrol.' He looked at his watch. 'There'll be nowhere open now.'

'*Ernest*. Calm down. Please.'

He rubbed his forehead and tugged at his earlobe.

'Now, tell me,' she said.

He leaned against the bannister at the bottom of the stairs.

'How do you know where Raymond is? Who told you?'

He picked up her hands and held them. There were flames in his eyes. 'I don't know.'

'You're going to have to explain.'

'It's in my mind. I asked and it was *put* there. I prayed. Not in the church but by the river, where Bryn was attacked. I was led there, but I should have known where to go, shouldn't I? Deborah, this is *not* something I've imagined.'

'I'm going to call the doctor.'

He held her hands tighter and said, as steadily as he

could, 'No, I don't need a doctor. There is no time now, but please believe me.'

'I don't know what you're asking me to believe. Shouldn't you go to the police if you're so certain?'

'The police? So they can ignore me again? And what would they think of a vicar who says he's been hearing voices?'

'Are they voices, Ernest?'

'No, not voices, that's what they'd say. I'm not hearing things but, however I'm being told, I can't ignore it. I'm going to find Raymond, Deborah.'

'You're frightening me now.'

'I'm sorry, I don't mean to.' He let her hands go. 'Where is the torch? I might need it.'

'In the cupboard.'

He went into the kitchen and found it. He switched it on and off. 'At least there's some life in the batteries,' he muttered. 'I have to go now.'

'Don't go on your own.'

'I called for Bryn but he wasn't there.'

'Then let me come with you?'

He stopped and turned. 'No, Deborah,' he said.

'Why not?'

'No,' he said again. 'In this, Deborah, no.' He opened the front door and went out. Dusk, and the last of the sun was beneath the horizon. The sky was a clear blue, darkening above the vicarage as the light receded.

He opened the garage doors and got into the car. He

put the key in the ignition. He gripped the steering wheel in both hands and stared over it toward the gates at the end of the gravel drive.

He turned the key and started the engine. At the end of the drive, he stopped and looked both ways. The road was deserted.

In the growing shadows, Deborah stood with her arms tightly folded.

'Keep me safe, oh Lord,' said Reverend Elwiss. 'Into your hands I commend my soul.' Never, however many times he had said those words over the years, had they been so literal or in the first person.

It was nearly closing time in The Red Lion. The pub was empty except for Maynard and Prosser, who had been banished to the table behind the piano. The landlord looked at the clock over the bar. 'Last orders,' he announced.

Maynard's head was nodding. His whisky chaser was untouched and his pint was only half empty. Every bloodless vein of his shrunken frame was full and he was done.

'Ellis?' Prosser nudged him. 'Ellis? We're being chucked out.'

'What?' Maynard mumbled, briefly opening his eyes before they drooped shut again.

'Why are you the Grim Reaper? Who were you talking about?' Prosser asked.

'I'm not stupid, am I?'

'No, you're not stupid. Tell me then. Quickly now.'

'About what?'

'Jeffries.'

'Who?' Maynard tried to pick up his unfinished pint and knocked it over Prosser's legs. The glass fell off the table and onto the floor where it bounced but didn't break. Maynard stared. 'Look,' he said.

Prosser tried to brush the beer off his trousers.

The glass stopped spinning. Maynard tried to reach for it but couldn't. 'Can I have another pint?'

'Right, that's it,' said the landlord. 'Out, the pair of you.'

Maynard started nodding again, still bent over, with his fingers outstretched. He toppled forward, banged his chin on the edge of the table, 'Ooof,' and slid off the chair. A trickle of vomit ran from the side of his mouth.

'Get him out of here,' said the landlord.

'Why should I? I only came in for a drink,' said Prosser.

The landlord came from behind the bar and stood over them with his hands on his hips. 'Now, be a good policeman and make sure he gets home or locked up.'

'Be careful who you're talking to,' said Prosser. 'I could have this pub shut down.'

'We'll see what Sergeant Phillips thinks about you coming in here talking to reporters and drinking with this miscreant.'

'Miscreant,' murmured Maynard from under the

table. 'Who is?'

'Get him out of here,' said the landlord, crossly, 'or I'll call the police myself.'

'I'm working on an important case,' said Prosser, indignantly.

'Of course you are,' said the landlord, holding open the door. 'Then you can work on it on your way home, can't you?'

Prosser got Maynard to his feet and they began to weave their way out. The door slammed shut behind them.

Prosser sat Maynard down on the bench outside the indoor market with his head resting against the metal grille and was going to leave him there when he realised he was in full view of the police station at the top of the hill. 'They'll know it was me.' Prosser heaved him back up. 'You stink,' he told him.

Maynard didn't answer.

Step by step they staggered to the tree-lined river next to the bridge and Prosser let Maynard fall with a thump. Maynard groaned and rolled down the slope toward the water.

'Not yet, butty-boy,' said Prosser, grabbing him by his lapels and hauling him away from the edge. 'I've got plans for you.' He propped Maynard up, sitting against a tree with his head on his chin and poked him with his foot.

Maynard twitched.

'Now you stay there,' Prosser told him. He looked around to make sure he hadn't been seen and climbed up the bank to the bridge, hurried across it and was gone.

Aled dreamed of sandcastles and the sea: 'This is all you will ever need,' and stirred.

In the next bedroom, Gwen slept.

'Mummy's asleep,' said Huw, looking up at her window from the moonlit garden.

'Yes, she is,' said his father. 'She is sleeping peacefully for the first time in a long time.'

'Is she happy?'

'As happy as she can be without you or me.'

'Oh,' said Huw.

'But not everyone is a good person, Huw, and we are going to have to be vigilant.'

'I know what that means,' said Huw. 'It's a word in my *Big Book*.'

Gwen thought it was the draught from the window that turned the pages.

Nesta dreamed of Jean when she was younger and lively, growing up at the top of the Rhondda Valley, her sister's child.

Huw walked with his father through the moon-cooled fields to the top of the cliff path that ran down to the beach.

'The whole world is ours,' said his father, 'but too soon,' he thought.

'*All* of it?' asked Huw.

'Yes, Huw, all of it. We can go anywhere we want.'

'Can we go to Broadway?' asked Huw, with wonder in his voice. From Bridgend to Cardiff to Broadway to Hollywood. It might have been; it wasn't impossible.

'We can't leave Mummy on her own with Aled. Not yet.'

Huw frowned. 'No,' he said, trying to sound grown up and responsible. 'No, we can't do that. But I would like to visit to see a show one day.' To cheer and clap. Huw was too young to have regrets. His father kept those for him in a knot of pain.

'As soon as we are sure Mummy and Aled are safe, we will go.'

'Until then, we must be vigilant,' said Huw.

'Yes, we must,' his father laughed and ruffled his hair. 'I promise we will and I always keep my promises don't I?'

They walked along the beach at the edge of the sea where the waves hissed on the sand, feeling neither warmth nor cold, remembering sunny days, rain and snow, howling gales and still nights, like this. Nowhere was forbidden and time and distance had no meaning. But Geraint wished only for his country, his wife and son, no more, no further.

16

SERGEANT EMRYS MOSTYN 26
ALBERT POHL OBERST 39

Deborah Elwiss' hand hovered over the telephone. If Ernest didn't want to call the police, she would. 'My husband, the vicar, is out alone looking for Mr Tanner. He's asked me to call you.'

And they would ask, 'Does he know where Mr Tanner is? Does he have new information? Why didn't he come straight to us?'

And would she say, 'God told him?'

'Pardon, Mrs Elwiss?' She could already hear the muffled laughter.

'I'm worried about him, he's not… himself.'

'In what way, Mrs Elwiss?'

Unless she made something up, there wasn't a sensible answer she could give. She couldn't even tell them where he'd gone.

She went out into the garden and looked up at the

sky where the moon was resting in a tree like a giant egg, its light falling softly onto the immoveable, patient church, radiating kindness like a holy battery. Good men had preached there. It was the stone pivot around which Heaven revolved. And the vicarage, too, where their wives had been just as important, if unrecorded. The stained-glass window reflected the moonlight like a kaleidoscope and, from the edge of the flowerbed that ran along the garden wall, she could see the gravestones, some of them leaning and almost flat to the grass. Even on the darkest winter nights, she had never been afraid to get some fresh air in the graveyard before turning in. The dead were glad to see her: *Elias Jacob Browning September 15th 1879, Martha Ruth Edwards October 18th 1901…* she had her favourites, but would not reveal who they were. 'If you lay amongst them, Ernest, and me alongside you, perhaps your calling would have been better appreciated in another lifetime.' What date would be on their headstones? 1782 for him, 1791 for her (she would live longer). An eighteenth-century vicar and his wife, who enjoyed weekly lunches with the squire. He could have been himself and they would have listened to him then; he was not made for this age of disbelief. She loved him for his kindness, forgave his pedantry and pitied his search for affirmation: the torture of doubt that he was not good enough. 'That's it, isn't it Ernest?' she told herself, 'but this is Bridgend not Jerusalem, you hopeless, pompous man.' But he had gone off into the night with a passion in his eyes she had not seen before. Ernest's voices would have to be from the Old Testament of bellicose men with straggly, grey beards and stony wildernesses. But he wasn't equipped for the sacrificing of goats. 'Please come home and we'll talk about it over a cup of tea. Be happy and let us be unremarkable.'

Gravid night.

She heard the sound of a heavy door being closed. She hoped it was Ernest coming back, embarrassed and trying to sneak in. 'Please come home, I'll never mention it, I promise.' But she hadn't heard the car on the gravel and, when she looked in through his study window, he wasn't there. The sound had come from the church, the big door into the tower.

'Someone's trying to steal the lead,' she thought, feeling relieved. 'Now I've got a genuine reason,' and went inside to call the police. She waited in the hall with the front door open to keep watch. How absurd, how foolish, how noble, the vicar's wife, defying criminals, possibly more than one to help carry the lead, fumbling around in the vestry, and her husband, summoned by the comic divine, searching in the night for his missing friend and not there to protect her.

It wasn't long before she saw headlights coming up the lane and a police car appeared. Dewi got out and put on his helmet, looking tall and reassuring. There was another policeman with him she hadn't seen before.

She went down the path to meet them. 'There's someone in the church, I heard them,' she said.

‘Have you seen anyone since you called us?’ Dewi asked.

‘No, I haven’t.’

‘The vicar hasn’t gone into the church on his own, has he?’

‘No.’

‘If you wait here, we’ll have a look around.’

She saw their torches flashing inside.

When Dewi came out, he told her, ‘There’s no one there now, but someone has been. I’m afraid it’s a bit of a mess.’

The front pew where Reverend Elwiss always sat to hope for answers had been tipped over. The tall brass flower vases were on their sides and the flowers were trampled and scattered over the floor. The wooden Christ lay snapped in two on the altar next to the pewter cross which had been bent.

‘I don’t know what they were trying to do,’ said Dewi. ‘It looks like they were using the pew to stand on to reach up for something, but I can’t see what.’

‘The figurine,’ Deborah said, picking it up.

‘What would they want with that? It’s not valuable is it, Mrs Elwiss?’

‘No, it’s not valuable, not in that way.’

‘Can you see if anything’s been taken?’ Dewi asked.

‘I don’t think so. The cross is still there, but that isn’t worth anything either. The figurine was on the wall above it.’

'I've been up in the tower but I couldn't see any lead missing and there was no sign anyone's been up there in a long time.'

'It's not safe,' said Deborah, guiltily. 'I'm sorry, I should have told you.'

'I didn't break my neck,' said Dewi. 'But we won't be able to look properly until the morning. I'll make sure I take more care next time.'

'I heard a door being closed,' said Deborah, 'but nothing else. They must have been careful not to make a noise, even if it doesn't look like it. I don't think whoever it was wanted the lead.'

'Don't you? Where's the vicar? You're not here on your own, are you?'

She waited until the other policeman had gone out. 'He's gone to look for Mr Tanner.'

'In the dark? Does he know where he is?'

'Not exactly. He is a vicar, Dewi. He believes in the power of prayer and the guidance of God.'

'I see.'

'Do you, Dewi?'

'Sort of,' said Dewi, slowly. 'He's not in any danger, is he?'

'I don't know, from himself perhaps, in the dark.'

Dewi frowned. 'He was close to Mr Tanner, wasn't he?'

She sighed. 'Was close, Dewi? That's what they're saying about Raymond isn't it, that he's had some sort of breakdown? Neither of them have, I promise you. My husband is a spiritual man, but let's not confuse that with a lack of judgement.'

'I would never suggest it, Mrs Elwiss, any more than I would say it of Mr Tanner.'

'I know you wouldn't, Dewi,' she looked around the church, 'but this seems like a deliberate insult, if that's the appropriate word. Ernest would call it sacrilege.'

'Well,' said Dewi, 'I don't know about that, but it is vandalism. I won't be able to report it as anything else unless we find something missing.'

'I understand.'

'He might find Mr Tanner, Mrs Elwiss. There is that possibility.'

'With God's help? Is that what you mean?'

'It's almost certainly just kids that did this, Mrs Elwiss.'

'I hope it is, Dewi. But why would they? It serves no purpose, not even mischief.'

'Neither does vandalism. Would you like one of us to stay with you until the vicar comes home? Or you could come down to the police station and I'll wait for him?'

'Thank you, Dewi, that's very kind, but I must stay here.' She tried to fit the two halves of Christ together. 'They should glue,' she said. 'I have some in the house. Ernest will be very upset to see it broken.'

It was dark but Eve would not turn on the lights. It was late, or very early, she didn't care which. She hadn't opened any windows even though it was a close night. The mugginess rose up the stairs and cloyed there. She slept in the armchair, but not because her bedroom was hot.

They were solid little houses to raise a family, not like the ones that had been built on Gwyn's fields that were perfunctory attempts to expand the growing town, advancing over the nearby farms as if Gwyn and the rest had never been.

She listened to the clock, italicising the silence from the sideboard, and didn't move, afraid to disturb the stillness. 'I am the only person awake in the whole of Wales,' she said to herself.

She thought about her father who had worked underground and shared the same disease as Alan's father. She was an only child and he had adored her. He died when she was eighteen and his death had rent her. She searched for someone to replace him and was taken in by Roy's promises and did not look beyond what she saw until it was too late. By marrying Roy, she had let her father down, more so because she knew he had never particularly liked him: 'There's something a bit sly about him,' he told her, 'but I know you will make up your own mind. Just be careful, though, won't you?'

'Look how it's turned out, Dad. I'm so sorry.' She longed for his voice and to feel his arm around her.

The apparition bent close to her ear and said, in its hoarse whisper, 'You could have saved those boys.'

Night after night it came.

'Dad?' She screwed her eyes shut. But he could not keep her safe. His powerlessness to save his little girl was a torment that screamed in the unlit roadways, disused and so deep underground they could not be heard.

'You were his *wife,*' it hissed.

'I didn't know,' Eve said.

'You told them you did.'

'I didn't, not the first time.'

'You've told them now. You knew.'

'I didn't. It wasn't true. I didn't know.'

'You could have saved those boys.'

'No.'

'What did the headmaster tell you, Eve?'

'Nothing.'

'Nothing? What did he tell you, Eve?'

Eve got up and went into the kitchen. The streetlamp at the end of the alley framed the door with a dolorous light.

The apparition followed.

She braced herself against the edge of the sink. Let it impregnate her while making its accusations. If that was the price, she would pay it. She would bear the incubus' child and nurture it secretly in the shadows even if she could not feel or see it.

'So you knew, didn't you?'

'Yes.'

She leaned forward and felt her skirt being lifted up and folded over her back. She presented herself.

The air moved as the door opened and was quietly closed. It had gone.

Eve pulled her skirt down and stood straight. She went back to the front room and slumped into the chair next to the window.

'I could find a man and offer myself. Once or twice and it would be done.'

Eve's mother had told her, a year after she married Roy and not long before she died, 'We wanted children, three or four, but we were only blessed with you.' He had been younger than Alan's father when he died. 'He always had a weak chest. The colliery was the worst place he could have worked, but what else was there?'

Eve's brothers and sisters had been sprites, riding on his labouring breath, seeking to find issue and form, but not strong enough, his heart and lungs rotting and turning black before they could. Eve's mother grieved for the children she never had as much as she mourned her dead husband. And Eve was her mother's daughter, but without a child to live her life through. That was what Roy had been for, to fill the emptiness and provide the children. For a short while, at least, there had been Huw, Jack and Aled.

How Eve cried, heaving with spasms that grew into wails of pain for her father, for her mother, for herself, for Jack and Huw, for her imagined, yearned for children. She cried as Jean had cried for Jack and Gwen had cried for Huw. Eve's memories flickered with the images of everyone she had loved. They weren't worth anything except to her, but they dwindled pitilessly, and she along with them, until all that was left was the fading afterglow of a young woman's life, the vestige of Eve.

The back door opened and someone came in.

'Why have you come back?' she asked. 'Why can't you leave me be?'

There was no reply.

'I've told you, I didn't know.'

A figure appeared, faintly backlit. 'Eve Brown,' said a low voice.

'Who are you?'

'What have you been saying, Eve?'

'Nothing. I haven't said anything.'

'You said too much.' The figure came closer.

Eve shrank into the chair.

He bent over her. 'You won't say anything more.'

'I won't.'

'No, you won't.' Hands reached for her neck.

'What are you doing?'

They tightened around her throat.

'No,' she gasped, 'Stop.'

They began to squeeze.

'Please.'

Tighter.

She looked into his face.

His thumbs were on her windpipe, crushing it.

'I know who you are.'

'I want you to know.' His fingers came together at the back of her neck. He lifted her from the chair and held her there until there was nothing left. Carefully, he placed her back down and straightened her head so she could see the children going to school. He left the way he had come.

Eve Brown – Guthrie – had gone. If her father and mother waited to greet her, they would laugh together, swapping the memories they shared that could not be deleted and Eve could love the many children. They would be hers for eternity. Her dream would come true. She would not be allowed to regret her life and its unrealised possibilities. Eve's worth would be the same as everyone's. This woman had been made more human than she deserved. By the mercy of God, she would forget her end.

Her last words had been, 'Yes, squeeze the life out of me.' That final syllable had popped from between her lips in a tiny bubble of spit that ran down her chin. '*Me.*'

Dawn was far behind him like a shadow less stark but, to the west, it was the blackest night.

The clouds of steam rolling out of the steelworks were faintly orange and puckered. High above, the fiery eyes watched. When Reverend Elwiss came over the top of Stormy Down, they saw him and demanded, 'You have dared to come here?' He had crossed an unseen threshold and, for the first time in his life, it had not gone unnoticed. In his mind, imagined or put there, he saw the place.

He turned off the dual carriageway into the quarry

where the headlights were dulled by hanging grey dust left by dump trucks on the haul road. The car whisked through and they were crisp again. The headlights grew bigger, rushing to meet him against the tall hedges of the lanes and sprang forward as thin as snooker cues where they opened out onto the fields bordering the dunes. They juddered over their uneven slopes, leapt through a gap and were fleetingly lost over the sea before finding them again with two bright jabs into the sand.

Reverend Elwiss slowed down, trying to recognise what he was looking for without knowing what it was. When he came to a track leading off the road, he turned onto it. The car lurched in the potholes. He came to a gate, half closed and couldn't go any further so he stopped and switched off the engine. The silence was abrupt. The headlights were as round as portholes on the wooden planks of the box-car. Its doors were shut.

Here it was, fabled but real, the place he had been led to or knew about from reports and pictures in *The Herald* (Lloyd's on a cold, rainy morning), the old railway car in the dunes where the police had found Jack Harris' jumper next to the body of a black and white cat, strangled, or so it was rumoured.

Protheroe had told *Herald* Andrew, 'Include the animals but don't say how they were killed,' so, in his reports on Alan's trial, he avoided the gory detail and tugged instead at readers' emotions: the floppy-eared rabbit was *someone's much loved pet*, and Alan's father's dog was *Sam the gentle labrador... Were they connected to the dead cat? It is impossible to be sure.* Which neatly made the connection. But, by then, Alan was guilty.

Reverend Elwiss reached for the torch on the passenger seat and opened the car door, feeling for the ground with his foot. It sank into the layer of sand under the grass. He swivelled on the seat and eased himself out. He tip-toed to the box-car and stood between the two headlight beams as if they were the handles of a sedan chair. He felt for them, but his hands passed through like moths.

Before the doors to a dream or the front page of *The Herald,* a minute passed by.

Behind those doors.

He remembered the day when God called him. A dove had been cooing in a tree, a soft entreaty that flooded him with joy. It was unmistakeably a calling. He opened his arms wide and embraced a different path. He told Deborah the story. 'I know it sounds unlikely,' he said, 'but it's true.'

She smiled and thought, 'It was probably a pigeon.' They were married soon after.

Was this to be its culmination? 'If I fail now, I have failed. Why have you offered me this choice, Lord?'

'Because you asked me for it.'

'Yes, I did, didn't I?'

'You must be careful what you wish for.'

'You're not mocking me, are you, Lord?'

'No, Ernest, I'm not mocking you.'

'I'm trying to understand. A man is alone when the moment of truth comes, when the outcome is unknown and cannot be predicted. There is no triumph; no one knows or sees. This is my battle, although I don't know what with… only God can protect me from the Devil.'

'It is too late to turn back. It knows you are here.'

'What knows?'

'Do it now.'

'I can't.'

'You can, Ernest. You must do it for your friend.'

His hand was shaking as he reached for the door bar. 'You have guided me here, Lord.'

'You came of your own free will, Ernest.'

'Then protect me now, I beseech you.'

The headlights went out. The car's battery had given up or been drained by unearthly powers.

Reverend Elwiss let go of the handle and jumped back. He grabbed for the torch in his pocket and dropped it. Feverishly, he searched for it on his knees by sweeping his hands through the grass. A foot scrunched on the sand. Someone was standing over him. He found the torch and fumbled to turn it on. Its feeble beam shone straight up. A face was looking down at him…

But the torch light bled away, barely reaching the top of the box-car. There was no one there. He fell forward onto his hands. Sweat ran down his neck. He tugged at his dog collar to loosen it and it came away completely. Disarmed. The cross around his neck fell out and swung against his forearm. He clutched it and closed his eyes and counted, silently, with his lips, 'One, two, three…' Slowly, he looked up. The torch made the metal door bar shine with a grubby lustre, still smudged with fingers.

'I must.'

He stood up and grasped the bar again. 'Please God, please God?' He pulled the bar up and felt the latch inside release. He took hold of the two handles.

He didn't fling them apart, this mockery of the dark sultan, shorter and timid, like an imp to a demon. The rain was not driving in off the Bristol Channel and breakers were not crashing on the shore. He was not surrounded by police cars and a circle of blazing lights. A vicar, alone with a torch.

Unseen, beyond the dunes, the sea was singing the lullaby of small waves, 'Hush… hush…'

The doors slid apart. A smell of old sacks and mustiness came out, disturbed from its foggy languor near the floor and filling the air with spores, followed by an acrid draught, the reek of diesel. Reverend Elwiss lifted the torch to see inside.

17

PRIVATE *STEVEN OWEN* *19*
EMIL ROTH *HAUPTMANN* *41*

Howell held the binoculars in his hands. 'I can't sleep,' he said.

'Look through them and you will see Aled,' Gerhard told him.

Howell did. He smiled and said, 'I can, even if I'm imagining it.'

'It's not your imagination.'

'Isn't it? If little boys are asleep at this time of night, why not old men? What's keeping me awake?'

'You know what it is, Howell. The same as always. Little boys are only afraid of the dark.'

'If I knew he was going to be safe and happy, that would be enough for me. I wouldn't ask for more. I've lived long enough.'

'A little longer, Howell. We must watch over him until we can be certain.'

'There isn't any certainty, is there, Gerhard?'

'No, we can only try our best to do all we can for him.'

Howell put the binoculars back on the windowsill. 'I'm glad that Aled will have these one day,' he said. 'They will remind him I existed.'

'That we both existed,' said Gerhard.

'How will he know about you?' Howell asked.

'You might be surprised what little boys know.'

'Go home, Bryn,' Laura told him. 'Go and get some sleep. You can't stay here all night.'

'I don't want to leave you,' said Bryn.

A nurse appeared behind him. 'Mr Hughes, your wife needs to get some rest. They'll both still be here in the morning.'

'There,' Laura said, 'now you don't have any choice.'

Bryn kissed her and gazed at his tiny son.

'Don't expect him to be like that all the time,' said the nurse. 'He'll soon let you know when he's hungry.'

'He's perfect,' said Bryn, quietly.

'They all are, Mr Hughes.'

'I'll see you tomorrow,' said Bryn.

The town was silent, but he thought he could hear a faint roar, which could have been the opencast mine, miles to the east, snarling over the carcass, or the air sizzling in the pent-up heat; and his footsteps, singly down the empty street and coughing from an open window. A baby was crying somewhere amongst the rooftops. 'Soon to be familiar,' he thought. 'But I must be in school first thing. I don't think I'll be able to make it back to the hospital until lunch break. Rose will have a lot more to do, she'll enjoy that. There's no one else now without Laura.'

He had been looking forward to telling Mr Tanner they had named their son after him and asking him to be a godfather. It had been decided weeks ago. Mary if it had been a girl, after Laura's grandmother. Now, he didn't want to think of it at all. 'He is already named,' and wished he hadn't tempted fate and blurted it out to Laura's father in that heady moment.

He came to the bridge and stopped to look over. The river was very low, only a thin ribbon of water at the centre of its channel, winding out of the town like a silken rope, with the smell of baked mud rising up. Bryn squinted. It wasn't a branch, it was a man, sitting against a tree at the top of the bank.

Bryn scrabbled down and squatted next to him. Maynard was even thinner than he remembered, nothing but a pile of loose sticks. But, in lieu of death, he was snoring.

The river was still deep enough to drown a helpless man. One easy push of this atrophied drunk and he would be gone. There would be almost no splash, no more than a small salmon leaping to free itself of sea lice.

Bryn was not sure if he was seriously thinking about doing it.

He stood up. 'I can't leave him here,' he thought. 'Don't

fall in, will you, Maynard.' But Prosser had pulled him far enough away from the water not to, even if he tipped onto his side. 'I'm not touching him. He smells.'

He went back to the road and looked up the hill to the police station. 'I'll have something to tell you when you're old enough. On the day you were born, I found a drunk asleep by the river.' Just a drunk, not who or what he was, a funny story, that's all.

Laura would say, 'You should have left him there.'

'I couldn't, not on my son's birthday, with Mr Tanner still missing.'

As he wearily climbed the hill, feeling overwhelmed by tiredness, a big, black car came out of the police station and turned in the opposite direction.

It was early and the air was as fresh as it was going to get. The sun was rising, the sky was an unblemished blue and the car threw a long shadow ahead of it on the road. Dewi said, 'He wants to see what we do. He knows how much we hate it.'

They reached the top of Stormy Down and came down the long hill on the other side, past the long span of dunes, then the reservoir. The fiery eyes were impassive, waving slowly over Port Talbot. The smell from the refinery grew stronger and a thin yellowy smog hung over the terraced houses. Dewi wound the window up, but the smell was already inside the car and leaking in through every gap. The road hugged the mountain as if it was afraid to go too close to the edge. Dewi drove faster and, gradually, the light from the sea grew brighter and whiter. They breathed again and felt braver, freer, the further away they got from Bridgend.

'So let's defy him,' said Dewi.

'Isn't that doing what he expects us to do?' asked Brenda.

'Then we've got nothing to lose, have we? Try not to get grass stains on your uniform this time.'

'I'll do it on purpose,' said Brenda, but it wasn't a joke.

Dewi parked the police car behind a hedge and they waded into the long grass and sank down into a sensual, immersing sea. Afterwards, they lay side by side, warmed by the growing heat of the sun, shimmering through stems like eyelashes.

'Perhaps I'll ask for a transfer instead,' said Dewi. 'I don't want to leave the police.'

'He's going to move you anyway.'

'Before he does,' said Dewi. 'I'm not going to wait.' He sighed. 'But Bridgend is my home.' He rolled onto his side. 'I think we'd better go.'

They left a strewn, interlaced bed of grass to mark where they'd been and what they'd done.

When they were back in the car, Dewi asked, 'What are we going to say to them?'

'I don't know,' said Brenda.

Dewi slapped the steering wheel. 'We've got no right. They're doing their best for him. What's it got to do with us?'

'It started with Eve Brown,' said Brenda, quietly. 'He was warning her off and letting them know.'

'It started a long time before Eve.'

'If you look at it like that, then yes,' said Brenda. 'I've been trying not to.'

'But she's in Bridgend, not Carmarthen.'

When Aled saw them coming down the lane, he stopped running and stood in the middle of the lawn with his arms by his sides. Gwen and Nesta came out.

'Hello Dewi, Brenda,' said Gwen. 'I'd like to say it's nice to see you, but I know why you've come. He's sent you, hasn't he? Nesta told me what he said.'

'I'm sorry, Gwen,' said Dewi.

'It's not your fault,' said Gwen.

'We'll tell him that we've seen you and that Aled's safe and well and that's all. It's true, what else is there to say?'

'If that's all you're going to tell him,' said Gwen, 'then why did he send you?'

Brenda shook her head. 'Because that's what he does.'

'That's Constable Dewi,' said Huw. 'And Brenda. Are they visiting?'

'Yes,' said his father, 'they are.'

'Are we being vigilant?' Huw asked.

'We are, Huw. We are being vigilant.'

Aled looked up at Dewi with his mouth open.

'He's growing,' said Brenda, and smiled. 'Hello Aled.'

'Not another one?' he thought, 'and this one's a police

lady.'

'After what he said to Eve and me, he can't do anything to us now, can he?' asked Nesta.

'No,' said Brenda, with emphasis, because she couldn't be sure. 'You're his guardian and you're doing what's best for him.'

'He's starting school here soon,' said Nesta, 'and I'm going to stay until he's properly settled in.'

'It's what Alan wants too,' said Gwen, looking at Dewi. 'He told me you'd been to see him. I admire you for that, Dewi. Thank you.'

Brenda looked at Dewi, her eyes shone.

They had a cup of tea and watched Aled playing. They talked about the unceasing heat and how much the farmers needed rain. Gwen said, 'I feel so sorry for Eve.'

'How many children are at the school?' Nesta asked.

As they walked down the track to the car, Gwen plucked at Brenda's arm to hold her back. 'You and Dewi,' she whispered. 'Well done.'

Brenda giggled and blushed. It was liberating for them both. When they had gone, Gwen realised how much she missed the frivolousness of a happy life. 'It will come or it won't come at all. It mustn't be hoped for.' She wouldn't admit to the spark of joy that Aled might bring, but she didn't try to put it out either.

As they were driving back to Bridgend, Brenda said, 'If he knew you'd been to see Alan Harris, I don't know what he'd do.'

'I think that's why he's doing it,' said Dewi.

'I hadn't thought of that.'

'Nor had I until just now.' Before they reached the fiery eyes, he asked, 'I wasn't wrong to go, was I?'

'We are both tempting fate.' Brenda spoke so quietly he could barely hear her over the engine.

'Both?'

Brenda looked straight ahead.

The smell enveloped them and the fiery eyes towered, regarding them warily as if they were ants biting their metal ankles.

When they were nearly back in Bridgend, Dewi said, 'I don't know if I can face it.'

'Yes, you can,' said Brenda, and patted his knee.

'Careful,' he said, 'he might see you.'

What he saw had no substance, the vicarage seemed to melt. The sounds of the waking town were far away as if he'd put a shell to his ear and imagined the sea. His thoughts would not gather; time did not pass. He had been separated and watched through glass.

Reverend Elwiss waited on the step, pale, wide-eyed and scavenged, dishevelled, without his dog collar, dirt on his knees and down his jacket, holding the cross hanging from his neck.

When Deborah opened the door, he looked up slowly and felt his way into the hall and sagged into the chair.

'Ernest, where have you been? I've been worried sick.'

He didn't answer.

She looked at him and his muddied suit. He still held the cross. 'What have you been doing? Your clothes are filthy.'

He shook his head.

She dropped to her knees and held his hands. 'You have interfered, Ernest. What have you been meddling with?'

'Meddling?' he murmured, as if he didn't understand.

'You're tired. You've been out all night.'

'The police are there.'

'The police, Ernest? Have you been into the church?'

He looked at her blankly. 'It's too late, Deborah.'

'You're a vicar,' she said, 'a vicar, with a parish full of ordinary people. Be one of them. Be normal. You have nothing to prove. Behind that dog collar, you're just my husband.'

He reached up to his neck. 'I lost it,' he said. 'It was dark.'

'It doesn't matter about that.'

'I don't think I will be able to sleep, ever.'

'You must try, Ernest,' she told him. 'Go to bed and I'll bring you up a cup of tea.'

He stood up and steadied himself against the bannister. He put his foot on the first step of the stairs and, one by one, went up to their bedroom.

She watched him go, as white and vulnerable as a child's fingers and his exhaustion came into her like a germ. She couldn't imagine what he'd seen, or if he'd seen anything at all. 'Why can't you leave God alone, he's got plenty of other holy men to boss about. It's not a price worth paying.'

She took the now glued together Christ from the kitchen drawer where she had hidden it. She listened but there was no sound from upstairs. Quietly, she slipped out of the back door and through the gate into the churchyard. The church was full of God in the morning but Deborah was having none of it. She hung the wooden Christ on its nail above the altar and stood back. 'Stay away from my husband,' she told him, sternly.

Detective Prosser waited nervously for Sergeant Phillips.

Sergeant Phillips' big, black car pulled into the car park. He got out, yanked his tunic straight, pulled on his gloves and smoothed his moustache with his thumbs. The peak of his cap was low over his eyes.

'Sir?'

'What do you want, Prosser?'

'Can we go into the interview room? I have important information for you.'

'No. Tell me here.'

Prosser's head ached, but there was no turning back.

'Now, Prosser, or go away.'

'Ellis Maynard murdered Darren Jeffries. I made him confess.'

'What use are you, Prosser?' growled Sergeant

Phillips.

Prosser gulped.

'I know his mind,' said Sergeant Phillips. 'I can see what is there. If it was there, I would see it. He didn't confess it to you.'

'He did, Sir. I'm not like the vicar.'

'You are no use to me, Prosser.'

Prosser saw Maynard stumbling into the car park out of the door that led to the cells, still drunk.

'You are no use, Prosser.'

'But Sir?' he pleaded. But Sergeant Phillips was already striding away. 'Please?'

In The Red Lion, just opened, Prosser sat down on the stool next to Maynard who was already there. The landlord served him with wordless contempt.

'I'm the Grim Reaper, me,' said Maynard, and they resumed their treacherous convenience.

18

CORPORAL *GORDON PRICE 21*
HERSCHEL RICHTER GEFREITER 19

A Detective Symonds called *Herald* Andrew. He warbled down the telephone like a schoolboy, but he might have been nervous, given his first important job to do by his new master and he was obviously reading from his notebook because he ended with, 'Tell that reporter to tell Protheroe to print it. Do it.'

'Very useful,' said 'that reporter'. 'I've seen you down the station, haven't I?'

'Have you?'

'So you're working for Sergeant Phillips now?'

'Yes.'

'We should meet up for a pint then.'

'Should we?' asked Detective Symonds, doubtfully. He had been told about reporters.

'When you're off duty, of course.'

'Well, it wouldn't be when I'm on duty would it?'

Symonds bridled.

'Not yet, anyway,' thought *Herald* Andrew, and said, 'No, I'd never suggest something like that, no, what I mean is that we could be useful to each other. That's the way it's always worked between Sergeant Phillips and *The Herald*.'

'Has it?'

'It certainly has. I think we might be seeing quite a lot of each other. He must trust you or he wouldn't have asked you to speak to me, would he?'

'I suppose not.'

'Keep up,' thought *Herald* Andrew. 'How about the Raven Arms?' he asked, to avoid Maynard at The Red Lion (that was to come. *Herald* Andrew almost felt sorry him).

'I'll think about it,' said Symonds, 'but I don't see why we should.'

'It'll be worth your while,' said *Herald* Andrew.

'What do you mean by that?' demanded Symonds.

'Nothing. It will put you in tight with him, that's all, I promise,' and he put the phone down and went upstairs to report.

Protheroe listened, without surprise, half expecting it. It would fill the front page, probably more than one as the story unfolded and there were lots of other angles they could pursue. He swivelled the chair to face the window and harrumphed to himself.

'Boss?'

Protheroe swivelled back. 'Is there anything else?'

'That's about it, boss. I'll get some more later, but

that's all I've got for now.'

'Who is this Symonds?' Protheroe asked. 'What do you know about him?'

'Not much. I've seen him around, that's all.'

'And you're sure this came from Sergeant Phillips?'

'I'm certain of that, yes. He's too wet behind the ears to do anything by himself, even if he dared.'

'Thank you, Andrew,' Protheroe said, trying one of his conspiratorial smiles of old which contorted into a strange grimace. 'Play this one with dollops of sympathy. The town has lost a great servant, much respected, irreplaceable.' Whatever *The Herald* had printed in the past had done nothing to diminish Mr Tanner's standing – the reverse – and it was too late now for the newspaperman's apology: 'It's nothing personal.'

'Right, how about...' Protheroe thought for a moment and said, 'Mmm,' to himself. 'Right,' he said, again, and began to compose out loud, once the pleasure of a master declaiming to his young reporter, but the words turned on him as if they knew they were being used fraudulently. 'And that recent pressures... no, *events*, relating to... *following* the discovery... no, start again. The discovery of the body of missing boy, Rhodri Mitchell may, *may*, Andrew, have contributed to Mr Tanner's confused, uh, no, *troubled,* state of mind, uh... yes, troubled state of mind... as it is believed he never fully recovered from the traumatic effects of the loss of the three boys – include their names – three years ago, two of whom were pupils at his school and may, *may*, explain the reason for his recent disappearance and add… no, finish with, and the police are not looking for anyone else in connection with their enquiries.'

'What about the bit about his breakdown?' asked *Herald* Andrew.

'Don't use the word breakdown and make sure you stick to *may* not *did*. Include condolences to his family. Has he got any family?'

'I don't know, boss.'

'Well, that can wait for now, but go down there and see what else you can find out, but don't barge in, Andrew.' Protheroe made a calming motion with his hands. 'Tread carefully, yes? And, after that you can write the… no, I'll do that.'

'The obit?'

'Yes, the obit.'

Protheroe shook his head as *Herald* Andrew left. 'Dear God,' he said, under his breath. 'I didn't want to see this in print, not in this or any paper.'

'Come on Lloydy-boy,' said *Herald* Andrew in the office downstairs.

Protheroe winced when he heard the glass door slam. He couldn't bear to let Andrew write Mr Tanner's obituary and have to endure unintentional – or intentional? – comparisons in every sentence. At least, if he wrote it himself, he would know what was coming.

Bryn locked the door to Mr Tanner's office so that it would remain undisturbed and gathered everyone in his classroom: Paul Rees, Rose and Mr Topliss. Laura was still in the hospital with the baby and he was hoping to bring them home tomorrow.

He couldn't hide his feelings; he thought they must know what he was going to say by the expression on his face. But they looked at him unsuspectingly. He was going to have to tell them. A more experienced man would have said, 'I have the most dreadful news…' and then they would surely have guessed. The soon to be experienced man said, 'Thank you for coming in at short notice.' He tried to control himself but it came out in a rush. 'Mr Tanner's body was found in Kenfig Pool by Reverend Elwiss in the early hours of this morning. They think he might have drowned. I'm afraid I don't know anymore. I'm sorry.' There was a moment of shock, then Rose started crying, Mr Topliss too: silent, big, soldier's tears. Paul Rees looked confused as if he'd been told of the death of a great-uncle.

Bryn took deep breaths. 'I haven't told Laura yet. I'm going to the hospital directly, visiting hours or not. She mustn't find out from a stranger.' He looked out of the window at the empty playground. 'The school will not close, not again. That's the last thing Mr Tanner would have wanted.' He looked up at the ceiling, with tears running down his cheeks and dripping off his chin onto his shirt collar. 'We've called the baby Raymond,' he said.

'We were going to before any of this. I'll never be able to tell Mr Tanner now.'

Mr Topliss gripped Bryn's shoulder and nodded.

Bryn wiped his eyes and tried to be purposeful. 'There's not going to be a right time to talk about this but, until they appoint another headmaster, perhaps you would let me organise things, only because I've been here the longest – as a teacher, I mean,' he added, quickly, looking at Mr Topliss. 'I feel I owe it to him to keep the school going and somebody has to.'

'Of course you should,' said Rose, wiping her nose with a dainty hankie.

'It will be in the newspaper,' said Bryn. 'But I'm going to put a notice on the gates to tell everyone the school's going to stay open and I'll tell *The Herald* so they can include it. I'm going to ask Reverend Elwiss and Mrs Elwiss if they will help out. This will have affected the vicar very badly, but I think he will want to, they were close friends.'

'If anybody should have found him, it should have been Reverend Elwiss,' said Mr Topliss. 'There's not much left after, except friendship. But what was he doing there at that time of night?'

Bryn shrugged. 'I don't know.'

Bryn pinned the piece of paper with its short message in capital letters high up on the school gates so the children couldn't read it. 'Term starts on Monday,' he thought, 'and I'm going to have to take assembly from now on.'

Aled wriggled in his new school uniform. 'You do look smart,' said Nesta. 'Doesn't he, Gwen?'

'Yes he does. He's a big boy now.'

Aled wasn't convinced. It was the first time he had worn a tie and the shirt collar was too tight; he didn't understand why he had to wear a cap and the jumper made him hot.

'Take them off,' Nesta told him, 'and we'll put them by ready for when you start.'

'Do you think the collar is too tight?' asked Gwen.

'Yes,' said Aled.

'I can always move the button,' said Nesta, 'or perhaps we should get him a bigger size.'

'Can we take it back?'

'I don't know. We've unwrapped it now.'

Gwen started undressing him.

'Do I have to go to school?' asked Aled.

'Of course you do,' said Nesta. 'All big boys go to school.'

'You'll be able to learn Welsh,' said Gwen. 'Everyone speaks Welsh here.'

'Welsh? What's that?'

'It's a language. It's your language, or it soon will be,' Gwen told him. 'I speak Welsh.' She folded the shirt and jumper. 'I think we'll have to move the button. There we are.'

Aled put on his old clothes which were less complicated.

'You need a haircut,' said Gwen.

Aled wrinkled his nose and pulled at his fringe.

'Go out and play.' She smiled.

He ran into the garden.

'He reminds me so much of Huw, except Huw was fair like his father.'

'He's settled down nicely, better than I expected,' said Nesta. 'Children are so adaptable, aren't they?'

Huw was sitting on the stone wall, waiting.

Aled climbed up next to him. Another year and they would be the same age. 'I've got a school uniform,' Aled told him. 'Auntie Nesta says I look very smart but I'm not sure I like it. It itches and it's too hot. And I've got to learn Welsh.'

They banged their heels against the wall and didn't say anymore for a while. Aled leaned back on his hands and closed his eyes. The sun made the insides of his eyelids bright pink. They listened to the seagulls. Two little boys in West Wales, a stone's throw from the river and not far from the sea.

Geraint watched them from under the trees at the end of the garden. 'We will be needed closer to home soon,' he thought, because he knew everything that would happen but not if he could change it.

'Let's go over the field,' said Aled, suddenly coming out of his reverie. 'Come on.'

They jumped down on the other side of the wall and ran off laughing. It was a big field, still green in the parching sun, with sheep dotted about grazing. Huw and Aled scattered them and didn't stop running until they reached the hedge on the other side. They crawled through. Aled had to untangle himself from the prickly branches. There was another field that sloped down to the river that was filling with the incoming tide.

They threw stones at a floating log and then tried skipping them over the water. 'That was seven,' said Aled.

'No, it wasn't, it was six.' Huw's stones flew through the air from an invisible hand.

Then they walked along the river until they came to a bend where the water had undercut the bank. It was deep and swirling.

'You don't want to fall in there,' said Huw.

'I can swim,' said Aled. 'I'm a good swimmer, especially in the sea.'

'You still don't want to fall in,' said Huw.

'Shall I jump in then and swim over to there?' Aled pointed at the far side of the bend.

'You'll have to take your clothes off first,' Huw told him.

'I can leave my pants on though,' Aled said.

'I don't know what my mum would say if you came home with wet pants.'

'Your mum?' Aled frowned. 'Who's your mum?'

'What?' Huw looked puzzled. 'In the cottage.'

'Auntie Nesta is your mum?'

'No.'

'Is your mum Auntie Gwen?'

'Yes,' said Huw. 'Of course she is. Didn't you know? Well, now you do.'

Aled looked at the river. 'I'd better not jump in then. Why didn't you tell me your mum was Auntie Gwen? She'd be bloody cross if I came home with wet pants.'

'You could take them off too,' Huw suggested.

'But someone might see my willy.'

'That's true,' Huw agreed. 'You might get arrested.'

They abandoned the idea and began walking back to the cottage. 'Next time I'll bring my cossie,' said Aled.

'And a towel,' said Huw.

'I prefer to swim in the sea. I like waves. Do you think your mum would take us to the beach?'

'Ask her,' said Huw, and they started running.

Aled burst into the cottage, hot and out of breath. 'Auntie Gwen,' he cried, 'will you take me and Huw to the beach?'

Gwen stared at him. 'Huw?'

'Yes,' said Aled. 'He said to ask you. Can we? Please?'

Huw was waiting outside. Geraint came to stand next to him. 'What have you said to Aled, Huw?'

Huw looked up at his father. 'Nothing.'

As Gwen packed a bag with towels and a rug to sit on, she asked Nesta, 'Did you tell him about Huw?'

'No,' said Nesta, 'but he might have heard us talking.'

Gwen shook her head, 'How very strange.'

'Has he met one of the boys from the village called Huw, do you think?' Nesta asked.

'I don't think so,' said Gwen. 'I don't know another boy called Huw.'

'Then he must have heard us talking,' said Nesta. 'It can't be anything else.'

Gwen rolled up a towel. 'But why did he say it like that?'

'Little boys are always making up new friends to play with,' said Nesta. 'He'll soon have some real ones when he goes to school.'

As they waited at the bus stop, Aled said, 'Huw and his dad are going to meet us at the beach.'

Protheroe refreshed the hole in the dirty window with the tip of his finger (the dust would quickly fill it in again). The river was gasping. There was no water coming down from the mountains, the slopes were bone dry, the grass was brittle and the sheep were bleating.

'I have made my life in this town,' he thought. 'A big fish in a little pond.' He peered through the hole at the trickle of a river, 'A very little pond... not such a big fish.' He leaned back in his chair and laced his hands together on his tummy and was irritated to find there was an even bigger shelf there to rest them on. 'Narrow-minded like all small towns everywhere...' a small figure ran through his mind like a fragment of memory and disappeared. 'What?' A sentence began to appear, like they did sometimes when he was trying to come up with a headline... *amongst us* and faded away. He shuddered. 'Stop now. I'm seeing things which are not there to be seen. Am I?' He wanted a whisky.

He was a wily old spider, plotting and watching from his lair. He looked around his office: screwed-up papers everywhere, like the husks of dead flies.

Herald Andrew's article was on his desk. He scored through *had a breakdown* and changed *emotionally disturbed* to *may have been troubled* and crossed out *one of his teachers who had previously been interviewed by the police in connection with the disappearance of the boys.* When he finished, *Herald* Andrew's insinuations were gone.

'He's defying me on purpose now,' Protheroe thought. 'He's trying to provoke me,' and imagined the scorn on *Herald* Andrew's face. He had looked at Jeffries like that, then at Prosser, 'And now at me. He thinks I've gone soft and I'm not up to it anymore.' His protégé was a legacy that would endure; a distilled version of himself, something to savour.

A whisky – two, three. Large ones.

As he walked to the Raven, shambling, as he was painfully aware, he wanted to make amends, even if it was only one sincere, well-intentioned act. The age of regret had suddenly collapsed on him like an old wall, but he did not tell himself, 'It comes to us all in the end,' because he had never imagined it would, as he lay under the rubble unable to move.

'We were almost there,' she lamented, 'a few more days, a week, and we could have told everyone,' and, then, if he had to die, she would have been comforted by his circle of friends (not many, but loyal; a select few) as someone who had shared his intimacies, who knew him in ways they did not. They would have encouraged her to find someone new, and helped with introductions, because that's what friends do. 'Life goes on,' they would say. 'He would have wanted you to. You know he would.'

Then she could choose; what would she give to be able to choose: she would not have to fade away, she would not have to be anonymous, her dreams would not be bitter, her remaining life would not be time itself, with few distractions, forcing her to take comfort in simple things, like a pot of tea in the morning, scones with jam and cream in the afternoon, with an unchanging routine, forgetting what day it was, because nothing marked one from another and afraid to change anything because it was change. When the sun came out, she would think of her parents and her childhood, her husband, her favourite places she no longer visited (but could? No, she wouldn't) but when it rained, that would be too much. She would talk to people in the street she didn't know well enough and try not to notice their impatience. They would be sorry for her, but couldn't spare the time. Rose could not grieve because no one knew she had a reason to.

In the mirror, she pulled at the sides of her eyes and under her ears to smooth the lines and lift up her jowls and turned her head from side to side to manage the shadows. But she could only look the way she wanted to if she sat very still in the morning sunlight when it was a quarter past eleven precisely and only in front of the hall mirror (it didn't work in the bedroom) with both hands holding back the skin behind her neck, without breathing.

Headmaster's Body Found

The body of headmaster Raymond Tanner was found in the early hours of yesterday morning in Kenfig Pool by Reverend Elwiss, vicar of St John's Church, who had been out looking for him.

Mr Tanner had been missing since last Tuesday when he left Bridgend Primary School saying he had an 'errand' to perform.

There were concerns that he may have been troubled following the recent discovery of the body of Rhodri Mitchell, 7, who disappeared together with two other boys, Jack Harris, 6, and Huw Evans, 6, three years ago. The body of Huw Evans was found but Jack Harris remains missing. Both boys were pupils at his school and Mr Tanner was deeply affected by their disappearance and, in a state of distress, may have been searching for Jack Harris in the dunes around Kenfig Pool where his jumper and sandals were found during the original investigation.

Mr Tanner had been headmaster at the school for many

years and was described by friends and colleagues as a pillar of the community. Teachers at the school said he was 'irreplaceable'.

He was unmarried and is believed to have no close family, but he was a much loved and respected figure throughout the local community and taught the fathers and mothers of many children who attend the school today. The Herald *wishes to be among those who extend their condolences to all who knew him. He will be sorely missed.*

The police have told The Herald *they are not looking for anyone else in connection with their enquires and, although investigations are continuing, the early indications are that Mr Tanner drowned as a result of a tragic accident.*

The school has confirmed that it will be open for the start of the new term and classes will continue as usual. Bryn Hughes, a teacher at the school said, 'It would be what Mr Tanner wanted.' Mr Hughes has named his newly born son, Raymond, in Mr Tanner's memory.

It was the first day of term and the roads near the school were full of children walking with their mothers. For many it was their very first day.

Eve watched them through the bay window as they passed from where she sat in the armchair at the other end of the front room.

One little girl noticed her because the sun from the

back garden fell across Eve's face. 'Why is that woman looking at us like that?' she asked her mother.

'Where?'

'There,' said the little girl, 'in that house.'

'Wait here,' said her mother, and she went up to the bay window to see in.

The back door was unlocked. 'Eve?' Dewi called.

She was cold. Her skin had a bluish tinge and her nostrils were purple with dried blood.

Dewi drew the curtains. Then he went outside to wait for the ambulance. Bryn was taking assembly and the road was deserted.

Brenda arrived with the young constable who had helped Dewi search the church. 'Is she?' Brenda asked.

Dewi nodded. 'Yes, and for some days.'

Brenda went in. When she came back out, she said, 'Something's gone on here, hasn't it?'

'Yes, it has,' said Dewi.

A big, black car pulled up at the kerb.

'Talk of the devil,' said Dewi.

'Has he said anything to you yet?' asked Brenda.

'No, but he sent me here on my own when the call came in. I think he wanted me to see her like this. God knows why.'

Sergeant Phillips got out. He yanked his tunic straight and flexed his knuckles as he pulled on his gloves and smoothed his moustache with the outside of his thumbs.

Detective Symonds got out of the passenger side and trotted after Sergeant Phillips as he strode, unhurriedly, down the drive.

'Two unexplained deaths in a week,' said Dewi under his breath. 'All we need now… and here they come.'

19

SERGEANT CYRIL PARRY 28
ADEL SCHAGER LEUTNANT 29

Salute: 'Good morning, Gerhard.'

'It wasn't a long life, but it is all my memories are made of. I have spent longer here than I was alive.'

'You have missed so much. It was taken away. I'm sorry,' said Howell.

'No, there is nothing to be sorry for, Howell. You came home and I did not. That is how it happened and there is nothing left to say.'

'You are a long way from home, Gerhard.'

'I am, but time does not weigh on me as I think it weighs on you. Here I am, in Wales. It is very different from where I grew up. It has been so unexpected.'

'None of us knew whether we were going to live or die, did we?'

'No, we didn't. But that is not the unexpected part. This is. You are. It could not have been imagined.'

'No, it could not.'

'One day I will take you to my home, Howell. Would you like that?'

'When? I will have to be dead.'

'It's not so bad,' said Gerhard. 'Perhaps you will meet my mother and father. I am the same now as the day we said goodbye. I am…' he smiled, 'well preserved. But they are long dead too.'

'If Aled is safe, I am prepared,' said Howell. 'There is little more I can do now.'

'You have contributed much to this life, Howell.'

'Have I? Is that you telling me, or is it what I want to think?'

'It's been too long for that, Howell. Don't doubt yourself. You know I can't offer you any proof and, if I could, would you want it?'

'You're right. I'm not sure it matters, now,' said Howell. 'You've been with me all these years and for that I'm grateful.'

'The boy doesn't question what he sees.'

'No,' said Howell, 'he doesn't but, then, boys don't.'

'I watched you take the binoculars from around my neck. Then I knew I was dead. Do you remember the trees? The only living things for miles except for soldiers. It doesn't matter if they were German or British, does it? You carried me in the binoculars for the rest of the war, together with the horrors they had seen. I came home with you because I chose to, Howell.'

In the morning, Reverend Elwiss felt like he hadn't slept at all or he was still asleep and dreaming he was awake. He got up and looked out of the window at the back garden and the churchyard. Deborah was not there. She must have already got up or he had slept alone.

Alone? Was she still alive? Did he have a wife called Deborah?

He didn't know what time it was but the sun was already warm. It was bright enough to hurt his eyes that were still searching in the darkness by the light of his torch.

He stared at the church. Stone upon old stone. In the shade of the tower, the mildew was as dry as green dust after the long hot summer.

'I had a church,' he thought.

He sat on the bed in his pyjamas. 'I don't remember putting these on.' He felt for the cross around his neck. It wasn't there. 'Did I lose it?' Then he saw it on the dressing table and put it over his head.

Deborah came in.

'Oh, thank God.'

'You're awake,' she said. 'How did you sleep? Are you feeling better?'

'No.'

'Go back to bed, Ernest,' she told him, gently, 'and don't get up until you feel fully recovered.'

'Is that my church?'

'Yes, Ernest, it's your church.' She sat down next to him. 'Shall I make you a cup of tea?'

He nodded. 'Thank you.'

The Herald was on the doormat where it had been pushed through the letter box by the paperboy. It had fallen neatly and squarely with the headline facing her. She put it in the bin behind the garage.

When she went back up, he hadn't moved. His hands were limp, resting on his thighs, palms up. He stared at them, perplexed, as if something was missing.

She put the tea on the dressing table and put her arm around him. 'Ernest,' she said, 'I am so sorry.'

'Yes,' he said, 'he was my friend. I mustn't forget him.'

'How could you ever forget him, Ernest?'

'I think I'll get dressed now,' he told her.

She took his black suit out of the wardrobe. 'You'll have to wear this one. The other one was filthy. It's gone to the cleaners.' She laid it on the bed with a neatly pressed shirt. 'I'll make you some breakfast.'

He sipped the tea as he dressed, holding the cup and saucer together because he was trembling.

'I'm not hungry,' he told her, as he was coming down the stairs. 'I'm sorry, but I'm not.'

'You must eat, Ernest. You haven't eaten for days.'

'Days?' He frowned and looked at her. 'I will have something to eat in a while.'

'Bryn came to see you,' she told him.

'Bryn Hughes?' He pressed the heel of his hand into his forehead. 'This will be awful for him.'

'It is awful for you, Ernest.'

'I cannot think of it that way. I have no right to.' He went through the back door to sit on the bench in front of his study window.

'Would you like some more tea?' she asked him.

'Yes please.' The little boy's white face seemed lit from within. His small hand tugged at his and he stumbled through the sand to the glassy pool full of stars and, swimming amongst them, girls with long green tresses smiled at him from beneath the water. Beyond the dunes, the sea ended its song, 'Hush, now… hush…'

Deborah brought him more tea.

He opened his eyes. 'Thank you. I think I'll sit here for a while.' He looked at his church.

'Do you want me to sit with you?'

'No,' he replied, 'let me think.'

'Don't think too much, Ernest. Bryn said he'd come back this morning.'

'Did he? I'm sorry I missed him.'

'I didn't want to wake you.'

'Wake me? He must have come very early.'

'No, Ernest, yesterday afternoon when you were asleep. You have been asleep for two days, a whole day and a night since you got home yesterday morning. Don't you remember?'

He thought. 'Do I? I'm not sure,' he said, uncertainly.

'Laura's had the baby.'

'The baby?' He put the cup and saucer on the bench.

At the water's edge, he could see, by the reddish light

of the fiery eyes, a dark shape. He knelt in the water and turned it over. The girls' hair coiled around his wrists to stop him from falling.

He looked up at his wife. 'I have to go into the church,' he said.

Reverend Elwiss went through the little gate, through the churchyard and into the church. He was greeted by the mended Christ, back on its nail above the altar, with its head to one side and the delicately carved sinews in its neck as taut as wires.

'I am your servant,' said Reverend Elwiss.

'Now you know,' Christ said, without moving his head or lips. 'You know what your friend knew. He is with me now. There is no other way you could know; there was no other way you could be told.'

'I understand.'

'Because these are not wholly the affairs of men.'

'I understand.'

'Do you?' Christ was standing before him. He put his hands on Reverend Elwiss' shoulders and looked into his eyes.

Reverend Elwiss looked into the eyes of God.

Christ said, 'You made your choice.'

Reverend Elwiss sank into the front pew next to one of the tall brass vases filled with newly picked flowers, placed there the day before by Mrs Wright. He rubbed his forehead. When he looked up, Christ was a wooden figurine again, with a hairline crack across its middle.

Reverend Elwiss stayed in the church for an hour.

As he was leaving, Christ said, 'I will love you no less if you fail.'

Reverend Elwiss turned. 'Is there more?'

Bryn was in the kitchen with Deborah. He stood up as Reverend Elwiss came in and held out his hand.

Reverend Elwiss took it and pulled him into his arms.

'Aw, come on, Dewi.'

Dewi glared at *Herald* Andrew who was loitering at the end of Eve's drive with Lloyd at his side.

'Come on, Dew, you can tell us what's what, can't you?'

Sergeant Phillips came out of the house.

Herald Andrew and Lloyd scuttled away down the pavement.

Detective Symonds followed, taking two little skips to Sergeant Phillips' one long stride.

When Sergeant Phillips reached his big, black car, he looked down at Symonds and said, 'Tell that reporter. Do it.' He got in and drove away, leaving Symonds dawdling at the kerb.

'What does he want us to know, then?' asked *Herald* Andrew. 'Why don't you tell us down the Raven where it's more convivial – if you're off duty, of course?'

Dewi listened. 'Don't go,' he thought, 'don't go.'

Alan's house was to his left, Gwen's was to his right, where strangers lived, and Eve's was in between, now empty.

Early September had a contemplative light, but still no rain. Aled walked between Nesta and Gwen holding their hands. He was quiet and wide-eyed. He felt trussed up in his new uniform even though Gwen had moved his shirt collar button to make it looser. The children's voices got louder.

The school was a small Victorian building in the middle of the village. The playground was to one side and surrounded by a metal fence. The school had less than thirty children, most of them from nearby farms, and three teachers.

Aled looked up at Gwen and Nesta. He was one of only four new children beginning school today.

'Go on, Aled,' said Gwen. 'We'll wait here while you go in.'

Aled clutched their hands tighter and didn't move.

One of the teachers saw them, a comfortable lady in her fifties. She came over and squatted in front of Aled. 'Hello,' she said, 'and who is this? No, let me guess.' She smiled. 'You're Aled Morgan, aren't you?'

Aled nodded shyly.

'I'm Mrs Bevan. It's so lovely to meet you, Aled. Would you like to come and play with the other children?'

Aled twisted, Gwen let go his hand and Nesta did too. As Mrs Bevan led him away, they passed some girls playing hopscotch. 'What are they doing?' Aled asked.

'They're playing a game,' said Mrs Bevan.

'Can I play too?'

'It's a game for girls,' she told him.

Aled looked back. Two boys ran up and spoke to him in Welsh.

'You'll understand what they're saying in no time at all,' Mrs Bevan told him.

Aled would never remember Bridgend; his life at the shop in Trebanog became remnants and his aunties and uncles were soon too old to make the trip to Carmarthen, but none of it mattered, he would have eternity.

Gwen didn't think they needed a car, new or old, and the van was left to settle on its tired axles in the corrugated garage with flat tyres and clotted oil until, one bitter winter morning, the rust ate through a bulkhead and it fell apart.

'He has new friends, Huw,' said Geraint.

'What about me?' Huw asked. 'I'm his friend too. Can I go and play with them as well?'

'Not today, Huw. He has to make new friends now he's started school.'

'Do we still have to be vigilant?'

'Yes, Huw,' his father replied. 'More than ever.'

'When can we go to Broadway?'

'A little while.'

'*Ohhh*, you always say that. You promised.'

Geraint laughed. 'I did, and I always keep my promises.'

Geraint watched Gwen walking up the road back to the cottage. 'I love you,' he whispered. 'I will always love you.'

'Did you say something?' Gwen asked Nesta.

Aled was lost amongst the children running excitedly around the playground. He already knew three or four words of his new language. Mrs Bevan rang the bell and, soon, the playground was empty.

Detective Prosser told himself, 'I'm nothing like Jeffries was. I just need to think of a new plan. I was never cut out for the police. I know that now.'

Maynard was skulking outside The Red Lion, waiting for it to open, holding a cigarette between his finger and thumb, shiftily glancing from side to side for no reason except who he was.

They sized each other up, as usual, but no words were exchanged before the bolts were slid back and they filed in. The landlord regarded them with jaded irritation and wished they weren't there. They sat side by side on the stools that were never moved and had the exact money ready as two pints were poured. This was when the day began.

Hours passed. Other customers came and went, lacking the dedication and application of the two gentlemen at the bar.

Prosser said, 'I'm looking for a fresh start. I've wanted to forever, really. I don't know why I ever joined the police. Well, that's all over now and good riddance to it.' He raised his glass in a toast to fulfilment, free from the yoke.

Maynard was looking at him with a puzzled expression

as if he was trying to remember what he meant to say.

'What?' asked Prosser.

Maynard saw a man floating face down in a dark river being carried away. 'I tell you what,' he said, slowly, as he tried to arrange his words. 'When they shut, right, we should get some take-outs and go down to the river until they open again. We can get some chips on the way too.'

'Drinks by the river?' Prosser mused, tapping his front teeth with the rim of his glass, as if it was a genteel prospect. 'With chips?'

'There we are then,' said Maynard. He would have company for the first time in a long while. His eyes narrowed and his tongue flicked between his lips. He took a big gulp of beer and delicately picked off the flecks of foam from the corners of his mouth.

'What time is it now?' asked Prosser, looking up at the clock over the bar. 'We've got a couple of hours so we can have three or four more, at least.'

'Aye, aye,' said Maynard, 'get it down you, then.'

Bryn and Laura walked home from the hospital. Bryn was pushing the new pram his parents had bought for them. Little Raymond was asleep under the hood with a woolly cap on his head and a shawl pulled up to his chin. 'The pram's first outing,' he said. They got to the traffic lights opposite the cinema and waited to cross.

'Did you go to see Reverend Elwiss?' Laura asked. 'How was he?'

'Not as I expected. I was the one that went to pieces. If I hadn't seen him, I don't think I would have. I was trying to keep it bottled up.'

'What did he say to you?'

'Nothing. He hugged me.'

'He hugged you? I can't imagine Reverend Elwiss doing that.'

'Well, he did,' said Bryn. 'After what he must have seen, he was only thinking of me. He is a good man, Laura.'

'Did he tell you how he found him?'

'No, he didn't say anything. I meant to ask them if they'd help out at the school, but I didn't in the end. I think he was exhausted so I didn't stay long.' The traffic lights turned red. The cars stopped and they crossed the road.

'What did Mrs Elwiss say?' Laura asked.

'Nothing. She was concerned about him, not surprisingly.'

'Has he told the police?'

'About why he was there? No, I don't think he has. I don't know why I should think that.'

'People have drowned in Kenfig Pool,' said Laura.

'It's shallow,' said Bryn. 'You'd have to wade out to get into water that's deep enough to drown. Why would he do that? It doesn't make sense.'

'Right, boss,' said *Herald* Andrew, coming into Doug Protheroe's office through the always open door and sitting on the rickety old chair.

'What have you got, Andrew?' Protheroe asked.

'I've just been down the Raven with Symonds. Straight from the horse's mouth he told me, although he didn't quite put it like that. But, whatever.' *Herald* Andrew grinned.

'What did he say?'

'Top story, boss. Tragic.'

'And?'

'She topped herself. It was all too much for her.'

'Are you telling me that's what he said, Andrew?'

'No, it's the story, boss.'

'Did Symonds specifically tell you she killed herself?'

'Yes.'

'How did she do it, Andrew?'

Herald Andrew shrugged, 'I know there was a rope, so she must have.'

'A rope? I see. What else?'

'She wanted to get the aunties looking after Alan Harris' son to give him to her and they wanted to because they're getting on – which is how she got a record in the first place wasn't it, trying to get hold of him – and her husband's still banged up somewhere up north, so Sergeant Phillips stepped in to put a stop to it and protect the boy and it was all too much so she topped herself. Tragic.'

'Yes,' Protheroe said, slowly rolling his forefinger over his bottom lip.

'Tragic.'

'What happened to the boy?'

'I don't know,' said *Herald* Andrew. 'He must still be up in the valleys somewhere.'

'Do you remember Gwyn Roberts?'

'Boss?'

'Andrew, let me write this one, will you?'

'*Boss*?'

'If you don't mind, Andrew. I need to keep my hand in. You know what it's like?' He smiled in a way that said there was nothing more to talk about. 'If you don't mind, Andrew.'

Herald Andrew got up and left without another word.

'I know how you feel,' thought Protheroe, who would have been furious in his younger days if an editor stole one of his stories. 'So fuck off down the pub and get over it.' The exact words he had once been told. 'You're not sitting in my chair just yet, Andrew.'

Maynard and Prosser sat under the trees with a clutch of bottles and a bag of chips each. The bank fell steeply away to what was left of the desperate river. The shadows were lengthening.

A big, black car stopped on the bridge above them. Maynard saw it but said nothing. After some minutes, it pulled silently away.

Protheroe walked up the drive to where Dewi was still standing in the porch outside Eve's front door and said, 'I'm the editor of *The Herald*.'

'Yes, Sir, I know who you are. Your reporters have been and gone.'

'Yes, they have.' Protheroe replied. 'I'd like some information if you wouldn't mind. I have no other agenda here, Constable, except the truth.'

There was a wink of lightning and thunder rolled up the Bristol Channel like a rock fall.

20

PRIVATE ARNOLD ROBERTS 18
ARNO STEIN FELDWEBEL 27

The sky to the west was so black it was purple. The storm rose over South Wales in fitful gusts that quickly grew stronger. A curtain of rain followed, like an army beating its shields, charging up Cardigan Street, thrashing the road and making the gutters run in torrents. Lightning flashed and thunder shook the houses. Summer fled, clutching its skirts. The new air was steely and cold.

Rose was forced to duck into the Raven Arms, shaking the rain from her hair. She looked around, embarrassed. 'Do you mind?' she asked the barman, sheepishly.

'No,' he said, not understanding why he should. 'What can I get you?'

'That's very kind,' she said.

'It is a pub,' he told her. 'What do you want to drink?'

'No, thank you…' but thinking it might be required as payment, she changed her mind. 'A pineapple juice –

actually, no, a gin and tonic. I don't usually.'

'Don't you?' the barman said. 'Have whatever you want,' and he stuck a glass under the optic. 'Large or small?' he asked, without turning round.

'Small, thank you.'

A man was sitting in the corner on his own. He was in his late fifties or early sixties, (her target age, she couldn't help but note). He was slim and dapper, wearing a damp blazer. She didn't notice that the cuffs were frayed and the elbows shiny or that his shirt was faded and his tie had been knotted so many times it had shrivelled like a withered plant.

She felt his eyes on her and, unconsciously, plumped herself.

He stood up and came over. 'We are both sheltering from the storm, it would appear, or are you in the habit of frequenting public houses unaccompanied?'

Flustered, she tried to push her hair back into place. 'Oh, I'm sorry, I didn't see you. I only came in to get out of the rain. I don't usually go into public houses.'

'Don't you?' He smiled. 'I think the rain is set in, listen to it. There's no one else here and it can be so tiring not speaking, don't you think? If I promise you won't be approached by any strange men, will you join me? I can be your chaperone. Please.' He gestured toward his table and she followed. He pulled out a chair.

Still fiddling with her hair, she sat.

'Let me,' he said, and collected her gin and tonic from

the bar. 'No, a lady never buys a drink when she is in my company. It's one of my strictest rules.' He leaned over her as he placed her drink on the table and said, in a conspiratorial whisper, 'It's probably *the* strictest.' He sat down opposite her. 'Rum and coke,' he said, nodding toward his drink, 'that's my poison. But, please, let me introduce myself. I am Denzel Arbuthnot. Yes, that really is my name. I'm not sure which bit I dislike the most, the beginning or the end, but I have learnt to live with it and have acquired a thick skin. And to whom do I address myself?'

'I'm Mrs Rose Davies.'

'Ah. May I call you Rose, Mrs Davies, or would that be outrageously presumptuous?' He waved his hand at the room. 'Don't worry, it is the lounge and not the public bar. And, of course, please call me Denzel.'

He was right, the rain showed no sign of stopping and, unless she went to another table taking the free gin and tonic with her, here she was: 'Rose.'

'I am honoured to meet you, Rose.' He clinked his glass against hers. 'Tell me about yourself, won't you? I'm sure you must have led an interesting life.'

'Oh no,' she said, 'unless you consider teaching to be interesting.'

'But I do,' he said. 'It is an honourable calling, one of the most honourable. Where would we be without teachers? What do you teach?'

'I'm a primary school teacher.'

'Just as they are beginning to learn about life, you are

there to guide them.'

'I've never quite thought about it like that.'

'What did Ignatius Loyola say? Wasn't it, *Give me the child for the first seven years and I will give you the man*? Or something very similar. His purposes were somewhat different, but it is difficult to argue with the sentiment. Those seven years are so precious.'

'I've never heard that,' said Rose. 'Yes, they are precious. Who was Ignatius Loyola?'

'A Spanish Catholic. Rather a fanatical one. Tell me more, Rose. Where do you teach?'

She told him about Mr Tanner.

'I read about that in *The Herald*. What a dreadful thing, deeply shocking and a great loss to the community. He was much respected.'

'Yes he was,' she said, almost betraying herself.

'Can I refresh your drink?'

To her surprise, she had almost drunk it all. 'No, thank you, that's very kind, but one is more than enough.'

'It's still raining, Rose.' He picked up her glass. 'More ice?'

'Well, let me then?' She reached into her handbag.

'Rose, my rules are not made to be broken,' he told her, with mock sternness, clasping her hand. 'Now, put that away.'

She told him about her life: beginning with the facts and soon the dreams and disappointments (but not that one).

To and fro he prompted, until he had the whole map of her to navigate by, with the creases smoothed out, lying on the table between them. Carefully, he turned her back to the times and places where she had been happiest, as if he had been there all along.

The rain stopped. The evening lengthened and she did not leave.

He caged the butterfly between the tips of his fingers and watched as it coated them with its silvery scales.

'Thank you for agreeing to help out,' said Bryn.

They were sitting in the kitchen at the vicarage. Outside the rain was stopping.

'If you could take assembly once or twice a week,' he continued, 'that would be an enormous help.'

'Assembly?' asked Reverend Elwiss, as if he had to think what it was.

'He hasn't been sleeping,' said Deborah.

'I didn't mean straightaway,' said Bryn, 'only after he's had time to recover.' It was an awkward word.

The vicar shifted. 'I am here,' he said. 'I think I can manage the occasional assembly, thank you.'

Abashed, Bryn turned to Mrs Elwiss. 'Would you be able to help Rose and Paul at break times and perhaps take a class for reading?'

'I'd be delighted to,' she said. 'I'm quite good at mathematics, too, if that helps?'

'It certainly might,' said Bryn.

'You were right to come, Bryn,' she told him. 'He needs something to occupy him.'

Reverend Elwiss ate his cake slowly and dabbed at his mouth with a napkin. He finished his cake and sighed. His eyes strayed toward the window as if he was alone in his study.

Bryn leaned forward.

'September is one of my favourite months,' Deborah said, 'September and May. But the nights are drawing in already. There's going to be an enormous crop of apples, which is surprising after such a dry summer. Isn't it, Ernest?'

He didn't reply.

She turned to Bryn. 'You were lucky to miss the worst of the rain, but it's almost stopping now. When it does, I think I'll pick a basketful, the storm has knocked a lot of them off, and I wouldn't want them to rot, so they shouldn't be left. Would you and Laura like some?'

'Thank you.'

'He hasn't told me anything, Bryn. I know that's what you're thinking. If I knew, I would tell you.'

Bryn looked at her and then back at Reverend Elwiss, who was still staring out of the window and would not be prompted.

'I don't know what was on Mr Tanner's mind,' Bryn said, speaking to the vicar. 'But I think he had found something out, or even suspected someone.'

'Is that true, Ernest?' Deborah asked him.

'It wasn't a breakdown,' said Bryn. 'He didn't drown himself and it wasn't a tragic accident.'

'Ernest,' said Deborah, in the quietly emphatic way she had, 'Bryn has a right to know.'

'Yes, it will be a good crop this year,' said Reverend Elwiss. 'Take some, won't you, Bryn?'

'He didn't stumble into Kenfig Pool and drown. That didn't happen, did it?' said Bryn.

'Then what do you think really happened?' asked the vicar, looking directly at Bryn for the first time.

'I hoped you could tell me.'

'What do you think could have happened?' the vicar asked.

'I don't know.'

'Yes, you do. Say what you think. And you, Deborah, what do you think?'

'You think there is foul play, don't you, Ernest?' she replied.

'There, you've said it,' said Reverend Elwiss.

There was a knock at the door.

Protheroe would not admit that he was better placed to see the truth more clearly than Mr Tanner, Reverend Elwiss, Constable Dewi or anyone else. So why hadn't he? Once, he pompously told a young *Herald* Andrew, 'You mustn't let your feelings get in the way, be *objective*.' (It was of little value, *Herald* Andrew was unafflicted.) But his feelings were bothering him now. Either he was not as clever as he thought or he was guilty of the sin of omission (sin was not a Protheroe word, but he was adrift in great waters). Nightmares woke him from his whisky-drowned sleep in the middle of the night like front pages bowling down empty streets in the wind that never settled long enough to see the headline clearly… *amongst us*. But, as he lay in the darkness, he was afraid he already knew what the rest of it said and answered the unasked question evasively and unconvincingly with another newspaperman's excuse – 'I can only report the facts' – hiding behind a rigmarole of denial and sources he wouldn't reveal: his conscience edged to the front like an estranged relative he had once wronged.

After speaking to Dewi, who was as guarded as he should be, Protheroe, who knew his job, had learnt enough. 'God loves a sinner,' he thought, with the bravado of old, because he could only face the man he had mocked in print as the fearless journalist. It failed him when the vicarage door opened.

It was Deborah who answered. 'Mr Protheroe,' she said, archly.

They looked at each other.

'I'm sorry to disturb you, but it's rather important. Is Reverend Elwiss in?'

'Yes,' she said, and didn't move.

'May I see him?'

It got worse when he saw Bryn Hughes was there too, looking daggers at him.

'Do not think badly of Mr Protheroe,' said Reverend Elwiss, making an effort to smile. 'I believe he is here for the same reason as you, Bryn. Please sit down, Mr Protheroe. Would you like some tea and cake? Deborah, would you?'

'I'm sorry to disturb you,' said Protheroe, 'but I'd like to ask you some questions, if I may. I am only seeking the truth.'

'You must forgive me, Mr Protheroe,' said Reverend Elwiss, with an effort, 'if my attention wavers but I haven't been sleeping well and these have been difficult times for all of us.'

'And I'm nearly deaf in one ear, so speak up,' said Bryn, caustically and, to Protheroe, unfathomably, who had to accept it as an odd statement of fact.

'Bryn, please?' Reverend Elwiss asked him, quietly. 'We are all seeking the truth, Mr Protheroe.'

'Yes,' said Protheroe, suddenly in two minds, his career of truth-seeking demolished by the resolute kindness of the vicar in this unfamiliar place. 'I believe there is more to this.'

'To Mr Tanner's death?' asked Reverend Elwiss.

'And to Eve Brown's.'

'Eve Brown is *dead?*' Bryn cried. 'How?'

The vicar held up his hand, swept with anguish.

'Yes, she was found dead at home.'

'A moment, please,' said the vicar. He was overcome, utterly weighed down.

'Ernest?' Deborah asked. 'Ernest?'

'No, Deborah, I can rest later,' said Reverend Elwiss. 'How did she die, Mr Protheroe?'

'I thought you knew,' said Protheroe. 'I'm sorry.'

'How could we know,' asked Bryn, 'if *The Herald* hasn't printed it yet?'

'She wanted to look after the Harris' boy because his relatives are getting on, but after her history with him the police stopped her, and they think she took her own life.'

'She took her own life?' Reverend Elwiss said. He took a deep breath, letting it out slowly and spread both hands on the kitchen table. 'But that's not what you believe, is it Mr Protheroe?' he said, spacing each word, very deliberately, both asking and telling him. 'Or you would not have come here.'

Protheroe shook his head. 'I have doubts.'

'Or that my friend met with a tragic accident?'

'There are more questions that should be asked.'

Now, the vicar was determined. 'Would you say so in print for the sake of a good man and a good woman, Mr Protheroe?'

That word 'good'. Protheroe picked up his fruitcake and put it back on the plate. Recant and repent? 'If new information comes to light…' he began.

'Hasn't it, Mr Protheroe?' asked Reverend Elwiss. 'Surely it has.'

'Then I will print… a different version of events.'

'You could have done that from the beginning,' Bryn said. 'What you put Laura through, my mum and dad, the school.'

'Bryn...' said Reverend Elwiss.

'It was what the police told me,' said Protheroe.

'No, please, Vicar,' said Bryn, 'Let me just say this, then I won't say any more. What you put Mr Tanner through, what you put the vicar through and Mrs Elwiss. What *for*?'

'It's a newspaper man's job, it was nothing personal.' Protheroe replied, with no conviction left that it justified his part, or that of his newspaper, in anything that had happened.

'If you came here seeking the truth, Mr Protheroe,' said the vicar, 'we have not told you anything you did not know and you have been the bearer of terrible news. Did you come to tell me what you suspect or to ask permission to print it? But you already know the answer to that, do you not? But I'm glad you came, sincerely I am.' The vicar got to his feet with an effort, exhausted once more. 'And now I will see you out.'

'Let me show Mr Protheroe out, Ernest,' said Deborah.

'No, I shall.'

'Thank you, Vicar,' said Protheroe on the doorstep. 'I'm sorry.'

Reverend Elwiss smiled.

Even to Protheroe, who was obliged to be an atheist, it fell on him like a blessing. As he walked down the garden path, the leaves of the shrubs on either side shone in the sun that had now appeared beneath a bank of receding clouds.

When Reverend Elwiss came back to the kitchen, he said, 'I think we are reaching a conclusion. I think Raymond knew and it cost him his life.'

'What conclusion, Vicar?' asked Bryn.

'In the midst of this, joyous news. You have a new baby, Bryn.'

'Raymond,' said Bryn. 'We've called him Raymond. We were going to before Mr Tanner went missing.'

'Missing. I hate that word,' said Reverend Elwiss. 'I'm sorry, but I am so tired and you, Bryn, have a family waiting for you at home.'

'What should we do now? We must do something.'

'When the time comes, Bryn,' said Reverend Elwiss. 'Now, Laura and little Raymond will be wondering where you are… little Raymond, well, my friend will be remembered in a new life, and that is something.'

'I wanted to tell Mr Tanner himself,' said Bryn.

'Unfortunately, Bryn, that isn't to be.'

When Bryn had left, Deborah said, 'Ernest, I don't know what you mean to do, but please don't do this alone again? Promise me?'

'I'm not alone, Deborah,' he told her. 'I will never be alone. And, now, I'm going up to bed to try to sleep for a while, although I don't think I shall, not now.'

She washed the cups and saucers, worrying about her husband and wondering why he hadn't asked her. She looked up at the ceiling but there was no sound upstairs. He had become a different man; he didn't need her to tell him if he was right or wrong. 'Will he again?' she wondered, out loud. 'Apples.' She went out and began to collect them. Her wicker basket was soon full and she looked over the wall at the graveyard and thought about their plot, where side by side, she and Reverend Elwiss could talk quietly long after their headstones had crumbled above them.

Eve's house was closed up: the curtains were drawn, the doors were locked and the back gate to the alley was padlocked. The house now belonged solely to Roy, in prison, and he could not look after it, so no one would. The garden was taken over by weeds; the grass on the front lawn grew long. The paint flaked off the window frames. In the row of neat pebble-dashed houses, it darkly reminded.

Sergeant Phillips was waiting for Dewi when he got back to the police station. 'Did you think I would forget, Jones?'

'I didn't think anything, Sir.'

'Yes, you did, *Jones*. I know your mind, *Jones*. I know what you want. I know what you both want.' Sergeant Phillips came closer to Dewi's face. In a low voice, he said, 'You know I do.'

Dewi felt a rush of fury. 'You don't know anything about me. You don't know what I think. You don't know what I want. You have no part in my life away from this uniform. You don't know anything about Brenda and me.'

'*Now* I have you, Jones.'

'No you don't. I'm going to leave the police so there's

nothing you can do to me. *Nothing*.'

Sergeant Phillips' nose was almost touching Dewi's. 'Wherever you are, whatever you are, I will know and I can do whatever I want, whenever I want.' Sergeant Phillips pressed his finger into the middle of Dewi's forehead. 'I will be in there.' He stabbed his finger. 'In *there*, Jones. You will need my permission to think, to act, and I will see everything you see through your two,' he stabbed, '*eyes*. Be a policeman or don't be a policeman, you cannot escape.'

Sergeant Phillips let his finger drop. It left a red mark above Dewi's nose, like a daub of paint on a sheep's back.

In the canteen with Brenda, Dewi said, 'I don't know what he knew, but now I've told him all he wanted to know. I shouldn't have said anything.'

'What did you tell him, Dewi?' she asked.

'I told him I was going to leave the police. I told him about you. I'm sorry. I was so angry.'

'You said you were going to ask for a transfer.'

'I'm not going to ask for a transfer and I'm not going to leave the police. Let him do what he wants.'

'He'll have to do it to both of us now,' she said.

In The Red Lion, anticipating a long evening but one they would forget, and their picnic by the river during closing time already done, Maynard was looking at Prosser as if he was the bag of chips he had just eaten. He was hungry for more. Even drunk, Maynard knew it was a strange way to feel. His tongue ran over his lips. 'I'm the Grim Reaper, me,' and he pawed at Prosser's shoulder.

Prosser pushed him away. 'What's your problem?'

'I'm not the problem,' said Maynard, with a leer.

As Protheroe walked from the vicarage through streets gently steaming, he was emboldened to write the article without delay. But, the closer he got to *The Herald's* offices, the more he was tempted to let things be. *The Herald* years: his growing paunch, his untidy grey hair; his sharp enquiry had become a squint. The hardbitten Fleet Street journalist of legend (he had only been there once to see what would never be) or the honest editor of a local newspaper? 'I am neither. So what does it matter?'

He didn't go back to the office, he went to the Raven for whiskies and then he went home and spent another restless night with his dreams taunting him to fill in the missing words.

21

PRIVATE *MERVYN TUDOR* 20
FRIDOLF TELLER UNTEROFFIZER 26

It could never be early enough. The people in the houses were just beginning to stir as Rose walked down the tree-lined avenue. She wished she could have waited until mid-morning when it might be assumed she was on her way out and not on her way home.

The air was crisp for the first time in weeks. Autumn was approaching; Rose was autumn.

He had charmed her with his undivided attention, like a stoat circling a rabbit, fascinating and deadly. He had led her from the Raven with promises she did not believe but had gone with him anyway.

She had succumbed eagerly, surprising them both. If she wanted to make up for Mr Tanner's death with an act of life, her body functioned but she could only ape it.

Afterwards, crackling between his polyester sheets, her hair standing on end and still not thinking clearly after three gin and tonics, she cried as he slept. Eventually, with the gin's help, she slept too.

When she opened her eyes, he was sitting at the end of the bed. He was older in the morning light. The hair on the back of his head was as sparse as a scabby lawn. She watched him turn his trousers the right way out and reach for his tie hanging over the back of the chair, still knotted (she remembered him struggling to pull it over his head before she changed her mind as they tangled together). She noticed how threadbare his shirt was and how shabby his blazer: a respectable, if tired, uniform on another man and a poor disguise on him.

It had been quick and he had gone straight to sleep without another honeyed word. But she was glad he had not thanked her – as if that was the polite way of leaving a few crumpled notes on the bedside table.

He was trying to be quiet so that he could escape before she awoke. He crept to the bedroom door circuitously, knowing the position of every creaking floorboard, and slid through. She heard him on the stairs. She heard the front door click and gently close. She heard him on the path outside and then she was alone in a strange house.

There was a scribbled note on the hall table. *Gone to work* it said. A lie. *Please let yourself out. My apologies for not being able to make you breakfast. We had a wonderful time, did we not?* He had added. *I frequent the Raven Arms on a regular basis.* Information as a question, with a throwaway insouciance: if you want some more? The piece of paper was dog-eared and finger-marked; the ink was faded. She didn't touch.

She went into each room. They were all untidy and the furniture was old. There were unwashed mugs and plates in the sink. He hadn't bothered: one room was all that was needed in the dark.

Perhaps she had misunderstood: the contract between them had been this only and he had assumed she knew. He had seen through her pretence of sheltering from the rain (even if it had been coming down in rods) and bought her drinks as the game required. Her acceptance had been acquiescence. He knew her sly smile: you can't fool me, Mrs Davies, Rose Davies, *Rose*. How many pubs have you been to before this one? Mind, I haven't seen you in here before. Fancy a change, did you? Slipping demurely into the lounge bar of the Raven. You can't fool me. Begging for it.

She tidied herself in front of the bathroom mirror as best she could. Not a second longer. So, as people were going to work, she made her way up the avenue, keeping close to the trees, with a thumping headache, certain she was being watched because he must be known for bringing home women of a certain age.

Some of the houses would have children at the school. She hurried on before they started coming out. She looked at her watch (a gift from her husband). There was no time to go home, she would have to go as she was, in the same clothes as yesterday, and wait in the playground for everyone to arrive, before ringing the bell to call them in for class.

But she still hoped she was mistaken about Denzel Arbuthnot.

By bus, by train, by bus to Cardiff Prison, with the now familiar faces decanted into the final bus until they were all waiting outside for visiting time to begin.

The door opened and everyone pushed through. Gwen hung back until the throng parted and there was Reverend Elwiss, looking at her from the other side of the entrance. He nodded and smiled, as if he expected to see her. 'Good morning, Gwen,' he said. 'It's been some time.'

'Vicar?' she stammered. 'Have you come to see Alan?' She couldn't think of what else to say but, even in her surprise at seeing him there, she was shocked at how sad and grey he looked, thinner too, his cheek bones were sharp and his neck was scrawny inside its gleaming dog collar.

'Yes,' he said.

'I've come to tell him about Aled. He's staying with me, with his Auntie Nesta.'

'Ah,' said the vicar. 'That sounds like a solution, Gwen.'

'He's started school so I wanted to see Alan to tell him. I didn't want to write.'

'I think we can go in now,' said Reverend Elwiss.

The warders apologised to Reverend Elwiss for making him wait and were solicitous to her as they went through her handbag.

Alan's face lit up when he saw her enter the visiting hall, but his eyes widened in alarm when he saw the vicar.

'Reverend Elwiss was waiting outside,' she gabbled. 'We didn't come together. I've told him about Aled.'

'Is it Jean? Has something happened?' Alan tucked his hands under the table.

'No, Alan,' said Reverend Elwiss, 'I think you would know before me if it had. As far as I am aware, Jean is as she was, sadly.'

'Yes, Alan, she is,' said Gwen.

'Have you come about Mr Tanner? The paper said he was looking for Jack. Is that true? Did he find something?'

'He didn't find Jack, Alan,' said Reverend Elwiss.

'Oh…' Alan nodded. 'I'm so sorry, Vicar. It was dreadful news about Mr Tanner. I know he was your friend. You found him, didn't you?'

'That must have been so awful, Vicar,' said Gwen. 'I can't say how sorry I am.'

'Gwen,' said Reverend Elwiss, 'perhaps you should tell Alan your news first?'

Gwen looked at Alan, mystified and fearful at what the vicar was holding back. 'Aled's settled down very well.'

'Your letter said so,' Alan said.

'Nesta's looking after him today. He's started school, Alan. That's what I came to tell you. He's really enjoying it and making lots of new friends. He's learning Welsh too.'

'Welsh? I suppose he'll have to now, won't he?'

They stopped and looked at Reverend Elwiss.

'I have some bad news. Yes, I did find Raymond and I am glad it was me and not a stranger, but he was not looking for Jack, Alan – at least, not directly searching in that way – and he was of sound mind, whatever the paper said. But that is not the reason I came to see you. I came to tell you that Eve is dead. She was found at her home, alone, two days ago.'

Gwen's hand leapt to her mouth.

'Eve?' Alan asked. He looked at Gwen. Tears were starting in her eyes. 'How? What happened?'

'I didn't know Eve very well but I knew about her circumstances,' said Reverend Elwiss. 'She had taken to calling herself Eve Guthrie.'

'That was her maiden name,' said Alan. 'That's what I knew her as in school.'

'She thought of Aled as her own, didn't she?' said the vicar. 'And, misguidedly, in those dark times, she thought she was protecting him by taking him away.'

'I suppose she did. I don't know what she thought.'

'She offered to take care of him again, recently, I understand? But you didn't agree?'

'It was nothing against Eve. She is one of our oldest friends. She would only want what was right for Aled but I thought I might lose him to her completely, as if it would make any difference now, but it would to me. How did you know? Did you speak to her?'

'You did what you believed was right for your son,

Alan.'

'What happened to Eve, Vicar?' Alan asked.

'You must not blame yourself in any way for what happened to her. You must not, both of you. The police believe she took her own life.'

'Alan?' Gwen cried. She slid her hand across the table before she could stop herself.

'Take comfort in each other,' said Reverend Elwiss.

Gwen blushed and pulled her hand back.

'How much more?' Alan whispered.

Reverend Elwiss waited until Alan lifted his head. 'Do you know the police told Eve she could not have Aled, Alan?' he asked.

'I did,' said Gwen. 'I didn't want to tell you, Alan. It wouldn't have helped if you knew. Sergeant Phillips told Eve and Nesta in the street outside the school. Nesta told me.' But she would not tell him that he had sent Dewi and Brenda to see them in Carmarthen.

'Sergeant Phillips told her? Why would he?' asked Alan. 'And to kill herself over it? It can't have been that, surely not? I didn't realise she would be so badly affected.'

'If that is what happened,' said Reverend Elwiss. 'Gwyn Roberts, Jack and Huw, Rhodri Mitchell, Raymond and now Eve. I don't think Raymond knew for certain, but I think he suspected someone. Do you understand what I'm saying, Alan?'

'Yes,' said Alan, slowly. 'I do.'

Reverend Elwiss looked first at Alan and then at

Gwen. 'Have faith in the truth and remember that God is with you, always, especially in places like this, where hope can seem so far away. I am sorry to bring bad news, but I have nothing else to tell you so, now, I will leave you to be alone, or not alone,' he looked around the dismal hall, 'but together.' He got up. 'You have done the right thing, both of you and, one day, I pray you find peace and justice and I will not rest, Alan, until you do.' He left.

'Now I know why I'm here,' said Alan. 'I didn't want to believe it was possible, but Reverend Elwiss has just told me it's true.'

Jean's perfect day was all the best days she had known, condensed into a single imaginary day that would never end. She saw Jack and Aled, Alan, the Rhondda where she grew up and visited on Sundays, the sea. The sky was blue, the fields were green and the breakers were white. But, with nothing new to sustain it, her mind was peeling away like strips of old wallpaper and, beneath, it was grey and lifeless. A few cells of light remained, but it was a decaying, dimming cluster of memories.

How long would it take? Within her shell, she could outlive them all. She knew only the joys of her former existence.

But there would be nothing left of Jean for Alan to take home. Time could not progress for her and, in time, it would stop her body too.

The world went around her without slowing as she

sat in the growing armchair next to the black and white television that showed the past and not the present and had no capacity for the future.

Protheroe got up early because he couldn't sleep. He didn't shave, but that wasn't unusual. His mouth was dry from too much whisky and his walk to the office was a weary lope. He was first in and climbed the stairs slowly, dragging his feet over the bare boards. He slumped into his chair and rested his chin on his fist. He didn't move until the glass door slammed and made him jump. Reluctantly, he searched for a pencil with an unbroken point amongst the papers on his desk, licked it out of habit, held it, poised over a blank page, slightly trembling, and began to doodle. When it was full of squiggles, he pushed it to one side and read the next edition's *Births, Deaths and Marriages*, which was curiously interesting. He spent an hour debating with *Herald* Andrew and Lloyd the best way to cover the proposed new housing estate; and, at lunchtime he went for a walk to 'clear' his head. By the end of the day, all he had were a few lines, in between doodles of bats (why?) some of which said *Eve Guthrie* and others *Eve Brown* who was married to *Roy Brown*.

He locked up the office early and wandered to the Raven, ordered a large whisky and sat in his usual chair in the corner. He held his glass by the rim and turned it in circles on the table. After a while, the whisky dulled the worst of it so he ordered another. Halfway through drinking that, his humours more equitably balanced, he felt able to concentrate and pushed the glass away: anymore and he would incline to the purple prose that always made him wince in the morning.

He pulled the small notebook he always carried from his jacket pocket. The first few pages were covered in drafts of old articles and notes. One of them was *Child's Body Found* followed by *painstaking efforts of Sergeant Phillips* and a reminder to tell *Herald* Andrew to emphasise it. He flicked over a few more pages and found *Headmaster Goes Missing... tragic accident.* It read differently now.

He had hundreds of notebooks going back years. Unable to resist, he took a gulp of whisky. It tasted of shame. 'No, that's enough, now,' he told himself. He found an empty page.

The headline? *The* headline.

He started a few more distractions but drew a line through all of them.

He could not get the words to say what he wanted them to. They flinched away full of distrust. He put the pen down and looked through the window. The bend of the river gleamed like a scimitar.

Protheroe snorted, picked up the pen and wrote the headline in one swift movement.

He was shocked at its brazenness.

Minutes passed.

The capital letters shouted back at him.

Heroically, he began to write. Under its newly

unfurled banner, the standard of a Crusader army, the words flowed as easily as the flooding river. Protheroe's thoughts did not guide his hand but it crabbed across the blank page of his notebook until it was full.

Catharsis… full stop. *Done.*

It read like a confession after many hours of relentless questioning. He was so startled he wanted to rip out the page and tear it into tiny pieces before anyone saw what he had written. It took revenge on him. Its existence alone was a mortal threat. *There.* Like his blood.

Under the trees, Maynard and Prosser were squabbling.

'What are we waiting for?' Prosser demanded. 'They're open now.'

'We've got these two bottles to finish,' Maynard said. 'So let's finish them first, right?'

'We can finish them later. Why do we have to drink them now?'

'Because I want to finish them now,' said Maynard.

'Well you can stay here, then, if you want, but I'm off back to The Red Lion.' Prosser picked up one of the bottles.

'That's mine,' Maynard told him. 'You've drunk all yours.'

Prosser stared at the bottle and tried to remember. 'No, it's not,' he decided, angrily. 'And I'm taking it.'

'Put it down, or I'll have you in the river, no problem.'

Something about Maynard's voice made Prosser stop. He sat back down on the bank.

Maynard said, 'We'll drink these first and then we'll go back to The Red Lion. I'll let you drink one. Say thank you.'

'Thank you.'

Maynard watched Prosser flip off the top and take a gulp.

'It's getting cold,' said Prosser.

'Is it?'

'There's no point in sitting here much longer if we're going to get cold.'

'I'm not cold,' said Maynard. 'Drink it, then.'

Prosser looked up the steep bank. They could not be seen and he was closer to the water than Maynard and the river was still rising.

'Alright, then,' Prosser said. 'But let's get these down our necks. There's a fresh pint waiting for us. I'll get us in a couple of chasers to warm us up. How about that?'

'I don't need warming up.'

'I'll buy them.'

'I'm not asking you to, am I?'

Prosser drank his beer. When he glanced up, Maynard was staring at him strangely again, the way he looked at women, with his eyes half closed and his mouth open. He was drinking his beer slowly.

Prosser jumped up and scrabbled up the bank.

Maynard's arm swung as he tried to trip him but he missed.

At the top, away from the water, Prosser bent over

with his hands on his knees to catch his breath.

In The Red Lion, not long after, Maynard came in and said, 'You were in a hurry, I wanted to finish my beer quietly.'

'I told you, it was cold.'

'Where are the chasers then?'

Protheroe tucked his notebook into his pocket and reached for his whisky.

The Rubens nude was sitting on her own at a table nearby.

Rose had spent the day making up excuses for Denzel Arbuthnot. But she had to know, so here she was, at his open invitation, in the Raven Arms.

The same barman served her. 'Gin and tonic?' he asked, and turned to the optics before she could say, 'pineapple juice'.

Every time the pub door opened, she looked up. A little bit longer, she told herself, then I'll go.

Her glass was empty. She distracted herself by looking in her handbag and fumbling about.

The door opened… No.

She saw the barman watching her and thought she was having a hot flush, her face was burning up. She would never let herself be humiliated like this again. She had just decided to leave, when a man's voice said, 'Good evening, are you waiting for someone?' He was so unmade, so crumpled and untidy, she looked past him before she realised he had been talking to her. Had she fallen so far? Without thinking, she took out her compact and tried to reassure herself in its small mirror.

His dubious allegiances soon to be squandered, his cynicism unwrapped, facing a similar decline and anonymity, but with no handbag or make-up, the naked Protheroe was before her (a much later work by an artist wearying of life and no longer vain).

Rose, realising how rude she had been, put the compact away. 'I was,' she said, and told him, with involuntary honesty, 'but he hasn't showed up.'

'Perhaps he's late?'

'No, I don't think he's coming.'

'If I knew you were waiting for me, I would have been early,' said Protheroe, without a hint of flattery. He seemed sad for her.

'Would you?' she asked, thinking, 'is this how it is for women in pubs?'

'Yes, I would. Would you mind if I talk to you, but I'll quite understand if you'd prefer to be on your own? If he turns up, I'll explain that we've just met.'

'If you want to,' she said, carefully, looking toward the door.

The barman pursed his lips. 'Doug Protheroe and a woman? That's a first. She gets about a bit, though.'

Protheroe held out his hand. 'I'm Douglas Protheroe,' he told her.

The name was familiar. 'I'm Mrs Rose Davies.'

'I take it you aren't waiting for your husband?' he asked, without insinuation. 'If he hasn't shown up?'

'No, I'm a widow.'

There was no glint in his eye. 'May I sit down?'

'If you wish,' she said, with the briefest flash of neon, like a fish turning its flank.

'I never married,' said Protheroe. 'I don't know if I regret that or not. Are you going to say it's too late, Mrs Davies?'

'Oh no, of course not,' she said, with more feeling than she intended.

'But it's what you're thinking? Never mind, I'm not seeking reassurance. I'm the editor of *The Herald* – not that the two are related, but perhaps they are.'

'Are you? I'm not sure I should be…' she stopped.

'I'm sorry, you're not sure you should be what, Mrs Davies?'

She meant to say, 'Talking to you,' but she shook her head. 'It's not important.' She would report back (the Raven Arms would be the café at the top of Cardigan Street).

'Isn't it? I've been sitting at that table writing the most important article I've ever written. Look.' He took his notebook out of his pocket and laid his hand gently on it. 'I've been stopping myself writing it ever since I've been in newspapers. I need to tell someone before I change my mind. May I tell you, Mrs Davies?'

'If it's helpful, Mr Protheroe,' she replied, intrigued, but still fearful it was a ploy.

Protheroe took a breath and was about to begin. 'No, first, I think I need another drink. What about you, Mrs Davies? Listening can be thirsty work.'

'Yes please,' she replied.

When he came back, Protheroe closed his eyes, took a sip of whisky, collected himself and began.

He told her without a pause, leaving out nothing, scarifying himself. Then he read to her what he had written. 'Do you think it is a truthful account of what I have just told you?'

Rose stared at him in disbelief.

'So far as I understand events and those involved in them, Mrs Davies, it is the absolute truth as I see it. You have my word and I mean to go to print.'

22

SERGEANT HAROLD UPTON 24
ARTUR VOIGHT GEFREITER 19

Salute: 'Good morning, Gerhard.'

'Do not look into the binoculars today, Howell.'

'Why not?'

'There are some days when they are best left alone.

'Why?' asked Howell. 'What will I see?' He picked up the binoculars. They felt heavier and colder than usual. 'They're empty now, aren't they?'

'Don't look, Howell,' said Gerhard.

But Howell lifted them to his eyes. There were mountains and a blustery sky filled with moodiness. 'There's nothing to see,' he said.

'Good,' said Gerhard. 'Put them down now, Howell.'

'Wait.' Howell saw a bank of fog and, above, two flames swayed from high masts and looked back at him. Howell let the binoculars fall to his chest. 'What am I seeing, Gerhard?'

'I don't know. Can you see beyond the mountains?'

'I can see straight through them.'

'Don't look again.'

'But I don't know what I'm seeing, Gerhard.'

'If I knew, I would tell you.'

'So why can't I look?'

'Because I think you might see something you don't want to see,' Gerhard said, quietly. 'Let them be. Today, at least.'

'And tomorrow?' Howell placed the binoculars back on the windowsill.

'Look then. That will be the time to look,' said Gerhard.

'I have to open the shop,' said Howell.

'It will keep you busy.'

'Not so busy to stop me worrying about what it is I'm not supposed to see.'

Gerhard faded into a weak shaft of sunlight.

Howell ran his hand down the side of the binoculars but he didn't pick them up again. As he went down the backstairs and into the passage, he thought he could hear the thump of guns rolling over the wasteland where he had found his friend.

A Killer is Amongst Us

By Douglas Protheroe, Editor

The body of a woman discovered at 18, Sycamore Road,

Bridgend has been identified as Eve Brown, 32, who had lived there for a number of years. In a statement, the police said, Mrs Evelin Brown had suffered a number of grave misfortunes in her personal life and, after becoming increasingly reclusive, she was unable to cope and, sadly, took her own life.

A tragic end to a young woman's life and there the matter would normally be closed. But is it?

Because, following an investigation by this newspaper, The Herald *now believes both Eve Brown and headmaster Raymond Tanner were murdered and the same person also abducted and killed three boys, Huw Evans, 6, Jack Harris, 6, and Rhodri Mitchell, 7, in late 1966 and that Alan Harris, father of Jack, imprisoned for the murder of local farmer, Gwyn Roberts, is innocent.*

But, firstly, the official story.

In December 1966, Eve Brown was prosecuted for abducting Aled Harris, Jack Harris' brother, who lived next door to her. Her defence was that, with Jack's abductor still at large, she had been trying to keep the boy safe because his mother, Jean, had suffered a breakdown and his father, Alan, was being held on suspicion of the murder of Gwyn Roberts whom he suspected of killing his son.

In handing down a probationary sentence, the judge said that Eve's actions had been well intentioned but misguided.

Recently, Eve Brown had contacted Aled Harris' relatives to try to become part of his life once more but the police had stopped her from doing so. With her husband in prison for unrelated crimes, and crushed by adversity, she committed suicide.

A week ago, in a distressed mental state following the discovery of the remains of Rhodri Mitchell, headmaster Raymond Tanner accidentally drowned in Kenfig Pool where he had gone to search for the body of Jack Harris, his former pupil which, he believed, is buried somewhere nearby.

Case closed? Not as far as The Herald *is concerned because we have a very different explanation.*

The police have never produced any evidence linking Gwyn Roberts to the disappearance of Jack Harris or Huw Evans, and Rhodri Mitchell did not go missing until after Gwyn Roberts was dead.

Did Alan Harris really believe Gwyn Roberts, a close family friend, had abducted his son and why would he go to such lengths to stage Gwyn's death as a suicide? Why such cold calculation if revenge was his motive?

No, because The Herald *believes this was an attempt by the real killer to divert suspicion and frame Alan Harris at the same time. The police's case against him is circumstantial at best.*

Mr Tanner never believed in Alan Harris' guilt. He visited him in prison and, after interviewing people who spoke to him shortly before he disappeared, The Herald *is convinced that Mr Tanner thought he knew who the real perpetrator was and went to confront him, intending to go to the police, and he was murdered to stop him doing so and his death was made to look like an accident.*

Shortly before he went missing, Mr Tanner was seen in close conversation with Eve Brown and The Herald *believes he told her what he suspected because of her close history with the boys and she was murdered to stop her revealing the truth.*

Sergeant Phillips has led the investigations throughout and has given Bridgend exemplary service for many years, but he should accept that mistakes have been made and take another look at the evidence.

The Herald *has reported on these terrible crimes over the past three years and it is to our shame that we did not pursue the truth as fearlessly as was our duty as your newspaper.*

There is a killer amongst us in plain sight who will stop at nothing to evade the law and we demand that the authorities do not rest until he is brought to justice.

It filled the front page as densely as a proclamation with no photographs and no space for adverts.

Bryn dawdled little Raymond on his knee, cupping the

back of his head in his hand and tried to imagine the image of his own face, pink and swimming, from beneath the watery surface of his son's purblind eyes. 'All you are is a lump of warm dough, but it isn't what you are now, it's what you will become,' the helpless potential he held, 'because we have invested our lives in yours,' Laura's fire and pain, 'from before she brought you into the world… what do I sound like?' He smiled and, for a moment, forgot what was beyond their net curtains that looked out on the rugby club.

Laura came downstairs. She looked tired. 'He found his voice, didn't he?' she said, thinking of her almost sleepless night.

'I would have got up,' he said, unable to turn away from the now contented, just fed wonder.

'You've got school,' she told him.

'I do,' he sighed, 'but I still didn't sleep.'

'So that wasn't you snoring, then? Don't worry, you didn't wake me up,' she said, testily. 'I wish I could go to school. I envy you.'

'He isn't going to be able to look after himself for a while, is he?'

'And neither can you, Bryn Hughes. I just don't want to become one of the mothers waiting outside the school gates every day.'

Bryn looked up. 'Then don't. We'll find a way round it. My mother can help out. She'd love to. Even if you only go back part time – and you could even ask your dad. I'm being serious.'

'No you're not. And who will decide if I can go back part time?' she asked. 'If there's even a part-time job for me?'

'Maybe I can,' he said.

'Give him to me, it's time you got ready.'

Bryn handed Raymond to her.

Laura held the baby's head against her shoulder and began walking up and down the front room (four steps between the settee and the armchair) patting his back.

She watched as Bryn did up his tie, looking at his reflection in the kitchen window and said, 'Why don't you apply to be headmaster, then you really could decide if I can come back part time?'

'I won't think about that now.'

'They will give it to someone, Bryn. Mr Tanner wanted you to be headmaster after him.'

'But not yet.'

'None of us can choose the time... *ohhh*, he's been sick down my shoulder.' She twisted her head and tried to wipe it off with a cloth.

'Give him to me,' said Bryn.

'No, he'll get you covered in it too. Go to school.'

'Because how old am I and how old was Mr Tanner? They won't, Laura.'

'You might be surprised and it will take them a while to find someone else, won't it?'

'It might.' He put on his coat. 'Until then, unless they

tell me otherwise, I'm going to be running things anyway and the longer it takes the more experience I'll get. There are other schools.'

'You deserve to be headmaster of this one, Bryn. You wouldn't want to go anywhere else, would you?'

He leaned past her to kiss the top of the baby's head. 'No, I wouldn't. Let's not talk about it, please?' He kissed her on the lips. 'Bye.' As he crossed the road at the traffic lights opposite the cinema, he looked back at their little house, 'They shouldn't be left on their own,' he thought, and wanted to turn on his heels.

He had to give Mr Tanner's eulogy and was dreading it. 'If Protheroe hasn't kept his promise, I will say it, I will.' But, as he went into the newsagent's, he saw the headline. 'He's done it. I didn't think he would,' and grudgingly wondered if he had misunderstood what an editor's job really was. He picked up the newspaper and didn't move until he had read it all with growing disbelief and horror. 'Dear God,' he said, out loud. He saw the girl behind the counter watching him with a frightened face and recognised her, still a child. She had left school not long after he started there and she would have known Huw Evans and Jack Harris in Year One.

'Hello, Mr Hughes,' she said. 'Do you remember me?'

'Of course I do, Anne.'

'Is it true?'

Mr Topliss was unlocking the school gates. He pointed to the newspaper under Bryn's arm. 'It's too much,

Mr Hughes,' he said. 'It's too much.'

Dewi spread *The Herald* out on the kitchen table.

They had spent their first night together in a real bed with no grass to stain her blouse. It felt like an act of defiance, in full view with the sheets pulled back.

Brenda saw the headline as she looked over his shoulder. 'What's this, Dewi?'

'He will know it was me,' Dewi said. 'Who else could have told *The Herald* about Eve?'

'Let me read it.' Brenda spun the paper round on the table and sat down.

'I know I shouldn't have said anything, but I didn't tell him all this. How did he know?' said Dewi. 'Perhaps I was wrong. Perhaps she did kill herself.'

'Did she, Dewi, I saw her too. I could have told *The Herald*. Why would he think it was you?'

'But you didn't,' said Dewi, 'and it's me he wants to suspect.'

'Why did you tell *The Herald*, Dewi?' she asked.

Dewi shrugged. 'I didn't think I did – not much, anyway.'

'You must have told him enough.' Brenda came round the table and put her arms around his neck and pressed her cheek against his. 'It's like a map from where we were to where we are now and you were brave enough to say it. If you told him about Eve, you were also telling him Alan Harris was not guilty, although perhaps in not so many words and, reading this, Protheroe had already worked a lot of it out for himself. You were just confirming some of it for him. That's what you were doing, Dewi.'

'He'll still be waiting for me when I get to the station.' Dewi reached up and pulled her head down. 'What do you think he'll do?'

'To you? I don't know,' she said. 'Whatever he wants, I suppose. Why does he have to care about what it says in *The Herald?*'

'He has in the past.'

'Only when they printed what he wanted them to,' said Brenda.

'I don't think I'll have much choice about staying in the police now, though, will I?'

But Sergeant Phillips was not at the police station and there were no copies of *The Herald* to be seen when, usually, whenever his name was mentioned, they were on every desk, face up, like tithes paid.

Lunchtime, and *Herald* Andrew was in The Red Lion at the table behind the piano with Detective Symonds, who was drinking on duty. They ignored Maynard and Prosser at the bar.

'Listen, now, will you?' *Herald* Andrew urged. 'I don't know why he wrote it. God's truth, I don't, but it's got nothing to do with me. You'll tell him, won't you? Make sure he knows I didn't write a word of it. I told Protheroe what you told me, honest, on my mother's life. I mean,

I can't stay at *The Herald* now, can I? There's a couple of papers in Cardiff that will give me a job. Tell him I can be even more help if I was working for one of them.'

Symonds didn't reply. He gulped his beer and stared into the corner.

'Do you want another pint?' asked *Herald* Andrew.

Symonds looked up. 'He told me what to tell you but that's not what's in the paper.'

'That's not my fault, though, is it?' said *Herald* Andrew. 'I told you, he made it up on his own.'

Symonds shook his head. 'Do you think he's going to believe that?'

'Now, you listen,' said *Herald* Andrew, his eyes narrowing, 'I told him exactly what you told me to tell him – if I can remember what it was, of course.'

Symonds looked as if he was going to start crying.

'But I wouldn't do that to you,' said *Herald* Andrew.

'It wouldn't work, anyway,' said Symonds. 'I wrote it down.' He started to reach into his jacket.

'I believe you,' said *Herald* Andrew. 'Look, we both want the same thing here, don't we? That's all I'm saying.'

'Do we?' asked Symonds. 'What?'

'Christ,' said *Herald* Andrew, 'I need something stronger than this. He's going to have us for fucking dogfood.'

In the Raven, at the other end of Cardigan Street, Protheroe was already on his second whisky. He was thinking about

Rose and desperately hoping he would see her again.

After reading to her what he had written, she had said, 'I think I should go now.'

'Must you? You haven't finished your drink. He's not coming, is he?'

She hadn't answered.

He walked – followed – her home. He wasn't sure which. It wasn't far.

'This I where I live.'

He stood on the pavement and watched as she went up the path, feeling in her handbag for her keys. 'Can I call on you?'

She had looked at him with the blank expression of someone in shock and closed the door.

But he was going to call on her. He was, and if she said no, what could he lose?

Bars of sun came through the clouds and lit up patches of sea as if they were searching; seagulls almost clipped the waves as they sped; and the tide rose up the seawall, each time heaving a little higher.

In his big, black car parked on the prom in Porthcawl, Sergeant Phillips read *The Herald*. When he finished, he folded it with great care and placed it on the passenger seat, smoothing it flat. He ran his thumbs down the outside of his moustache and pulled on his gloves, stretching them tight over his knuckles. He didn't look round as he pulled away from the kerb. He never looked round.

Gwen got Aled ready for bed. 'I've got an extra blanket for you,' she told him. 'It's getting chilly.'

He yawned.

The sky through the cottage window was virgin blue, with a sable hem, as if it was drawing up the east.

It was exactly three years to the day since Huw disappeared.

Gwen thought about him as she buttoned Aled's pyjamas: he was dark, Huw had been fair; he was lively, Huw had been thoughtful like his father.

'There,' she said. 'There.'

Nesta had gone home to the shop in Trebanog and left them alone with the years to come.

In the garden outside, Geraint and Huw looked up to the window. 'We must be vigilant as never before,' said Geraint.

'I see,' said Huw, seriously.

The upstairs light came on. It sprang into the garden. The day was eased away to watch over children in lands where the dawn was beginning and it was hot or snow was falling and glaciers cracked in valleys.

Gwen read to Aled until his eyes drooped and she closed the book.

He slept.

She pulled the extra blanket up to his chin and took one last look before turning off the light and closing the bedroom door.

'We must wait,' said Geraint.

After an hour, the downstairs light went out.

'Mummy's gone to bed,' said Geraint. 'Let's go and stand under the trees at the end of the garden.'

Leaves trickled down from the branches. It grew colder. They could hear sheep in the field. Then they were quiet too.

'Is that the sea?' whispered Huw.

'It could be,' said Geraint.

Or it could have been Aled's sleeping heartbeat and Gwen breathing like brush strokes on a drum's skin.

'Look,' said Geraint.

A stain was creeping along the whitewashed wall of the cottage. It filled the cracks between the stones and flowed over them.

Huw looked up but it was blacker than a moon shadow. 'What is it?' he asked.

'Wait now,' his father replied.

Reverend Elwiss prayed in the church before the altar. He looked up at the figurine. Its colours were dim and he didn't see it move when he heard it say, 'The time is now. You must choose.'

'I have already chosen, Lord,' said Reverend Elwiss. 'I am your servant in whatever is to come.'

Christ did not reply.

Deborah was in the living room.

For a moment, he watched her sewing. 'I have to go,' he said.

Her hands fell into her lap. 'Go where, Ernest?'

'Where I am guided,' he said. 'I knew all of it and I did nothing.'

She put her sewing on the chair arm and stood up. 'No, Ernest, you have done enough. You're worn out. You might think you knew, but you've been muddled.'

'I am not muddled. I can understand why you would think so, Deborah, but I have never been able to think as clearly as now. I knew where Raymond was. How could I have known if I was not shown where he was?'

'Oh my tired Christian soldier,' she said, wearily, worriedly. 'Shall I see if I can find something to help you sleep? Sit down and let me take a look.' She went into the kitchen and began opening cupboards. 'I really think you should see the doctor,' she called to him. 'It won't hurt. You've had such a shock. Let's go back to Hampshire for a few days... Ernest?' She went into the hall and saw the headlights swing in an arc and disappear down the lane. For a moment, she waited on the step, then she went angrily into the church and glared at the figurine but couldn't think of what to say. Its power began to enfold her.

23

PRIVATE TOMOS VINCENT 21
HANS WITT GEFREITER 22

Aled dreamed he was being lifted from his bed. It was cold and he shivered. He reached for the blankets but they fell away.

The arms that held him were not soft like Auntie Gwen's or firm like Uncle Howell's. He was gripped without love. He tried to arch his back and wanted to wake up.

Gwen's door stirred the air as it opened. She reached for the child next to her in the empty space where Huw had been, as if no time had passed. As the door closed, she whispered, 'Goodbye, Huw.'

A thin light of moon and stars came through the window.

Aled felt himself being carried down the stairs and into the hall, rocking in his cage of iron.

'Look,' said Huw.

'Wait,' his father said.

Aled's head was tilted back and his face and neck were like a wilting flower in his red and yellow pyjamas.

'Wait, Huw.'

Against the dark fields, the vivid child was severed by an arm around his waist and, briefly, it seemed as if he was sitting on the dry stone wall, basking in the moon with his eyes closed, bumping his heels as he had with Huw.

Through the gate and down the track to the road.

Geraint and Huw followed, keeping close to the hedge.

There was an old grey van pulled up on the verge. The back doors creaked in pain. It shook as the engine started and the fan belt squealed. It began to move, rolling off the verge, picking up speed.

Geraint and Huw stepped out onto the road and watched the two red lights growing smaller. They rounded a bend and were gone.

Aled dreamed of the back of a man's head, framed in speeding lights cleaving the windscreen. 'Uncle Howell?' There was no answer. 'Auntie Nesta?' but he was not asleep in her bed with the buses straining up Trebanog Hill. 'Auntie Gwen?' but he couldn't hear her coming to him from her room. He rolled amongst blankets that were as coarse as the diesel-stinking sacks that scraped his cheek and made him cough.

They passed the outskirts of Carmarthen, like a bank of pebbled lights. It was gone and then a swathe of blind fields. The engine's drone rose and fell.

The fiery eyes grew out of Port Talbot on metal spikes, towering like gatekeepers, their flames casting a probing glow through the sulphurous cloud that left a sticky residue around the wiper blades. They were let to pass. For a moment, Aled couldn't see them, then they reappeared like suns on the insides of his eyelids, stretching across the night sky like comets' tails with scarlet points and white-hot edges.

Along the dune-lined coast, barren Sker beach and the sea behind. The hedges were tall and the road narrowed. The van came out onto the golf links with the dunes like a mountain range with snowy peaks of sand.

The fiery eyes, now far down the coast, rose higher above their molten hearth.

The van reached a pot-holed track and turned onto it, bouncing and rearing. At the end and stopped. The engine died with a sigh, and ticked.

The door creaked and swung the stars. Aled was pulled by his feet, bunching the harsh blankets and trailing his arms. Heavy steps jolted him. The stars disappeared. The sides of his bed rose into a trough and rolled him into the middle. He dreamed he was in his den at the bottom of the garden where grass snakes hid under sheets of corrugated iron. They slithered out through the bleached grass and up his legs. He tried to push them away but they flicked at his fingers and slid inside his pyjama top and wound around him. The trough was as deep as a trench. It filled with a mist that wept diesel and formed droplets of stinging dew.

The sacks writhed with more snakes. He clutched at them and spat out the bitter threads. He pressed his head against the headboard but his hair was twisted into knots. The bed wrapped around him and rolled him up inside. He tried to shout for Auntie Gwen but his mouth was stuffed and no sound came out.

Reverend Elwiss would not rue what he had asked for, to be the safer man, disguised as a priest, prayerful over a dwindling flock and return to Hampshire and be forgotten. Deborah would know he was broken but she would not ask; he would not have to explain. But no matter where he went, he could not escape Christ's judgement. He had made his choice; he had promised. He told himself. 'I have to be afraid or there is no courage.'

The fiery eyes observed.

He drove slowly. As the headlights lifted out of a rut, they shone on the box-car.

The old grey van was parked nearby. Its doors were open. The headlights shone inside. It was empty.

Reverend Elwiss peered over the steering wheel. 'Why have you brought me back? My friend died here.' He got out. In the darkness, in the silence, he asked, 'Am I to die here too?' His feet sank in the sandy grass.

The heat from the fiery eyes was on him.

The box-car was as large as a tomb, estranged from its original purpose, leaking enmity, a lair, or the mouth of a lair, opening into a cavern, full with the echoes of cries and as still as a dungeon.

Its doors were shut tight but the metal lock hung loose. He thought, 'I don't remember closing them.' The light was dim from the falling moon, but he could make out the joins between the planks and even the grain of the wood. Reverend Elwiss steadied himself against the bonnet of the car. It was as warm as gloves.

'Do you see, Deborah? Do you see now?' Christ was waiting for him in the church. '*No*, be with me, here, Lord, *here*.'

A fox barked somewhere in the dunes or, loose-limbed, loped along Sker Beach at the edge of the sea.

His pounding heart.

Reverend Elwiss pushed himself up from the bonnet. He swayed on his feet and almost fell into taking a step, with his legs unwilling.

At the doors, he stopped and looked up: they were as tall as a cathedral.

His hand lifted to the lock, but he was not doing it. The metal was cold. He listened. There was no sound from within. He placed the flat of his other hand on the door and saw a child's face. 'There is a boy, a living boy.' But he could see nothing except the faint sheen of the planks. 'Will I be engulfed in fire? Will I be looking into blackness or is he waiting for me on the other side? But there is a child. He has a child.'

The tide was swelling…

'God be with me.' He closed his eyes. He whispered

the Lord's Prayer, hurrying to its plea, '… *our trespasses…*'

Rolling in from deep water and breakers rose…

'… *but deliver us from evil…*'

And tipped with a tremor he felt beneath his feet…

'… *for thine is the Kingdom…*'

And shuddered in the pit of his stomach.

'… *the power and the glory, for ever and ever, Amen, Amen.* Keep me safe and let me save this boy.'

Reverend Elwiss could smell the tar in the wood. 'Now,' he said, 'I must. God be with me and this child,' and he began to draw the doors apart. He heard them slide in their grooves.

'I came here with Jack and his grandpa,' said Huw.

'I know you did,' said Geraint. He looked at his ageless son who would never be a man. 'We have to help Aled, Huw. That's why we're here.' Geraint would be ever thankful Huw did not remember the mud.

'What do we have to do?' asked Huw.

'I want you to be his friend and then he can go home.'

'Then I will,' said Huw, feeling important. 'Is that the vicar? What's he doing?'

'He's saying his prayers. You must wait here now, Huw.'

'Where are you going? Can't I come with you?'

'No, Huw. I'm going to fetch Aled. Think about what we can go and see on Broadway.'

'A musical?' Huw asked, excitedly. '*Porgy and Bess*?'

'If that's what you want to see.'

'It is.' Huw looked up into his father's face. 'But Broadway can wait for a little while. We have to take Aled home to Mummy first.'

'Good boy.' He ruffled Huw's hair and left him in the shadow of a tall dune with the moon fading into the wings.

Diesel fumes tumbled from the opened doors. 'Beg,' said a voice.

Reverend Elwiss recoiled and was overcome. He grasped for the doorframe, with his head swimming, and fell to his knees.

In the corner of the box-car, as small and bright as a lure, the boy was sleeping.

Reverend Elwiss tried to get to his feet, but he could not. He shook his head and reached out with both hands. They hovered before him like naked partridges, flapping over the Christmas table. Curiously, he watched them trying to fly on featherless stumps. His father's cigar glowed; his mother kneaded cake mix with rounded shoulders.

He tried to get up, clawing at the planks, but his fingers kept slipping and he sank onto his haunches.

Someone stepped past him. In the blue tinted darkness, his fair hair shone like a halo.

The Reverend gasped and sucked the fumes in deeper. He tried to wipe his streaming eyes.

'I know you're here.'

Reverend Elwiss fumbled with his hands until they bumped together in a drunken clasp. He pressed his tangled fingers against his chin to feel his jaw move and began the fervent Psalm, '*The Lord is my shepherd, I shall not want...*'

The air quivered with each toxic breath.

'*... he leadeth me beside still waters...*'

The sacks scuffed along the floor.

'You took my son.'

The walls began to thrum.

'But you will not have this boy, not this boy.'

The sacks were drawn over the sleeping child. A bright pyjama arm slipped beneath as if it was the end of joy.

A small figure came running out of the dunes and stopped next to Huw.

'Hello, Jack,' said Huw. 'Where have you been?'

'Not far,' said Jack. 'I played in the dunes for a while and I went down to Kenfig Pool with Sam.'

'Is Sam with you?' Huw asked. 'I did wonder where he'd got to. Look, there's the vicar. He's praying.'

'I told him that you should never swim in Kenfig Pool because Grandpa says that every year people get caught in the weed and drown.'

'Aled's in there,' said Huw, pointing at the box-car. 'We're taking him home to Mummy.'

'Have you seen my mum and dad?' asked Jack. 'I think they must be up at the shop because I haven't seen them for ages. They promised to take me for ice cream.'

'At Alphonsi's,' Huw said, for him, because Jack could

never pronounce it properly.

'Yes, there. I'm going to look for them,' and he skipped away, back into the night.

Reverend Elwiss was an interloper in the battle for souls, a witness to good and evil beyond the sight of men. But he pressed on, with slowing words, hoping he could be seen to make the merest contribution, '... *I will fear no evil for thou art with me, thy rod and staff they comfort me...*'

The tar began to ooze from the wood grain like blood from a thousand cuts. The box-car erupted into an oven of sparking fumes and the air combusted.

The vicar's clothes began to smoke. He smelt himself burning. His face was scorched. He thought, 'What will Deborah have to bury if my body is gone? If I am already cremated?' But, soundlessly, his lips still moved, as if the prayer was life, '*Thou preparest a table for me in the presence of mine enemies...*'

In the distance, the fiery eyes roared with fresh gas.

The sacks boiled. Two heads rose up to face each other and sank back down.

The vicar's mouth twitched, '... *thou hast anointed my head with oil; my cup runneth over.*'

The sacks lifted and settled like flags. Their coarse weave reappeared. They formed into a ring as if they were towels to wrap up the boy from his bath.

'... *mercy shall follow me all the days of my life...*'

In his arms, emerging from the smog, Geraint held Aled.

The vicar stared. 'Praise be,' and fell on his side and mumbled into the sand, '*And I shall dwell in the house of the LORD forever.*'

A breeze came from the sea between the dunes. The diesel fumes drifted out through the doors and, slowly, the flashing lights in the vicar's head went out

Geraint slid down the wall of the box-car. He looked at Aled, resting across his legs, and smoothed his pyjama top. There were tufts of broken thread where the buttons had been, so he folded the two sides over each other. He curled over him and blew a playful, tearful raspberry into his tummy: Huw before he died; the boy he had never held. He could only imagine. He remembered the weight of the collapsing mine, barely time for a last regret, before, in an instant, he was a sliver of flesh and bone.

It was some time before he got to his feet.

He looked down at Reverend Elwiss, who was barely conscious and struggling to breathe. 'I'm so sorry,' he told him, but the vicar didn't move.

Geraint carried Aled into the dunes.

Huw was waiting for him. 'Will the vicar know we've taken Aled?' he asked.

Geraint stroked Aled's hair. 'No, he won't,' he said, quietly. He turned to let the fiery eyes see he had Aled in his arms, 'Look what you've done,' he told them, and then he looked back at Reverend Elwiss, still lying across the doors of the box-car.

'But how will the vicar know that Aled's safe with

us?' asked Huw. 'He has to know, doesn't he? Will Auntie Gwen tell him?'

Geraint pulled Aled tighter to him as if he was afraid to let him go. 'Perhaps we should let the vicar take him home.'

'I think we should,' said Huw.

Geraint sighed. 'Then we shall,' and he carried Aled back to the box-car with his son walking at his side.

'You take him home, Vicar,' he said, and gently laid Aled next to him. 'Open your eyes.'

'There,' said Huw.

Geraint slid an arm over his son's shoulder. 'You are so kind, Huw,' he told him. 'One day I will explain.'

'Explain what?'

'It doesn't matter. We had better go.'

Reverend Elwiss opened his eyes.

Geraint looked back at the vicar, with his arms outstretched, swaying on his knees over the boy.

Aled opened his eyes and pulled down the blankets. The bedroom curtains were silvering. He got up and looked out. There was nothing to be seen.

Quietly, he crept downstairs and into the garden. In his bare feet, the grass was wet and cold. He pushed over the planks, upturned the corrugated iron and wrecked his den.

He went back to bed and snuggled down in the soft blankets. His feet were soon warm again. For a while he watched as the room filled with pale light. Then he was asleep.

In the morning, Aled went into Gwen's room and got into bed next to her. She wrinkled her nose and sniffed. 'What on earth have you been doing?' she demanded, sitting up. 'You stink of petrol or something. And what have you done to your new pyjamas?'

'I had a bad dream.'

In his church, Reverend Elwiss prayed to the figurine. He gave thanks for His intervention and the certainty of Heaven.

Deborah found him sitting in the hall, eyes glazed and awed. She led him into the kitchen as the first light came through the apple trees.

24

PRIVATE ROBERT WILLIAMS 20
GOTTFRIED ZIEGLER VIZFELDWEBEL 28

'Good morning, Gerhard.'

'Good morning, Howell.'

'I'm sorry, but I'm too tired to stand.'

'Are you feeling unwell?'

'Just tired, Gerhard. I couldn't sleep, I kept wondering how many years and mornings it has been.'

'That we have greeted each other in the military way?'

'In the military way? Yes, you could put it like that. In 1918, when I came home, that's, I don't know, 51, 52 years, is it? And how many mornings? Too many.'

'It is 53 years since I died,' said Gerhard, 'but I haven't counted the mornings. We stopped being soldiers when the war ended.'

'We've never stopped being soldiers.'

'Yes, we have,' said Gerhard. 'I speak English with a Welsh accent. I even think my German has a Welsh accent, but how would I know? I haven't spoken to anyone in my own language since a few minutes before I died, to a young man called Jupp. I hope he saw his home again.'

'There were many bodies,' said Howell.

'There were always bodies. Let us hope he was not one of them.'

'Perhaps you should have taught me to speak German,' said Howell, 'then you could have had someone to talk to.'

'Perhaps, but I don't think it's often spoken in the shop, is it?'

'No, not too much.'

'Only part of our lives was as soldiers… our lives,' Gerhard smiled, sadly, 'or whatever it is my existence has been. Part, yes, part or all of mine. But I know it cannot be put away. Look at me, Howell.'

Gerhard still wore his uniform, mud-spattered and bloodstained, torn with the shrapnel that had killed him.

'You are still a soldier,' Howell told him.

'Only because I have nothing else to wear. I neglected to bring a change of clothes. I am your memory of me, as I was, as you found me, but I am not a man at arms any longer. If I can accept it, dressed like this, then it must be so. Where is my gun? Where is yours, Howell? The sounds of battle are long gone, all we can hear is the traffic on the road and the sheep on the mountain. Do you remember the smell, Howell?'

Howell nodded. 'Yes.'

'Can you smell it now?'

'No, but I can hear the guns sometimes.'

'No, Howell, it's your imagination. They're quiet now. There's nothing left there, I'm sure. The grass will have grown back, there will be cows grazing and fields of wheat. The land will have covered it all up. My grave too. I don't know if I have a grave. The land can't remember. It has its scars, but only we know what they are. Isn't that true, Howell?'

'Yes,' Howell replied, 'but we're not earth and grass.'

'No, we're not.'

'But it's as bitter now as it was then.'

'Is it, Howell?'

'Yes, and enough time has passed for me to know that it's impossible for it to be anything else. That's what I was trying to say. And, now, I haven't got enough time left.'

'You're very low today, Howell.'

'I am low, Gerhard. I can feel the weight of it on me. I want to be with you, to be like you, Hauptmann Albrecht, lighter than a feather. That's why I can't stand to attention.'

Alan lay on his bunk in his cell and listened, as he did every night, to the noises of the prison: crying, coughing, angry shouts, awake or in their dreams, the warders walking outside, talking and rattling, the snoring of his cellmate in the bunk above, and the ghastly light that seethed.

Alan was the pet rabbit with a stake impaled through its back on the top of the dune; he was the strangled black and white cat in the box-car; he was Sam, his father's labrador, its spine cut through in Gwyn's milking shed.

He had been told it would take weeks before his case could be reviewed and, in the meantime, he would be filed in a buff folder with his photograph.

He turned on his side and stared through the wall at the imagined streets of Cardiff, separated only by mortar and brick and wire. Offered the chance to escape, he wouldn't, not even if he could walk through them like a ghost, not even if he left there as a ghost.

His cellmate's snoring grew louder. Alan pushed his hand against the bottom of the bunk. The snoring stopped and started again.

'Raymond Tanner was a much loved, much respected pillar of the community. I feel his loss grievously as, I am sure, do we all.' Reverend Elwiss mourned as he spoke, words through tears, but not once did he hesitate, watched over by the figurine. The teachers, the children and former pupils now grown, almost the whole town, it seemed, filled the church and out through the doors into the graveyard.

When Bryn stood up to give the eulogy, he faltered but Reverend Elwiss caught his eye and smiled. Then Bryn's voice steadied and he became more than himself. He used that word, 'great', as of kings. It was the right word because it was true. He saw Laura in the front row, holding little Raymond in her arms, asleep, ticked 'present'. 'I will tell him he was here when he's old enough,' he thought.

After Mr Tanner's committal at the crematorium,

Reverend Elwiss stood at the empty catafalque. 'I came close, Raymond, but I don't know what I saw and it's by the grace of God that Aled is safe. I prayed, but your example was my strength. I could not let you down.'

Deborah came and stood next to him. 'He's gone,' she said.

'But never forgotten,' the vicar said. 'We don't make too many friends in this life, not real ones, and those are less as we get older. After all we went through, I would have liked to have spent our declining years together.'

'You're not declining yet,' she said.

'Neither was he. I pray Raymond is the last but I dread it is not yet resolved.'

'There is Eve's service to come,' she told him, gently.

'Yes,' he said, 'but I did not mean Eve.'

'I'm here, Ernest.'

He turned to her. 'Yes,' he said, 'you are, and I give thanks for it.'

The next funeral started to come in. They would have stayed longer, paying their respects to an empty space, but it must be filled by the next. Reverend James, the vicar who was officiating, jiggled his eyebrows at them.

'*Don't*,' Deborah hissed, feeling her husband bristle.

Later, in the Raven, Reverend Elwiss told Bryn, 'You will be the next headmaster, if I have some say in the matter, and I do. You won't be denied. There is no one more deserving to follow in Raymond's footsteps. You have done him proud today. You make me proud, too.'

Laura squeezed Bryn's arm.

'How will I ever be able to follow him?' Bryn asked.

'You will,' said Laura.

'Yes, Bryn,' said Reverend Elwiss, 'you will.'

The days were too long, now there was much less to do, and none of it interesting so, sometimes, usually, always, Protheroe went for a lunchtime drink to ease the afternoon away and give him the courage to go back to lock up in the dead-end alley where his body might not be found until the next day, or never if he ended up in the river, whistling as he scraped the key around the lock with one eye closed. Until he began locking up before he left and went home straight from the Raven.

Rose's husband had been a quiet man whom she had married to shine alongside. She reflected on his dullness like a glitterball and he was grateful and often told her so. She enjoyed it because of the jealousy of her many previous admirers.

Then he died, a wisp.

She had needed him more than she realised: he had been her setting, her framing, to set her off like a picture to be admired from behind a rope.

Purposely, Mr Tanner, accidentally Denzel Arbuthnot and, unexpectedly, Douglas Protheroe. She had no social life and few friends of her own and of men, where could she meet them, those that were suitable and unmarried, widowed, divorced?

'What do I want?' Rose asked herself. She knew the answer but could not specify it because her calculations began with an uncontainable urge. '*No*,' she scolded herself, 'whatever I want, I must stop wanting it; my happy times are over.' Had they been happy? Whatever they had been, she was determined to consign them to the past. 'It is better this way.' It had been a curse, a blight. She put away her bright clothes, her make-up, the lingering study of herself in front of the hall mirror before she left the house. She made herself look dowdy.

It was over.

School continued and she was much busier but, at the end of each day, she was left to the empty house where the presence of her husband was too timid to linger, when her only time in the world was the walk to and from school and shopping on Saturdays.

She was becoming everything she feared.

She read Protheroe's article in *The Herald* and felt important because she had been present at its writing, like a muse (failing to recollect they had been unaware of each other). She began to think about him. 'Hasn't he redeemed himself? After what he wrote about Bryn and Mr Tanner and the vicar, hasn't he made up for it? Isn't that what newspaper men do, see both sides of an argument and report what they see? I think,' she decided, 'that he is a better man than he has been given the credit for. A bit of a character, a rough diamond, possibly – but Raymond would have understood,' she added, hastily.

She opened the cupboard in her bedroom and had on a bright dress before she stopped to consider; shoes, that handbag; the hall mirror, turning from side to side, pushing her hair into place.

The Herald's address was under its masthead. Unexpectedly, she found herself at the end of the alley, peering into the dinginess (she put that aside). The downstairs office was dark but, upstairs, above the faded green sign, there was a light on. That was where she imagined Protheroe to be. She didn't want to be seen so she didn't stay long. She had only been passing. The alley came out at the bottom of Cardigan Street, not far from the Raven. The Red Lion was at the top end.

Protheroe was trying to distract himself by cleaning up the office. He didn't know what to do with the old newspapers strewn over the floor, so he rolled them up into a giant ball and shoved them in the corner (which the mice soon moved into, rustling and squeaking excitedly), and there they stayed, leaving a patchwork of dust on the lino like an archipelago seen from a great height. The window badly needed cleaning too but it was jammed shut. He looked at the patchy reflection of his face, gothic with decay: a cheek was missing, the skin on his forehead was peeling off and one eye was blacked out. He listened to the river. Every time he heard the door downstairs, he tensed. It was the wind and the loose glass. He had a call from a local councillor and promised to include a piece on the new housing estate in tomorrow's edition. The article was tedious but difficult, as biased even-handedness usually is, and he couldn't escape for lunch. Finally, in late afternoon, he looked at his watch (the wall clock had stopped working in 1959), and decided, 'That'll do.' He locked up and hurried out of the alley.

Rose was coming in the opposite direction down Cardigan Street. She was on the other side of the road and, possessed of a sudden caution-to-the-winds impulsiveness, he crossed over. There was no time to come up with a plan and his head was still numbed with phrases like 'desirable family residences'. He knew she noticed him because she pretended she hadn't and, so unerring was his course, like a car careering out of a junction, she was afraid they would collide.

'Oh, hello, Mr Protheroe,' she said. 'I'm sorry, I didn't see you. I didn't mean to be rude.'

'How are you, Mrs Davies?'

'I'm well, thank you,' she replied, primly, to the uninvited suitor, a man she barely knew, who was unexpectedly confronting her in the street.

'Have you moved house?' he asked. 'You didn't used to come this way? I meant to call on you.'

'Did you?'

'Yes, I did. I asked if I could. Do you remember?'

She bit her lip, as if she was trying to. 'Well…' her heart fluttered.

'I wanted to ask if you'd read my article in the newspaper.'

'Yes, I did, Mr Protheroe. I thought it was brave of you.'

'Is that true?' he brightened.

It was, she hadn't meant to be so candid, but found herself not regretting it.

'Why do you think that, Mrs Davies?'

'Well,' she began. She had gone over most of his possible questions, but not this one. She was annoyed at herself. 'Well…'

He wasn't going to interrupt. There was a little contest of wills.

'Well, it was quite a thing to say, let alone print in a newspaper.'

'Was it, Mrs Davies? Do you think I shouldn't have done it?'

'I don't know. If it was the right thing to do.'

'But do you think it was, Mrs Davies?'

She looked up and down the street.

'You're not afraid to be seen talking to me, are you?' He tried to smile, but couldn't. This was too serious, the future course of what remained of his life depended on what he said in these fateful moments.

'Mr Protheroe?'

'Forgive me, Mrs Davies, but I would like to know what you think. You knew Mr Tanner.'

She flinched.

'But, more than that, Mrs Davies, I would genuinely like to know because I value your opinion.'

'But we've only met once,' she said.

'It was enough.'

'That's very… Mr Protheroe?'

He took a deep breath, as if he had been summoning up the courage ever since their last meeting, 'But rather than stand here in the street, would you like to come for a drink at the Raven, where we met before? It's only over there.'

'I was on my way home. I haven't eaten,' she replied, teasing him with a glance at the open doors where the light was beginning to spill out, needing him to work harder before she could allow herself to say yes.

'They serve quite good food. We could have a sandwich, or something more substantial, if you like? Or just a quick drink then? Would you come for a drink, Mrs Davies?'

If she refused, that would be an end to it. She would have to walk home the way she used to.

'Please say you will, Mrs Davies.' There was a desperate tone to his voice.

That would do for now, the contest was over: the game was hers. 'As long as it's not for too long, Mr Protheroe.'

'This way, then.'

He opened the door for her.

The barman smirked.

Protheroe quelled him with a glare.

'A whisky, Mr Protheroe? Madam?'

'A gin and tonic, Mrs Davies?' Protheroe asked her.

'Yes, please,' she replied.

He pulled the chair out and she settled into it and folded her hands into her lap. It felt intensely pleasant.

'Why do you think it was a brave thing to do, Mrs Davies?'

She thought, and said, without artifice, 'Someone had to say he didn't drown. We all knew he didn't drown. But nobody would listen. The police didn't. So who was going to say it until you did? That's why I think it was brave of you, Mr Protheroe. It was brave to tell them what they said wasn't true. It was.'

'I didn't say what they said was untrue.'

'Didn't you, Mr Protheroe?'

'Yes, possibly I did. Thank you, Mrs Davies. I hope I did the right thing and I'm glad you think so too.'

The barman brought the drinks. Protheroe clinked her glass before she picked it up. 'To Mr Tanner,' he said.

She looked away.

'Would you like something to eat, Mrs Davies?'

She cleared her throat. 'I'm not sure I should.'

'My name is Douglas.'

'Perhaps,' she said, with the quickest hint of a smile, wanting him to know she still had the capacity and the desire for the right man.

Protheroe caught the barman's eye and mouthed, 'Menu.'

'We'll start with a haircut and then some new clothes,' she thought, as she slyly looked him up and down. 'And then we'll see.'

The barman brought the menu.

'My name is Rose,' she said.

The two services were only a week apart, but Eve's remembrance had been eclipsed like a shadow over the face of the sun that sent the birds to roost. Reverend Elwiss' words were not for her; he could think only of his friend.

There weren't many there: Gwen, Bryn, Laura, Dewi and Brenda, the Trebanog uncles and aunties, a few others from where she worked.

Roy Brown was given compassionate release from prison to attend. He stood apart with a plain-clothed policeman at his side. He was handcuffed, but not behind his back and the chains were hidden under his sleeves. He thought they blamed him for Eve's death because no one spoke to him but he didn't try to speak to them either.

When the service was over, Reverend Elwiss picked up a white rose and laid it on Eve's coffin to cover his shame. He heard sobs coming from the pews and felt like a fraud. For a moment, he stood with his back to the tiny congregation and tried to pay his final respects, but he kept seeing the face of someone he didn't recognise. 'We all deserve to be remembered,' he admonished himself, 'and Eve had many qualities.' What did that mean? She knew she would be remembered for the way she died and not for herself. 'How wretched,' came to him as if it had been chosen for her as an epitaph, but not willingly.

'I cannot make that judgement,' he thought, angry with himself, 'and I didn't know her well. But God bless you, Eve Brown or Guthrie.'

Her headstone said *Evelyn Brown*.

Roy Brown was the first to leave. Everyone waited while he was escorted out to begin the long journey back to Wakefield in an unmarked police car.

'Do you think we'll ever see him in Bridgend again?' Brenda asked Dewi.

Dewi shook his head. I don't think so,' he said. 'He doesn't belong here anymore.'

'That's sad,' she said. 'It's still his home.'

'Is it? In what way, now?'

At the bar in The Red Lion, repulsed by each other, Maynard and Prosser drank.

The trickle of lunchtime customers came and went.

Maynard was leaning on his elbows over his half-finished pint. He hadn't said a word for some time and his eyes were closed. Suddenly, he groaned and tipped forward. His arms splayed and his nose hit the rim of the glass and knocked it over. As he toppled off the stool and fell to the floor, his head bounced on the foot rail with a *clang*. Blood ran from the corner of his mouth and his leg twitched. The spilt beer dripped off the bar into his hair.

Prosser looked down at him. 'Grim Reaper,' he said. 'You better get him an ambulance,' he told the landlord, 'he's in the way of the toilet. But fill this up first, will you?'

and pushed his empty glass toward the beer pump.

At Maynard's bedside in the hospital, Reverend Elwiss sat, once more. He watched and said nothing, refusing to patronise him with any more prayers. Maynard must find his own way, whichever way, emptied, finally, of whatever had so improbably sustained him.

Time went by, but not long. The vicar thought of other things.

He didn't notice the moment when Maynard's life wobbled from him like a crane fly bouncing up a pane of glass, set free after a grub's life. It reached the top corner of the window and settled there, as flies do, its wire legs quivering and its abdomen throbbing, soon to be squashed by the nurse's duster.

Reverend Elwiss pushed back his chair and left.

Herald Andrew joined the *South Wales Tribune,* the big Cardiff paper. Sergeant Phillips told Symonds to tell him what to write.

Sergeant Phillips Corrects a Mistake

Sergeant Phillips told The Tribune *that, 'Justice must always triumph even if it means admitting the law made a mistake. Juries are not always right.'*

There was no apology. *Tribune* Andrew? Never. He didn't prosper there and it was not long before he was back as the editor of *The Herald*, grey and bushy-browed, crumpled, tummied, under the never cleaned window, listening to the mice; the Raven, whiskies, watching the door, desirous of a Rose, secretly weeping his alcoholic rheum and, like so many hundreds of thousands of words before, he could see the letters in his mind as they faded: Douglas Protheroe as he should have been.

25

A SOLDIER OF THE GREAT WAR
EIN DEUTSCHER SOLDAT

Alan stepped out on a warm April morning. The sun was shining and the shadow of the prison wall was stark on the road.

He was neither glad nor sad.

At the end of the street, just before the corner, he saw a big, black car. There was a dark silhouette in the driver's seat, motionless. The bus pulled up and Alan turned away. The prison visitors got out and he got on. Now, it was almost empty. He went to the back. 'Don't look round,' he told himself.

The train to Bridgend didn't take long. It went past the trading estate where he used to work. It hadn't changed. 'I don't have to be anywhere; I don't have to do anything,' he thought. 'Time is mine to do with what I want.' But it wasn't. It had been taken away and nothing could buy it back. He would die when he would die, perhaps living longer than if he had stayed in prison, but the years could not be tagged on as recompense. There was only a legal system that had wrongly convicted him, haphazardly corrected its mistake and had him released. But he could still be locked up and the Heavens would not fall if he was. There was no great hand of justice to put it right. He walked from the station to Parc Hospital.

Jean was as frail as a fledgling bird, shallowly gasping and dishevelled at the bottom of an abandoned nest. After nearly four years, he didn't recognise her. This had been his wife and Jack and Aled's mother, the girl he had been in school with. The cruelty of her fate made him inexpressibly angry.

He held her hand. Her skin was like paper. Her once beautiful eyes were dull and her hair was lank. Her clothes were too big for her and they were old. Not hers.

Alan looked around the day room. There were no nurses, but all the armchairs were full. They had nothing to look at so they criss-crossed each other with sightless eye lines. Alan leaned over and switched on the television. It took a minute to warm up and, when the picture finally came to life, it had a greenish tinge because the tube was giving out. No one moved.

Alan didn't try to tell Jean he was there. He remembered her torment as the kindly doctor, called in the middle of the night, tieless in his yellow waistcoat, slid the needle into her arm and her fleeting, lucid understanding before she tipped over the edge and fell into a chasm, disappearing smaller and smaller with a frightened white face, still falling, not so far to fall now.

'What were our lives for? Your life and mine?' he asked, to which she had no answer and could make no reply.

He thought about the brother his father had told him about in the moments before he died, 'It was the war, when I was in Eastbourne, before we went over.' He wouldn't try to find him. How could he explain their story? He thought about Jack and Huw; burying Sam in Gwyn the Milk's field; Rest Bay and Kenfig Pool, the dunes. 'I won't go there again.' Eve and his once friend Roy, fellow convict. Until his mind turned to Gwen and Aled with a hope he didn't trust to be true.

He placed Jean's hand gently back on top of its other and kissed her forehead. She was like a wood shaving, dropped to the floor with masses of others in a rush of selfish inspiration when she should have been part of something, indivisible from the revealed creation within.

He would visit again, but she wouldn't know he came and he wouldn't try to make her. 'A duty,' he sighed. He got up to leave but could hardly move for the burden of regrets. 'I let Jack down,' he thought. 'I should have watched him. I should have asked him to help me get the coal in, then he wouldn't have run out the front.'

He told the nurse on reception, who was young and new, 'Look after her, don't give up on her.'

The nurse looked puzzled. 'We never give up,' she said.

Alan wanted to say, 'You already have,' but no one there could be blamed.

Before he left Bridgend, he called at the vicarage. Deborah kissed him. He touched his cheek where her lips had been. He shook hands with the vicar.

'You're free, Alan,' said Reverend Elwiss. 'An injustice has been made right, finally.'

'Finally, yes,' Alan said, 'but at what cost? I don't feel anything. I don't know what to feel.'

'Would you like to come into the church to pray with me? It might help to clear your mind.'

'Would you mind if I didn't?' Alan replied. 'Thank you.'

'No, of course not, but I am always here for you, Alan, should you have need of me. for what I am worth.'

'Yes, we are,' said Deborah.

'We are,' the vicar corrected himself. 'Give Gwen my best wishes, and Aled too.'

Nesta sat in the armchair with the mountain by her side. 'What if we had left Aled with Eve?' she thought. 'What might have happened to him?' Nesta shuddered. After the funeral, Eve's name was never mentioned.

Without Aled, they were allowed to be old. They cheered themselves with plans to visit. It was all they talked about; their lives revolved around his absence and the stories they told about him and never tired of repeating.

Gwen telephoned twice a week and wrote, sending

them pictures of him, as Nesta had to Eve. They gathered around the table in the back room with her letters before the shop opened. Howell read them out loud and then Nesta put them away in an old Milk Tray box and it was Delia's job to make sure all the pictures were framed.

Howell's walks up the mountain were lonely; his legs didn't want to take him there. He stopped going and spent more time in his room, holding the binoculars and talking to Gerhard, leaving Idris and Emlyn to look after the shop.

When customers asked where he was, Idris told them, 'He's missing Aled.'

They nodded slowly and said no more.

Delia was bustling about.

Nesta snapped, 'Stop fiddling with everything.'

Delia was pained. 'But I've got to dust,' she protested, vibrating from the waist up. 'I've got to do the housework. Somebody's got to do it.'

'Not all the time,' said Nesta.

'Well,' said Delia, 'well. Who's going to sweep the step if I don't, then?'

'It doesn't need sweeping every morning.'

Delia was shocked. 'Of course it does. What will people think?'

'Does it really matter?' Nesta asked, holding up her hand at her sister's anguished expression. 'Just don't, will you?'

'Well,' said Delia, now tearful, 'well.'

Nesta leaned close to the bottom of the window to

look out and tried to see the sky above the mountain. Her breath fogged the glass. 'Please, not now, Delia,' she said.

Delia went into the kitchen, took the crockery out of the cupboard and exaggeratedly wiped down the shelves.

Nesta turned back to the fire, not lit, and watched the empty grate into the afternoon.

Idris and Emlyn closed the shop and pulled down the blinds.

Emlyn switched off the lights and they went into the passage. 'Howell's not right,' he said.

'He just needs a bit of time,' said Idris.

'Do you think he should see the doctor?'

'He wouldn't go,' said Idris.

'No, I don't suppose he would.'

'Then there's no point is suggesting it, is there?'

'Not really,' agreed Emlyn, who knew the answer.

There was foreboding in the narrow passage stacked with shelves of tins and primed mousetraps in the gloom beneath. 'Don't say anything to Nesta and Delia,' Idris said.

'They've got eyes,' said Emlyn.

Howell didn't come down for tea.

'I'll take some up,' said Delia. 'He must be a bit tired today.'

'Leave him be,' Nesta said. 'I'll make him something a bit later.'

'But he's got to eat,' said Delia.

'Let him alone,' Emlyn told her. 'I'll go up and see how he is when we've had our food.'

'Is there something the matter?' asked Delia. 'Isn't he feeling well?'

'Oh, Delia,' said Nesta.

Emlyn knocked on Howell's door. There was no reply so he went in. The room was in darkness and Howell was sitting on the windowsill holding the binoculars.

'Are you alright?' Emlyn asked.

Howell looked up. 'Yes,' he said. 'But leave me be, just for a bit, will you?'

'We're all missing him,' said Emlyn. 'Don't you think it would be better if you kept yourself busy?'

'The shop doesn't need the three of us,' Howell replied. 'It never has.'

'It's not about that, Howell, is it?'

'I'm going to give him these,' said Howell, and he put the binoculars back on the windowsill. 'But, if I don't get a chance to, will you make sure he gets them?'

'What are you talking about? Why don't we take them down on Sunday, all of us?'

'We could,' he said. 'Promise me, though?'

'Give them to him yourself.'

'Promise me? Just say you will?'

'That's daft…'

Howell looked at him piercingly from the shadows.

'I promise,' said Emlyn.

'Thank you,' said Howell. 'I'll come down later.' He did not.

At the end of the track to Gwen's cottage, Alan slung his jacket over his shoulder and stood to admire fields of freedom and, beyond, hidden in the valley, the River Tyfi, full with the tide and foaming, with a big, swirling eddy where Aled had told Huw he wanted to swim.

Colours surprised him the most; the prison was a colourless place. Why? Was colour a privilege to be denied? 'How long is it since I saw a cloudless sky and the horizon in every direction?'

Gwen was at the kitchen window. 'Come here, Aled,' she said, quietly. 'Come outside with me.'

'What?' asked Aled, disturbed from his concentration, lying on the floor, drawing. 'In a minute.'

'No, Aled, now. Come here.'

'In a minute.'

'Now, there's a good boy.'

'*Ohhh*.' Aled got up, holding his drawing. 'Look,' he said.

Gwen took his hand. 'Yes, very nice,' she said.

'*Look*, then.'

They went outside and stood together at the backdoor with Aled's drawing fluttering in the breeze as he tried to hold it up to her face.

Alan saw them but his smile was drained by the sight of his remaining son, grown so like Jack now.

'Who's that?' asked Aled.

'That's your Uncle Alan,' Gwen replied, without hesitation, because she had been waiting so long to say it.

'Another one?' Aled sighed.

'He's coming to live with us.'

'To live with us?' Aled's fingers crumpled the edge of his drawing. 'Why?'

'He's had to move out of his house and, because I've known him a long time, I said he could come and live with us.'

Aled looked up at her suspiciously. 'How long for?'

'I'm not sure,' she said. 'It depends.' His perspicacity always disarmed her, as if there was a question behind his question and he already knew some or all of the truth (and if it was being kept from him). In the excitement of Alan's release, she had not prepared as well as she thought.

'Will I still have my bedroom?' he asked.

'Yes, of course,' she said, looking down at him.

'Where's he going to sleep?' His expression was so perfectly guileless and accusing, she blushed.

'In the room where Auntie Nesta sleeps,' she told him.

'Where will Auntie Nesta sleep?'

'She's not here all the time and, when she is, Uncle Alan can sleep downstairs.'

'There isn't a bed downstairs.'

'We will think of something,' she said, quickly. 'Look, Aled, he's waving to us. Go on, wave back.'

Aled raised his hand and flapped his drawing slowly up and down, frowning at why this strange man should have a claim on him (and how did that other woman auntie know what his favourite squash was? Anyway, she'd been wrong, so she didn't know).

Geraint and Huw watched from the end of the garden. 'That's Uncle Alan,' said Huw.

'Yes, it is.'

'It's a small world, isn't it,' said Huw. 'Has he come to visit?'

'I think he's come to live here, Huw.'

'With Mummy?'

'Yes, Huw, with Mummy.' His wife would find peace with another man. His friend; always his friend. 'Deserved,' he thought. 'For both of them. I am the husband who was killed underground and, soon, she will say it was a long time ago. They mustn't wait to have a child of their own.' The pain at their imagined intimacy made him screw his eyes shut, knowing he could watch if he wanted to.

'With Mummy?' asked Huw, again. 'Without you?'

'We have the world to see, Huw.'

Huw nodded. 'Does that make you unhappy?'

'Yes, Huw, it does a bit, but all that matters is that Mummy and Aled are happy.'

'Mmm,' Huw murmured, wisely, looking up to the father he had never known: the husband and son to a wife and mother they loved inexpressibly. 'Aled will be glad to see his father again, won't he?'

Geraint couldn't explain. 'And Uncle Alan will be so happy to see Aled too. We should leave them together now, Huw.'

'Do we have to go?'

'Yes, we do.'

'When are we coming back?'

'There will be a time, Huw, when we must.'

'Hello, Gwen,' said Alan.

She touched his arm.

Aled watched, suspiciously.

'And you are Aled,' said Alan, looking directly into the eyes of his son. Aled's small hand was soft and yielding.

'Shall we go inside?' asked Gwen, turning away to hide a tear. 'Show Uncle Alan your drawing, Aled.'

'Look,' said Aled, holding it up. It was a drawing of the sea in a bay with a golden beach and, above, on a cliff, a farmhouse with a face looking out of the window. 'That's me.'

'That's very good,' said Alan. 'Did you draw that on your own?'

'Yes,' said Aled, affronted. 'I'm good at drawing. Can I go and play now?'

'Yes, go on,' said Gwen.

Aled dropped the drawing and Alan picked it up. 'This really is good,' he said.

'He's your son,' Gwen smiled.

Aled ran down to the apple trees.

'It's too nice a day to go inside,' said Gwen. 'You sit out here and I'll make us some tea.'

Alan sat on the bench against the cottage wall. 'I didn't think this day would ever come,' he said.

Gwen went into the kitchen. She sang softly.

Aled flickered in the sun coming through the

branches as he ran. Then, suddenly, he was gone.

Alan sat up quickly and shaded his eyes.

Slowly, Aled reappeared, as if materialising out of the light, but the sun still shone through him as if he was a chiffon scarf, airily floating between the dappling beams, to be swept out over the fields, up into the sky and over his sparkling sea of dreams, carefree of what might have been.

'Gwen?' Alan tried to call.

Aled came out from under the trees and stood looking at Alan, standing very still with his hands by his sides. He said, 'This is all you will ever need,' in a sad, deep voice. And then he was running under the apple trees, laughing.

A morning.

'I am tired,' said Howell. 'I am tired of remembering. It's too much.'

'You will not have to bear it any longer, Howell,' said Gerhard.

Howell raised himself in bed. The mountain had gone and rolling hills stretched to the horizon, radiantly green, their folds in shade, spilling mist. It was a painting of all he had ever wanted, his dreams during the war, a wordless emotion without the need to explain, as evocative as music, as cool as the breeze on a warm summer's day, the scent of flowers.

'You are smiling, Howell,' said Gerhard. 'You see, it is healed.' He held out his hand. 'We will remember them. It is time to go.'

Acknowledgements

Chapter 1, P7 *But dead or living…* XXII *A Shropshire Lad*
– A. E. Housman

With thanks to Judy who read it chapter by chapter and to Lisa for all her support.

And to my Uncle Eddie whose binoculars they were and on whose foot the lamb slept.

Robert David
April 2021

Read more about the author or contact him at:

www.athanpress.com

@writerrdavid

writerrdavid@gmail.com

Printed in Great Britain
by Amazon

82298653R00217